HOMER'S WIVES

HOMER'S WIVES: PENELOPE

By Naouma Kourti

© 2018 by Naouma Kourti

All rights reserved. This book or any portion thereof may not be reproduced or used in any manner whatsoever without the express written permission of the publisher except for the use of brief quotations in a book review.

ISBN: 9781796893656

"To my mother-in-law"

Preface

This book is about Penelope, the faithful wife of Odysseus. *The Odyssey* has been a great source of inspiration for many generations. Odysseus's ingenuity, cleverness, and determination, as well as his fights against all monsters, have been sung, played, and rewritten in many languages.

History has reduced Penelope to the faithful wife of Odysseus. Textbooks teach us that she stayed and waited for her husband to come back for over twenty years. If history says that, we have no reason to doubt it; however, history doesn't say anything about how Penelope managed to keep the kingdom intact over the twenty years of Odysseus's absence in the difficult years of the Greek Bronze Age—years when the rule of the most powerful prevailed; when women had little to say; when men were ready to kill, fight, and die on the battlefield to showcase their manhood and conquer kingdoms; when there was no justice system in place.

I wondered how Penelope managed to survive so long, ruling on her own. Her court was full of men wanting her kingdom and desiring her. Why, during those years, did none of those heroes try to take her by force and declare himself the new king of Ithaka? Instead, everybody was waiting for her to decide. There must have been something special about this woman after all. Why does no one talk about it? Why has nothing been saved about Penelope's intellect but so much about Odysseus, who, after all, carried out an atrocious act, murdering all the youth of Ithaka? The same youth who didn't dare to take Penelope by force but quietly waited for her to make a decision? It looks as if Penelope created a respected leadership structure in her kingdom, which Odysseus had to uproot in order to regain control over Ithaka.

It looks like the story of a gender fight to me, and one of megalithic dimensions.

What if Odysseus didn't kill those who were consuming his property but those who were faithful to his wife? What if Odysseus, when he came back, realized that all his subjects were now faithful to his wife and didn't miss him at all? What if the so-called suitors were Penelope's private army, and he had to take his kingdom back from her and not from the suitors? Penelope had become too important over the years of her reign, and he had to subdue her in order to subdue his country again. Killing her would have only enraged the people against him. So killing her army and ensuring she would become a loving wife was essential for his success. And for the success of the whole patriarchal system.

That sounded to me a more plausible explanation for what might have happened in Ithaka than what Homer sang to please the ears of the rulers of that time. So I decided to rewrite the story of Penelope to fit the above thinking. This opened to my mind a whole new way of approaching women of that period and explained a lot about the women of today. Penelope would have been a role model of female power if more had been said about her real story. Similar to Helen of Sparta (see my first book of the series, *Homer's Wives: Helen*), she suffered systematic mistreatment and diminution of her valor at a stage in which she received value only for her faithfulness to her husband, while Helen, the first woman to choose her man, has lost any value whatsoever.

Athenians of the classic period hated the Spartans and the freedom of their women. In order to keep their women quiet at home, they stripped away any value from the Spartan women—Helen, Penelope, and Clytemnestra—so as to ensure they wouldn't serve as role models for their women. Helen and Clytemnestra were treated as man-destructive monsters, and Penelope, the most intelligent, became the faithful. Then all intelligent Athenian women who were close to renouncing submission to their husbands would have identified themselves with that archetype of the faithful wife, thus creating no further concern for the patriarchal system. This Greek homemade reality survived until our day so well that still, after three thousand years, no one challenges it, not even women themselves.

Both epics of Homer that have survived to our time seem to talk about the valor of their male protagonists, Achilles and Odysseus, but in reality, they are about the two females who inspired the men's valor, Helen and Penelope—both Spartan and both very important and independent women who stood on their own and made their own decisions and led their people to a different way of being and thinking. They marked their times, and they still mark the fates of females in all the world. They deserve a better treatment and a better story to be told. They do sing it in our ears, if we can only listen to it.

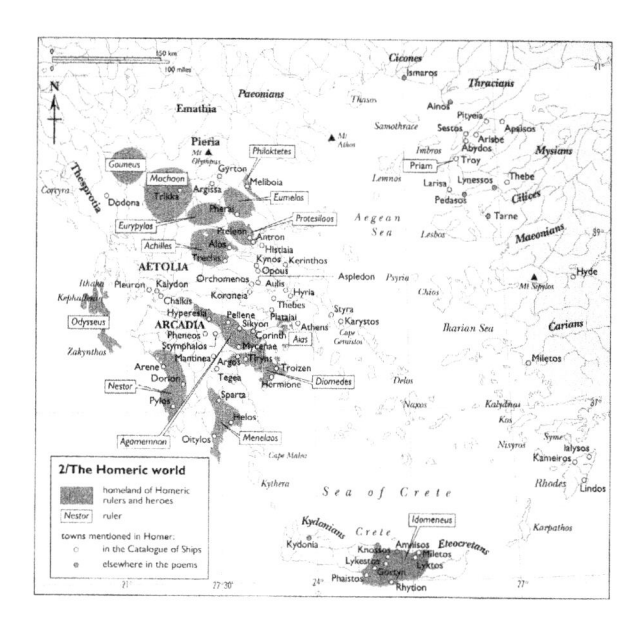

Figure 1. Main settings of the late Greek Bronze Age.
Source: College.Columbia.edu

xi

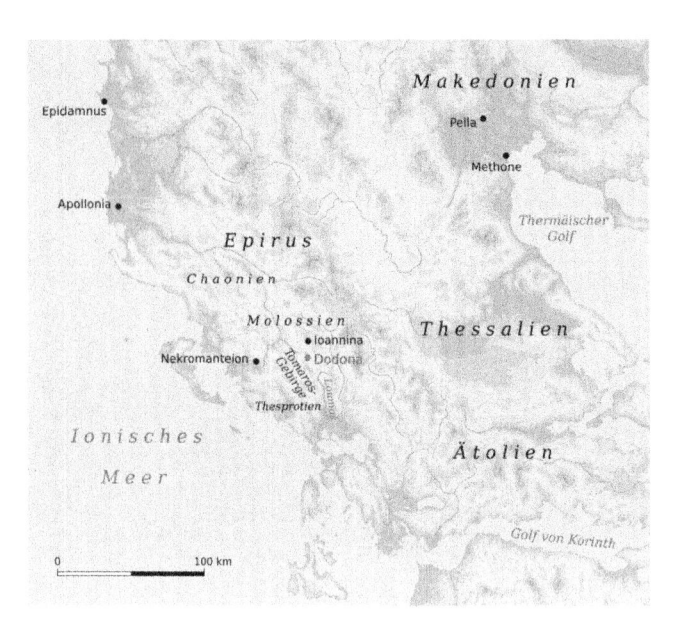

Figure 2. The Nekromanteion of Ephyra.
Source: Wikipedia commons

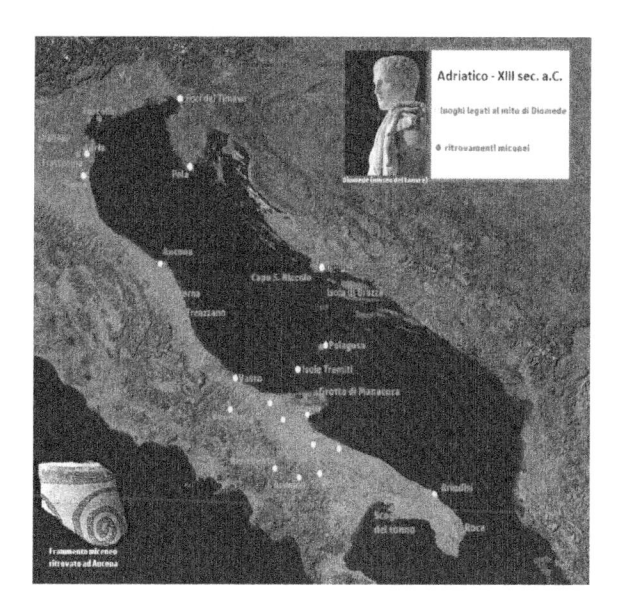

Figure 3. Diomedes's reign in Italia.
Source: it.wikipedia

"Oh, great you are, Spartan girls and women. Great were your accomplishments and your wisdom. The examples you gave to humanity are valuable and eternal. All the way along the development of human spirit, you have accompanied us; you have walked as first new paths of life and given all women after you the certainty of their deeds. Look at me, Penelope, daughter of Icarius, princess of Sparta, wife of Odysseus, and mother of Telemachus. Queen undisputable of Ithaca."

α′

I was intelligent. I could read the thoughts of people and understand their feelings. My thinking was profound, my mind was working fast and effectively, and I could sense its eagerness to get to work every morning with the rising of the sun. It was keen and pushy and wanted me to achieve things. My resourcefulness gave me confidence in my thoughts and determination in life. I felt free, independent, and empowered. Freedom of action and decision was important to me. Without it intelligence would only be a means to self-destruction.

As a child I was at my best when I was learning new things or meeting new people. I got bored quickly when I didn't have anything more to explore. My favorite place in all of Sparta was the top of the hill next to the palace in Amycles. I could watch the whole plain of the Evrotas River and the surrounding villages and fields. I could see the road coming from Gythio and the road going to Sparta, and looking up, I could see the top of Mount Taygetus on the one side and Mount Parnon on the other.

Oh, how I loved this land and its people. And more than anything my mother, the nymph Periboia, the undisputed lady of the whole region and great-great-granddaughter of Taygete, the nymph who gave her name to the mountain. I didn't live much with my mother, but I always remember her with great affection. She went back to the mountains from where she had come when I was still little. It was about half a year after my accident in the river when she left us. My father, Icarius, had always described her as a free spirit, as a completely independent woman who had decided by pure love to live by him and give birth to his children. At the end, she couldn't manage to live the life of a common woman and returned to the mountain, its woods, and its springs. Yes, my mother was a nymph. One of those women who dedicate themselves to Mother Earth, to the forest springs and creeks of the mountains, and live by the rules of nature.

Icarius was a great runner. He was able to go to the top of Taygetus running and come back in less than two days. Most people would take two days only to go up, walking with difficulty the swirling, steep, impassable mountainous paths. My father liked to go up to the small shrine of Zeus on the top of Taygetus. Like me, he liked the free view down to the sea and the overlook of the Evrotas's valley, which unfolded from the lakes in the north all the way down to the Gulf of Lacedaemon. And most of all, he liked hunting in the forests. His quick legs would take him chasing the wounded prey for kilometers, together with his dogs. He would come back with game much bigger and more valuable than any of the other lords of Lacedaemon.

On one of these hunting tours, my mother seduced him. She observed him for some time before she decided to appear to him. He was overwhelmed by the beauty of her naked body. He remained immobilized, thinking that he had ended up in a dream. She took him by the hand and guided him to a spring where the crystalline waters were forming a little pool before entering the creek down the mountain. She loved him there, and she kept him with her for half a year. Everybody thought he was dead, lost forever in some of the numerous precipices of Taygetus. It wouldn't be strange. Being killed while hunting was a common type of death for men in those days.

Coming back, Icarius was as if reborn. Full of energy and confidence. He was going around to everybody saying that he would marry a nymph. Oebalus, his father, was not happy. He himself had taken a nymph as his first wife; Bateia was her name. She had abandoned him after giving birth to a son and a daughter. He knew how difficult it was for a nymph to live the life of common mortals. But he didn't tell Icarius; instead, he offered him the palace of Amycles to host his new family. The palace in Amycles was the first palace of the family and was smaller than that of Sparta. But it was much more beautiful. It had a little megaron made of Krokean stone, with many decorations at the tops of the columns made with the harmonious synthesis of Krokean stone and wood from the forests of Taygetus. All the wooden reliefs were painted in vivid colors such as red and cyan, pink and turquoise. There was a painting on the wall of Taygete, the nymph mistress of the animals, being chased by Zeus, with the goddess Artemis watching them. There was also a painting of the doe with the golden horns that Taygete was turned into by the goddess, running free among the trees. It was the same doe that Heracles chased and caught and released as one of his labors.

It was as if my father were inebriated. He took a team of workers and fixed the old palace. He painted the walls anew. He refreshed the frescos, put new tiles in the yard, and made the stables bigger and the kitchen more practical. And most of all, he decorated their bedroom. He made a bed from the best oak tree in Taygetus and an armchair with soft woolen pillows and a beauty table with legs like those of a doe and a mirror with the most polished bronze on the top. He bought the most expensive mirror the traders had brought to Sparta from Egypt. The bedroom was painted with forest scenes to make her feel at home, and there was a fireplace on the wall to keep it warm in the winter. He asked the weavers to make clothes from exotic fabrics from Tyre. He was happy preparing and imagining a life with the chosen of his heart. There was nothing she would have asked that he couldn't deliver.

When he was happy and satisfied, my father disappeared again in the mountains for some time. He reappeared again with his pregnant wife. Periboia was not used to living among people and was very shy. So the Amycles Palace was fine for her, away from the frenzy in the palace of Sparta. The wedding had taken place in the mountains, according to the rules of the nymphs. My mother didn't wish any sacrifice of animals or any drinking of wine. In her world, animals had to be free to fulfill their reason for existence, their purpose of life. They had feelings and intelligence, and they liked music. She claimed she could speak to certain animals and could listen to trees. Although my father knew about her capabilities, I don't think he appreciated them.

They spent a wonderful time together waiting for their first baby and making preparations. But Periboia wanted to give birth in the woods with her nymph friends whom she trusted. Icarius was not happy about it, mostly because he wouldn't be able to participate, but he gave in under the promise that the second child would be born in the palace. She agreed and left.

She came back after three months, when all danger had passed, with a beautiful, rosy, fat baby girl who became moody every time she wanted to eat. Icarius called her Iphthimi, which means precious.

They were as happy as they could be. Periboia was making an effort to enter the life of a mortal royal woman. She was working in the palace, getting acquainted with the housekeepers and servants. She even learned to sleep on the bed, although she preferred the hard pavement. She didn't wish to have nannies for any of her babies, and she was very appreciative of the efforts of Icarius to give her a comfortable life. However, she often took the horse and disappeared into the mountains with her little daughter, sometimes for days—something that irritated Icarius increasingly.

When she was pregnant with the second baby—that was me—Icarius became more vocal against her riding in the mountains. As she had promised, she gave birth in the palace, and my father assisted throughout the process. He was the first to hold me and called me Alcestis, meaning the courageous. I guess he was commemorating his own courage in insisting having me born in the palace.

After five days, when my mother felt stronger, she took me to the mountains. She wanted to go through the rituals for strong and blessed babies that she was used to. As always, Icarius couldn't follow her, which made him even more sore. She came back after three months, happy and content with her second rosy baby girl. But my father was obviously annoyed. My mother swore not to have any other babies, to avoid another quarrel.

She started taking us all on excursions in the woods, where she would tell stories about each rock, each bend of the creek, and each spring. She was able to call the does, which came and ate from our hands. She taught us to listen to the murmuring of the tree leaves and to understand if they were signaling danger or inviting us to play. She knew the ways of the wolf and the boar and was able to find their traces on the ground and vegetation. She told us not to be scared but to start singing if we saw them. They usually appreciated a nice song from the humans and wouldn't attack.

It was so exciting being with her, spending hours doing the things she loved, such as collecting herbs, making flower garlands, and bathing in the crystalline, clear waters of the numerous cave pools of Taygetus. With her we felt free and fulfilled.

β′

As elegant as she was when moving among the trees and climbing the rocky sides of Taygetus, as electrifying as she was when talking of the movements of the leaves and the sounds of the water, so awkward and graceless she was when carrying out the palace chores. Icarius was carrying out all tasks, trying not to complain, with the hope she would learn to love her life in the palace. But her initial ferment was soon transformed into apathy.

I was five years old and Iphthimi seven. Evrotas was angry and had spread his waters over the valley. Everything was flooded, including the palace of Sparta. Everybody had moved to Amycles, where the palace was on slightly higher ground. As kids we were not aware of the danger and thought it was only a game. We were, as usual, playing in the yard of the palace. Most of the adults were busy containing the flood. None had slept the night before for fear the flood would reach the palace and drown us all. People had to be ready to move to higher ground if necessary. During daylight they were making canals and ditches to guide the water away from the palace. That was the third day of the flooding, and they had noticed the water was going back slowly, but they couldn't let their guard down.

We noticed everyone's agitation, but for us kids, playing had the first priority. Other kids seemed to be scared of the river, but Iphthimi and I were not perceiving any fear, probably due to our mother having taken us close to water so many times. So I went out of the yard thinking to find my mother, and I saw them working farther down the hill. I ran to them, and only then did I realize how angry the river was. It was not the usual crystal-clear water but all dark and brown and on its irate way to the sea, carrying the death of animals and trees and the destruction of the settlements around its banks. I felt betrayed by Grandpa Evrotas, as we were calling the river, and I wanted to find Mummy. I was crying and hadn't realized that I was too close to the brown mass when I felt the arm of my sister pulling me. "Come back," she shouted. And, like a dream, I remember the cries of my mother, who had seen the danger from far away. Everybody had seen what I was realizing only at that moment. The tree trunk hit us both, my sister and me, and a prolonged arm of the river grabbed us and took us with it. I embraced the trunk exactly where it had hit me, and I managed to keep my head above water. I saw Iphthimi fighting to keep herself aloft, and I murmured, "Dear Grandpa Evrotas, don't kill your grandchildren."

Exactly at this moment I managed to see Iphthimi standing on her feet with my father, who had already reached her, grabbed her, and taken her out of the water. I saw Mummy running after me, but then the river turned and I couldn't see anyone. All over was the angry dark-brown water, and the trunk was hitting on rocks and other things that were in the way. Every time the trunk went down, I swallowed water. Then the trunk entered a calmer part of the river, and it stopped. My feet touched the firm ground. I realized it was time for me to let go, but as I tried to escape, a piece of the bark broke off and remained in my palm. As I reached the land, I saw the trunk carried away again by the angry river.

I found fresh grass, sat there, and started calling Mum. I was so tired, and with my eyes full of tears, I realized that my mother was not around. I lay down and fell asleep still holding the bark.

In my dreams I saw my mother crying and my father looking for me. I was waving and crying, "Father I'm here," but he didn't seem to listen. When I woke up, dawn was breaking. It was a push from the beak of a duck that had woke me. I opened my eyes and saw the duck's eyes watching me. I sat and rubbed my eyes, and the duck was still there.

Other ducks started coming toward us. They were white with purple-green wings and a red stripe along the head starting from the beak and finishing at the white of the neck. They were tall with strong bodies and looked more like geese. My duck quacked and made a move as if to show me something. I turned and saw the eggs well hidden below the leaves. I don't know how the ducks had managed to save their eggs from the ravishing river. Their instinct had told them that spot would be spared from the catastrophe. My luck had driven me to this same spot of land, and I was blocking the way between them and their eggs.

I moved so that they could pass, and I saw them all go into the little caves made of leaves and sticks and sit over their eggs. They didn't seem to mind my presence, and I did not feel any fear.

I sat there watching them and talking to them for hours, and then I realized I was thirsty and hungry. I looked around, but there was hardly anything to eat, and there was no water either. The duck then did something I didn't expect: she freed one of her eggs and pushed it with her beak toward me. I knew the duck was sacrificing one of her little ducklings so that I could survive. I looked at her hesitantly but took the egg. She quacked approvingly, so I opened the egg from both sides as Mum had showed me and sacked it. When I felt better, I thought to go and find my parents, but I didn't know which way to go. The ducks quacked again as if to tell me to stay with them. This was what I did. I stayed with them, watching them and stroking them and telling them how I had arrived there and about how my sister had been saved and how my father was looking for me. They were talking to me, telling me about their travels to the south. Before dark another one of them gave me one of her eggs, and during night they slept around me to keep me warm.

Next day, the water of the river had retracted significantly. I heard lots of noise behind the bushes. It was as if a quarrel between ducks and swans had started. My ducks moved there, and I did the same. And then I saw it. The small pool was fed from one side by a source, and on the other side, some tens of meters was emptied by a creek flowing toward the river. I was next to a source of clear water so well hidden by the vegetation that I was not sure even my mother knew about its existence.

Despite the quarrel still going on, I ran toward the source and drank as Mother had showed me. As I was drinking, I realized that the reason for the quarrel was a loose egg. Both ducks and swans were claiming it. I went closer and looked at it. It was a different kind of egg, and instinctively I looked above me. There it was—the nest of the falcon; the egg had probably fallen from there. The soft grass of the ground had protected it from breaking.

I took it and realized all the birds were looking at me. I climbed the tree with the egg in my hand, and I managed to arrive at the nest. I put the egg in it carefully, and I noted the falcon mother watching me from a higher tree branch. The ducks and the swans that had been arguing before walked away to undertake their routine, as the issue had now been resolved.

The tree was full of little black berries, and I ate some. I was proud of myself and went to find my ducks again. They were washing their feathers in the lake, so I decided to have a bath with them. It was fun. We were playing, and when I got hungry, I got another egg as a present. That night was cool, and I could not sleep, so the ducks brought large leaves and fern branches to put on me, and they all slept around me, touching me with their warm plumage.

My father found me there after two days of running and searching the banks of the extended river. I was sleeping peacefully among the ducks, with all the empty eggshells around me. He understood immediately, and as he took me still asleep in his arms, he called me Penelope, which means little duckling of this special type of duck.

My mum cried from happiness when she saw me, and she stayed close to me until everything went back to normal. The river reentered its banks, and people went back to cultivate the fertilized land. I had forgotten everything and was happy playing again.

And then she was no more. Granny told me she had gone to find Grandpa and bring him back to her, and Daddy told me she had gone off to find her sisters in the woods and she would come back again. But she did not come back. Not after a day, not after a week, and not after a month. I was crying and asking for her all the time. My daddy was desperate, so one day he told me that Mother Earth had taken her and that she would never be back again. I didn't cry anymore after that, though something in me was certain I was to see her again. That certainty kept me quiet during the nights when I was missing her arms and her smell. I was not crying but thinking that she was happy and she would show me the way to her.

γ′

My father, Icarius, was the younger brother of Tyndareus. Both were the sons of Oebalus and Gorgophone. Hippocoon and Arete were their half siblings from Oebalus's first marriage with Bateia, also a nymph who deserted her family. When Bateia abandoned him, Oebalus took as his wife the widow of his cousin Perieres, king of Messini. So my grandma Gorgophone was the first known woman to have married twice. Apart from being brothers, Icarius and Tyndareus were also very good friends. They both suffered exile in Acarnania, imposed by their half brother Hippocoon, and they both came back when Hercules killed Hippocoon and reestablished Tyndareus and my father as kings.

During their time in Acarnania, Tyndareus married Leda, while my father took Polycaste as his wife. Polycaste died giving birth to her second son. My father had to leave his two boys behind when he left Akarnania to return to Sparta. Thus my mother was the second wife Icarius lost. He decided never to marry again.

When the two men came back to Sparta, they shared the responsibilities of ruling. My father was in charge of Sparta's production, trade, and finances. Tyndareus was in charge of the army, war, and the laws. When Tyndareus was going off with the army to protect the borders or to help any fellow king, my father was in charge of the whole kingdom. Moreover, they were both high priests and shared all religious ceremonies. They also shared the palaces. While Father took Amycles, the older palace, Tyndareus took the newer palace in Sparta, which Oebalus had started building before his death. Tyndareus extended it and decorated it. However, it always appeared a bit rough in comparison to the finesse of the palace in Amycles. The two kings were spending a lot of time together discussing and deciding the affairs of the state. They had only a few elder advisers. Mostly their cousins. People trusted that whatever their decision, it would be for the best of Lacedaemon.

My father, being in charge of production, knew every farmer by name. He knew what was produced in all corners of the kingdom, and he kept all tax books for each one. Each farmer and each trader had to pass some of his annual earnings to the palace, either in kind or in gold or silver. In this way the kings could keep the army fed and well equipped.

The river and the mountains, along with the Eurotas Valley, provided nourishment for the people. In the valley, farmers were planting crops, fruit trees, and vegetables. They had their little houses there, where they kept their equipment and slept during harvest, when work started with the first sunbeams and ended beyond dawn. Beyond the valley the terrain became hilly, and the herds of sheep and cows and pigs populated the slopes. Most of the villages were located there to avoid the river's flooding. The hilly region was best for olive trees, vines, and animal farming. Behind the hills were the mountain slopes with their black forests full of firs and oaks and creeks and streams flowing leisurely from the top, impatient to meet the river. Only wild animals lived in the mountains, countless deer and boars and the wolf and bear, who were better than man in hunting. There were glades where peasants brought their flocks to pasture. This landscape followed most of the river up to the gorges, where the river passed quickly and the terrain was rocky. After the gorges, it flowed free into the delta and the gulf.

Since the disappearance of my mother, our father was the only one left looking after us. Iphthimi, being older, responded well to the expectations of my father. So she became more conscientious and started taking up more responsibility. She was in charge of the palace and the people working in it and was slowly replacing my mother.

The growing process took me a little longer. I missed my mother. I could not yet control myself and was crying a lot when I thought of her. So Daddy decided to take me everywhere with him. He was a very busy man, since half of the responsibilities of the kingdom were on him. He was in charge of production and taxes, so he was often out to meet the farmers and checking on their needs. In the spring he would travel all over Lacedaemon to check on the condition of the land and talk to the people. That was his first estimate of the harvest. At the beginning of summer, he carried out a second check, and then he would go again if there were floods, storms, droughts, or any other disaster. People liked him because he showed comprehension. He didn't try to cheat or oppress them, and he made it clear he wouldn't accept it from their side. He was clear and transparent and always kept his promises, even if that would mean more work and effort. Throughout our travels we would stay in the houses of the people, often sleeping on hard mattresses and eating humble food. But that was all right for me as long as I was with my father.

One of my father's projects at the time was the expansion of Sparta's naval fleet. So we were often in Gythion, Sparta's seaport in the Gulf of Lacedaemon, to oversee activities. He wanted more boats for Sparta and the small shipyard could not keep up, so he was building a bigger one. He had to be there almost twice per week, since there were many decisions to be made.

This was how I discovered the sea and its magic. People of that time disliked the sea. It was a source of problems. Cities were usually built away from it to avoid pirates, looting, and storms. However, it was becoming more and more clear that days of traveling overland could be spared if one went by boat, so people started engaging more in sailing. The Cretans and Phoenicians were rich from trading their products by sailing everywhere with their mighty boats. The Greeks, with the guidance of Heracles, started making their first boats to cover their own needs. There was high demand for tin to make bronze and therefore weapons. Sparta had to build its own fleet if it was to reduce its dependence on Mycenae. My father felt strongly about it.

During his hours of discussing and working in the shipyard, I was playing on the beach. I had always a guard with me because Father was scared of sudden raids by thieves and looters. On the beach I would find beautiful shells and would put my legs in the water to cool myself on hot days. I loved the crystalline waters on calm, sunny days. I spent hours watching the reflection of the sunrays on the sand within the water and the little fish that were growing in the protected and warm, shallow waters.

At home he had to keep books, go hunting, look after his olive grove—he loved his olive grove—and train with his garrison. We had our own garrison, faithful to Icarius, that would follow him everywhere. He looked personally after the well-being of each single soldier, since he knew that they were there to protect him and us under all conditions, even against Uncle Tyndareus. His officers had lunch with us often, and they could even bring their families if they wished. I would listen carefully to what they were saying and to their arguments with my father. He never raised his voice, and through that, he was even more respected.

δ′

Icarius also traveled often to Sparta for the council of the elders and discussions with Uncle Tyndares. At the beginning, I was always with him, attached like an oyster on its rock. Uncle Tyndareus would laugh about the strange duo that was coming to see him, but my father had patience and love. During these meetings I met Helen, my cousin. Sometimes Uncle took her to his meetings. She was so white and beautiful that all stopped talking to watch her. It seemed that in her presence, Tyndareus achieved agreement swiftly.

I didn't have many friends, and I didn't want any during that period. Her strong looks put me off, and she noticed and didn't bother me in the beginning. After we had met and looked at each other several times, she came to talk to me. It was a rainy day, and the megaron was full of people from all Lacedaemon. Tyndareus had asked her to come, and she was playing her role brilliantly. She whispered the decision in the ear of Tyndareus, and he spelled it out loudly. None would dare to disagree with the daughter of Zeus. After that, she was free to go, and the discussion changed. She passed in front of me, stopped, and stretched her arm out. "Come; I want to show you my little animals," she said.

I turned and looked at my daddy, but he was busy with the discussions. I had to decide for myself, and I decided to go. She took me to her room and showed me her collection of clay animals. She had horses and cows and eagles and swans and bears and deer. She took one of her swans, one with open wings, and gave it to me. "Please have this as symbol of our friendship."

I nodded and took it. She had a magnetic power, and one could hardly oppose her. Then she showed me the places where she would hide and watch what the adults were doing. She had various posts all over the palace, which was huge in comparison to that of Amycles. When my father called me to go back, I was somehow unhappy to leave her.

After that, I was with Helen all the time when we went to Sparta. Helen was the first person I trusted besides my father after my mother left us. She was about a year older than I was. At times she seemed so irrational. She seemed guided by something beyond human comprehension, and of all the people in the palace, I was the only one who could see Helen's daemon, her guiding spirit. Not even her mother could do it.

This was how I started understanding my special talent. I could sense each person's secret motivations, passions, needs, and thoughts.

During this period we were invited to the big wedding of Thetis and Peleus. I don't remember much of this event except the endless days of playing with Helen and Philonoe, her younger sister. When Aunty Leda presented us to the bride, she told me that she was a nymph, just like my mother. I looked at her with respect. She was busy saluting the invitees. Her face was serious—I'd even say severe. Maybe she was not enjoying all this at all. I knew Mother wouldn't have done it.

I saw Daddy talking to the husband, and I immediately sneaked next to him. I pulled Peleus's robe, and as he looked down to me, I said, "You know that nymphs do not like home life. Bateia left my grandfather, and my mother left my daddy. It may happen also to you."

Daddy grabbed me and murmured that I should be quiet. A deathly silence fell over the room, with all looking at me. Aunt Leda looked at Thetis, but she grinned. "You have a point here, child," she said.

Peleus intervened. "Of course, my wife is free to return to the cold and troubled ocean whenever the palace gets too hot or too cozy for her. Now let's go on with our party."

Icarius felt a bit embarrassed. But I'm sure it was something he wanted to say himself but didn't dare, so he wasn't too severe with me. Indeed, some years later, we did hear that Thetis had abandoned Peleus for the cold and troubled ocean only a couple of years after the birth of their son Achilles.

The news of my cousin Philonoe's disease arrived. Philonoe was about a year younger than I was. She died after two days, and Father took us to Sparta for the funeral. We stayed a full week there. The palace was mourning the death of the little girl. But I was happy being with Helen, and Iphthimi was doing well with Clytemnestra, so my father decided to transfer us all to Sparta. I got the room of Philonoe, and Iphthimi got a room next to Timandra's, who was preparing for her wedding with the king of Arcadia and was going to live with him.

Icarius asked Aunt Leda if he could refresh the rooms, and Aunty, who was a very pragmatic person and had little interest in emotions and memories, agreed at once. So my room was painted with ducks playing on the water, making nests, and flying in the pink of the dawn sky over a blue lake. Iphthimi's room was painted with an olive grove, the insects and the birds eating the insects. Both were lovely.

At the same time, Leda asked Helen's nanny, Cyanea, to take care of me. Helen and I were becoming good friends, playing more and more together and sharing the same nanny. So I didn't need to follow my father everywhere. He felt relieved that he could leave me behind, and I could follow the learning program that all kids of the palace were following. Clytemnestra and Iphthimi were good friends, having less than a year's difference of age, and were doing many things together. They both had entered the club of Spartan virgins and had a lot to discuss about men, families, and children.

So for a while, we were all together—me, the youngest; Helen; Iphthimi; Clytemnestra; and Timandra, the oldest. We had a fine time whenever we met all together to play and talk next to the river, under the huge oak trees at the shrine of Artemis. We would also ride horses around Sparta's plains and toward the lakes in the north. My fears and self-pity disappeared, and with the new friendships and things to do and learn, I started forgetting my mother and the strange ways of the nymphs. A new era had started for me.

ε′

As my sister arrived at the age of ten, my father introduced her to the art of bookkeeping. She seemed to like the new responsibility, and anyway, we both wanted to make our father proud of us. She learned quickly to keep records of what was produced from which land parcel and what was traded in or out of Sparta. She noted that the way my father was keeping the records was very difficult for her, so she wrote the numbers and the names of the people on white cloth of very fine thread with black rock coming from Arcadia. The black rock was carbon that Tyndareus had brought back from his various missions. So my father had only to write the annual sums on the terracotta plates and store them in a type of library in the megaron.

Iphthimi's responsibility allowed my father to work more in the olive grove. His olive grove was one of the best in Lacedaemon. His trees looked beautiful, since he had brought pruning to perfection, and almost every summer the branches were bent by the weight of the olives. Every autumn he produced the best olive oil in the region, and he was putting it in huge jars stored in the cellar of the palace. We were using it for making soap, for massaging our bodies, as a medicine for a number of diseases, and, of course, as nourishment raw or cooked. Every year he made a selection of olive oils that he then would trade all over the Mediterranean. With his new ships, he started going to various places to taste the olive oil produced there. He was saying that before Athena went to Athens to give the olive tree, she passed by Lacedaemon. She planted her trees there, and then she took a branch and went to offer it to the Athenians.

I loved to follow him to the groves. It was a fantastic walk colored by the blue of the sky, the silver of the olive tree leaves, and the bright green of the grass. The smells of the olive groves in spring, with the wildflowers, freshly cut grass, and wetted earth, accompanied me all my life. During harvest, we kids had specific jobs, such as going to the spring to bring water and collecting the olives that had fallen outside the length of cloth unfolded under the tree for collecting them. When we were fed up working, we would organize races, lie on the grass under the sun, or count ants or grasshoppers, which could be found there in millions.

While my father was becoming a trade man, I was following the lessons and training with my cousins and sister. We had different teachers; some were just older Spartans who had been around for a while, and some were foreigners who had established themselves in Sparta's royal palace. For a while, Gorgophone, our grandmother, was teaching us the sacred songs, but she soon become too old for that, and a priestess of Artemis came twice per week to teach us. The songs were beautiful, and her voice was magical. They talked about the deeds of Artemis, our virgin goddess of the forests, and they included many details of our tradition and history. I particularly liked the stories of the nymphs of the region, such as Kleokhareia, Taygete, and Bateia, and there was even a sentence dedicated to my mother. These women had contributed to making Sparta what it was, and singing about their lives was one way to remember them.

More than singing existing songs, the priestess was teaching us how to compose music in order to remember our stories. Since writing was not widespread in those days, music was a way to remember history and stories. And both were intertwined, and no one knew exactly what were facts and what was fiction. Anyway, playing the lyre or flute along with narrating the story helped us remember the story. So the priestesses were training us in both these instruments. Often the drums joined in to emphasize some parts of the story, but these were rare occasions.

We had a Sidonian teacher whom we all liked and who was teaching us his language and Egyptian. His name was Paltibaal. He was a former trader, and my father had hidden him and helped him escape his lenders. So he was with us six months per year and with his family back in Sidon the other six. He was always happy and had great stories of pirates to tell us, and we couldn't wait to go to his lessons.

We had an Athenian who taught us Greek dialects and logic. The Athenian was a former priest of Athena who had taken up as his duty teaching children "her wisdom," as he would say. His name was Euarestos. He had been in Thebes for some years and then in Argos, and now he was in Sparta. "Understanding how to use your own mind"—that was his purpose. He taught us to separate emotions from thinking and make decisions based on facts. It was strange, this lesson, because I couldn't exactly understand how to do this separation. I would go to war because I loved my homeland and not because of some mental considerations. "Yes, Penelope," he said, "but you can win the battle only if you think strategically, position your soldiers cleverly, and exploit the weaknesses of the enemy. If you throw them into the battle based on love, chances are they will lose." It made sense, what he was saying, and I must say his lessons used practical examples of life, and I liked it a lot. My cousin Pollux and I were his best students. Cousin Castor had only fighting in mind, and Helen didn't need to reason in the first place. Her strength was exploiting the emotions her looks caused. Clytemnestra was in continuous war with him about the traditions, and Timandra was mostly absent, preparing her wedding. Indeed, we celebrated her wedding some months later. She then left, and it would be many years before I would see her again.

For his intelligence, love of logic, and beautiful manners, I started developing an interest in Pollux. He was the same age as Helen, but he seemed older and more mature. His body was developing quickly. He was becoming strong and beautiful. His appeal was as strong as Helen's, and at the same time, he was witty and playful. He didn't like the palace jobs and was always around with his brother, Castor, training and hunting and talking about future adventures. Helen adored him and was spending time with him. But I was very shy, and I was trying to avoid crossing eyes with him because his beauty was making me become red, and I was losing my words. Whenever I got an opportunity to watch him without his knowing, I did. Yes, Pollux was my first love, but no one ever knew. Not even Helen.

Something more than a year had passed when Helen was abducted by Theseus. Tyndareus, Castor, and Pollux prepared the army of Sparta to go and get her back. My father's aims to build a bigger fleet had paid off. Now the ships were needed. "I think you just go in front of the palace and ask her to come with you," I said one day after listening to the troop positioning and various strategies for attack.

"I don't think he'll want to give her back," Castor replied quickly.

"How can he keep someone who wants to go? I am sure Helen knows how to be nasty," I was fast to say.

"Helen is a worthy trophy, even if nasty," Pollux patiently said.

"If nasty, even more so," added Castor with a smirk.

I continued my line of thought, mainly worried about Pollux getting hurt. "But why fight? Just steal her back and bring her here."

"Well, little cousin, in order to steal her, we need to enter the palace. He will hardly invite us in, so we have to enter by force. This means fighting our way through," Pollux said, seemingly willing to discuss this with me.

"And if you get in by the back door? The one used by the servants. You know, the one they use to take the laundry and the rubbish in and out."

"Yes, we considered this, but it is difficult to know where it would be."

"You just follow the girls with the biggest baskets of laundry from the river," I said. "The biggest baskets are always the royal ones."

The brothers looked at each other with interest. Then Pollux tried again to get me to understand. "You are right with that, Paps." That was what he used to call me to avoid the long name. "But we can hardly leave the old fart unpunished. After all, he offended Helen and made us look like hopeless fools."

I was surprised to hear how personally the men were taking the kidnapping of a woman. It was not an issue for Helen and Theseus, but it was for Castor, Pollux, and Theseus. This was how they saw it.

Some days later, Uncle Tyndareus sacrificed his big bull to Zeus, imploring him for support and guidance for the expedition to retrieve Helen. The army of Sparta and Tegea, Timandra's new home, departed for Gythion, where there was support also from Pylos and Messina awaiting. My father was proud to have prepared the big Spartan ships and dressed them in deep-red colors. They sailed off to Athens, and we all waited for news of war with Athens.

ς'

Without Helen and Pollux, the palace seemed empty. I tried to spend more time with Clytemnestra and Iphthimi, but it was not the same. Besides, they both seemed to condemn Helen for her own abduction. "She was so provocative," Iphthimi told me.

"No, she was not," I replied angrily. "She is just beautiful. It's not her fault she is beautiful."

"But the way she treats men and dresses...the best thing would be for her to immediately marry Theseus," Clytemnestra said.

"Helen is just herself. It is men who have to respect her, not she who has to change," I said. I slammed the door as I left, running and crying. I was angry. I couldn't understand why Helen should change herself and reduce her freedom so as not to provoke.

I went to find Aunt Leda in the temple of Zeus, where she spent most of her time.

"Don't worry! They will bring her back," she said when she saw me there, guessing why I was searching for her.

"But Aunty, Clytemnestra is so strange. She thinks—"

"That Helen carries the blame. I know."

I nodded and started crying.

"Don't worry, little girl. Clytemnestra never managed to forgive Helen for being beautiful and me for giving birth to her. Maybe sometime." She took me in her arms. "She'll be back soon. I know it," she said with a calm voice. Aunt Leda always made me feel good, although I got to see her very little.

The subject of freedom kept me thinking the next few days. I asked Paltibaal in one of the lessons, "What is freedom, Paltibaal?"

"I guess it is the ability to do and say what you want without fear of being punished. But I believe freedom is very different from kingdom to kingdom."

"Are we free here in Sparta?"

"Tyndareus and Icarius are good rulers, and men are happy. But other kings have other manners."

"And what about women, Paltibaal? Are they free?"

"Men or women—if one has debts, he is never free," he said, avoiding an answer. "Come, little girl. We need to do your Egyptian now."

Then I asked the logic teacher, "What is freedom? Is there a god in charge of it?"

"No one is free, girl. Not even Zeus in front of the duties that keep Olympus and the fates of the mortals running."

"But Zeus never gets punished, whatever he does or says," I said, based on what I had learned from Paltibaal.

"We mortals live too short to judge what may happen to Zeus. Don't forget that Zeus deposed Cronos, his father, who had ruled from the beginning of time but became mad, reckless, and violent, making all suffer." Obviously he thought duty was before freedom. But who assigned the duties? "Each god has his or her duties, and he or she cannot ignore them or start doing the job of another. That wouldn't be good, because each one was born with special qualities, and their duties were assigned according to those."

"And what about humans?" I asked with expectation.

"The only difference between gods and humans is that gods are free to choose their duties, and they carry them out in complete freedom, since they do not interfere in one another's jobs. Mortals are often assigned their duties without being asked, and often they are hampered when they try to accomplish them, by the interests or deeds of others."

That night, lying on my bed, I was thinking. "Freedom means choosing your duties, scope of life, and mission. That's freedom. And a society that allows each to accomplish her duties and achieve her mission—that's a free society." Did I know anybody free, then? Icarius hadn't chosen his duties; they had been assigned to him. Only Aunt Leda had chosen the job she was doing, helping and healing the people who were going to her. She had managed to keep her activity going despite the complaints of Tyndareus and the criticism of other noble ladies who usually did nothing and despite the allegations of other priests not as gifted as her. No one in Sparta had ever prohibited her from doing her job, but did Sparta qualify as a free society? Many questions and few answers.

"No need to think so much, little lady," Cyanea would tell me every time she noticed I was busy thinking. "The questions are too big for your little head."

"Oh, Cyanea, why are things so complicated?"

"Things are easier than you imagine. Sleep now, and you'll see how all questions will have vanished by tomorrow." She smiled at me with caring. Cyanea was amazing. She had beautiful blue eyes, and she claimed that she had seen the goddess Athena with all her armor in front of her. She said she looked the goddess in the eyes, and that was how she had gotten her blue eyes.

"But why did she appear to you?" I asked.

"Because I asked for help when a soldier was about to rape me in front of her temple," she said. "And she granted it to me. She helped. The man was hit by lightning, completely carbonized in front of my eyes. Then I raised my eyes, and I saw her. She was a sight! Absolutely intimidating! Fully armored, tall to the sky, and shiny like the sun. Her blond hair was covered by her helmet, and she was holding a spear. I managed neither to move nor speak. Since then no man has come close to me, and I have never wished for the sweet caresses of love. She has made me one of hers," she told me.

"What does it mean—one of hers?" I asked.

"Well, this goddess, similar to our lady Artemis, doesn't wish to be touched by men. She is a warrior of her own making, a keen strategist who takes her path and makes wise decisions and victorious moves. She lives in virginity, and love is manipulative. No one can manipulate wisdom. Those whom she favors are usually victorious, but she wants them to work hard. She will never grant any of her thoughts to lazy or cowardly people. She wants you to take risks, to try hard, and to dare to go beyond your limits, no matter what it takes. Then she helps. See our hero Heracles. She was always by his side in all his endeavors. And still she couldn't help him with Deianeira's poisonous chiton. Because love was involved."

"So love excludes wisdom?" I asked.

"In a way, yes, my dear. So make sure you choose your husband wisely and not under the influence of love. Then you'll live with him for many years."

"Why are you here, Cyanea?" I asked.

"She asked me to," she replied. "'Go to Tyndareus's palace,' she told me. 'You are needed there.' When I arrived here, Tyndareus told me that he didn't need anybody and told me to try another palace. But that same evening, Helen's nanny disappeared. She went off to join the nymphs, and Tyndareus looked for me. So I joined the palace. When Leda met me, she knew immediately that I was sent by the gods, and she fully entrusted me with Helen and Pollux, kids of Zeus. Now I also have you to look after. And you know what? I am really pleased."

I hugged her. I liked the way she was talking to me. She was making me feel different. She was instilling in me the voice of logic. I felt free for the first time, since my mind was growing, my thinking capabilities were evolving, and I was becoming ever more independent. Cyanea taught me little by little to trust my own thinking, a capability that always followed me after that.

When my cousins brought Helen back, I was extremely happy but at the same time scared of her change. All other girls wanted to know how it was with Theseus in bed, but I wished only to go out riding with her or go to the river for a swim. The funny thing was that she wanted just that herself, so next the morning, we departed. Tyndareus had forbidden her to go anywhere without her guards, so three soldiers were following us everywhere.

We sat at the riverbank and put our feet in the cold water of the river. "That's good," she said. "You know, Penelope, they thought I talked to the gods!"

"And…do you?" I asked, thinking that it wouldn't be surprising.

"I had never considered that before, but maybe I do talk," she said.

"Lucky you!" I said, and we didn't say anything more.

Helen had brought back a real queen for nanny—the mother of Theseus, Aethra, another very important lady who had attracted the love of none less than the god of the seas, Poseidon. So Tyndareus's palace was full of important ladies during that period—Leda, who had attracted Zeus; Aethra, who had attracted Poseidon; and Cyanea, who had been chosen by Athena. Leda was fully occupied by her service to the community, Aethra was fully occupied by Helen, and Cyanea by me.

My relationship with Helen was maturing. The adventure with Theseus had changed her. She didn't like to talk much about it, and I was about the only girl who was not interested in boys. So we spent a lot of time together. We were learning together, and we were going riding together. Helen was also used to training herself, so she introduced me to her training regimen. We were running, jumping, and exercising with the bow. Tyndareus didn't allow Helen to go out of the palace unguarded, for fear she would be kidnapped again. So we were doing everything in the palace, and mostly we were using Castor and Pollux's gym in the north part of the yard.

ζ'

Clytemnestra was to be married soon, and the palace was all excited. People and presents started arriving, and the palace was surrounded by the tents of the suitors. Tyndareus and my father were doing everything to keep the strangers content and cherished, as was the custom. Leda was spending more time in the palace now, since Clytemnestra's wedding was an important event and her guidance was needed. It was clear to everybody that Clytemnestra had to be the queen of Mycenae, since the city was now in the hands of the sons of Pelops. She was a representative of Perseus's family, and balance required one of us to be in Mycenae. Perseus was the founder of Mycenae, and the presence of his descendants in the royal house was sacred.

But, of course, as was tradition, men had to bid for a royal woman. And so it was. Thyestes was bidding a lot for his son Tantalus. During the time of Clytemnestra's suitors, we stayed inside mostly, which was pretty boring. From our windows we could observe the suitors and what they were doing. We usually had lunch before them, and then we were off in our rooms. During the evening banquets, our presence was requested only for a short time, and then again back to our rooms.

With so many kings and warriors around, it was scary. Clytemnestra was happy so many had come for her, and she was spending a lot of time talking to Iphthimi about those guys. I couldn't understand why Clytemnestra was so excited about them. I couldn't imagine what she could find of interest among those rough faces with so much hair and the horrible smell that accompanied them.

"Do you really have to go with one of them?" I asked her. "Isn't it better here, despite all the boring history and language lessons?"

"Cousin, a woman has other things to think about. Besides, I'll soon be a queen. I can't waste my time any longer in Sparta."

"Other palaces are not necessarily better than this one," said Helen, who had already had the experience of Athens.

We were closely watching the men and their exhibitions from the upper floor, and I noticed the young Menelaus, brother of Agamemnon, following Helen with his eyes wherever she was. I found him disturbing, and I told Helen so. But she only laughed and said that I shouldn't worry and that she knew how to deal with him. The house had been liberated only after Tyndareus had announced the lucky Tantalus, son of Thiestes, to be the winner, upon which decision Agamemnon left the palace offended and speaking out threats against Mycenae and the new couple. Tyndareus and my father were really worried about the behavior of the young Atreides, but that didn't stop them from celebrating the wedding in Mycenae and making rich sacrifices for the protection of the couple. Since Mycenae was the most important city of the Achaeans, representatives from all the city kingdoms arrived, so I met some of my cousins from Messene, Argos, Thebes, and other places.

It was some months after the wedding when I received my first menstruation, and thus the time arrived to enter Sparta's virgin club. Helen stayed by me, explaining the ritual and what I had to go through. She was a real friend and in that much better than Iphthimi, my sister, who was too busy with the work that Icarius was entrusting to her.

Tyndareus was busy resolving the conflict between Agamemnon and Thyestes, which led to the death of Tantalus and the establishment of Agamemnon as king of Mycenae. Icarius was running the country now with the help of ever-present Leda, and Iphthimi was in charge of all the accounting, which she was doing with sacred dedication.

I was enjoying riding with Helen, always under the careful attention of guards, and we were training and having endless discussions about our concerns for the future. Helen enjoyed sharing her thoughts with the priestesses of the shrine, but I was more reserved. I didn't like much to talk about my feelings and emotions. I was trying to seek a rational answer and hated the blather about Mother Earth, the goddesses, and Artemis herself. Mother Earth had deprived me of Mother, and Artemis had taken away Philonoe. What was so good about them, then? I was little trustful of the advice the priestesses were giving about successful marriage, and I enjoyed more watching how Aunt Leda was managing her husband. She had achieved maximum freedom and high respect by all, not through her prudery but through her dedication to her cause and faith in her abilities and wit.

Two years later, the whole circus of suitors restarted—this time for Helen. All these men, big names at that time, came to Sparta just for Helen. I was somehow envious of Helen's capability to attract all these people, but at the same time, I could understand her embarrassment, and I was thankful the whole circus was not happening to me. The irrationality of men in bidding for a woman hit me this time stronger than Clytemnestra's bidding. Their proudness and vanity were revolting, and I only wanted to be as far away as possible. So I was spending most of my time in Amyclaes with Cyanea. Icarius agreed that I could stay there for the months of the bidding, only under the watchful eye of my nanny, which was all right with me. I spent most of the time playing music and singing hymns. I always found this activity very liberating, and often I composed my own music, which I played at ceremonies.

The loom was not my first priority, and a lot of my dowry was prepared by Cyanea. When I was singing, the gardeners and service people would stop their activity to listen to me. Very few of the suitors were losing their way toward the Amyclaes Palace, so I was left mostly in peace to enjoy my walks or rides on the slopes of Taygetus. It reminded me of my time with Mother. I was often standing to watch the same ant hole or the same creek turn, or to listen to the same sounds that she had drawn our attention to when we were little. Now that I was becoming older, I was missing my mother more and more.

It was during one of these walks that I felt a presence watching me. I didn't give it any attention, but I hurried back to my horse and left quickly for fear that it might have been a bear or wolf. The next day I took my bow with me, which made me feel a bit more secure. When I arrived at the creek and stopped to drink, I again noticed the presence, and I turned to watch. Nothing advanced from the bushes, and I turned my horse behind the rocks. I took the horse into a little cave that I knew was there, and silently I climbed up the rock, holding my bow. There she was. A woman, not short, not tall, with black hair and almost naked, was coming my way. I moved back, took the horse, and disappeared in the forest.

The next day, I decided to go again. Now I took the lyre with me, and when I arrived at the creek, I rode off and started playing the hymn of the nymphs. She came out of hiding and stared at me from afar. I stopped singing and stood, but when I took one step farther, she turned and disappeared.

I was shaking. This woman had skin painted like bark, but she was beautiful and, I thought, very similar to me. I took the horse and ran straight to Sparta. Entering the yard, I almost fell on a young man with a clever face and a short, carefully trimmed beard. He said something like "My pleasure, madam" as he helped me up. But I ignored him completely and ran to see Icarius. The man followed me, but I entered the room that Icarius was using as his office and closed the door. I was shaking from anger when I shouted, "Tell me the truth about my mother. Is she alive? Tell me now."

My father was reduced within two seconds like a man struck by lightning. "Did you meet her?" he asked with a trembling voice.

"Is she alive?" I repeated. "What happened to her? Why did you let me think she was dead?"

"She abandoned us, Penelope. She was not up to her duties," he murmured.

"I don't believe you," I shouted. "She wouldn't have left us if you'd loved her as much as she loved us."

He looked pale. "I loved her, but she kept on with her mountain life. She was the reason for your almost drowning."

"You lie!" I shouted back. "I hate you."

And I left. I didn't notice that the man I had bumped on before was following me as I rode away. I went back to the creek and starting calling my mum, crying. Then two strong hands were holding me by the arms. "Whatever it is, it doesn't deserve the tears of such beautiful eyes," he said.

I looked back and saw the same young man. I made a move to liberate myself, and he noticed I didn't like to be touched. "You know nothing of me," I said. "And anyway, it is my cousin's bidding, not mine. Go back and leave me alone."

"I'd never leave a young woman alone in the mountains in such a condition," he said. "I'll go back if you allow me to take you home."

I realized he was right, and besides, I wanted to get rid of him as quickly as possible, so I agreed to be escorted up to the palace in Amyclaes. I didn't speak at all on the way, and I ignored all his attempts to start up a discussion. I left my horse in the yard to the horsekeeper, and I asked him to show the stranger the way back to Sparta. I went to my bed and fell asleep almost immediately, as a kind of physical response to the psychological stress I had been exposed to.

I woke up from the sweet caresses of my sister. I opened my eyes, and I was happy to see her.

"Did you see her?" she murmured.

"Yes, I did. She is as beautiful as ever," I said, and I started sobbing. "Why did you tell me she was dead? I have been so unhappy all my life. Thinking I had no mother. But she is alive. Why did she have to leave us?"

"She is different…a nymph," she replied.

"But why did Daddy always lie to me? And you. Did you know it?"

"Yes," replied Iphthimi. "I was there when they argued. I was listening behind the door. He accused her of being irresponsible. Of always exposing us to risks. She said she wanted us to be strong and know the secrets of nature. He said that nature is wild and rough, and she should teach us how to be good housekeepers. She said that she would prefer to leave if she was making him unhappy. And he reaffirmed that this was probably the right thing to do.

"I was crying behind the door because I didn't want her to leave, and I knew even Daddy didn't want her to leave. I knew Daddy wanted her to change, but I also knew she couldn't change. When she came to put me to bed, I asked her not to leave us. She said that whatever happened, she would always guard us. She said that whenever I looked at a tree, I would be looking at her. Whenever I listened to the water of the creek, it would be her voice. Whenever I lay down on the warm grass of the summer, it would be her hug." She was talking without watching me, and now she turned her eyes to me. "You were little, Penelope. You wouldn't understand, so Daddy told you she was dead and made me swear I'd never tell you."

"How could he? I hate him," I said with sobs. "How could he deprive us of Mother?"

"Maybe it was better for us to grow up with Aunt Leda and our cousins. Mother would have been different. She wouldn't fit with anybody."

I liberated myself and stood up.

Cyanea entered to bring me breakfast. "Don't be bitter, my child. Your mother loves you. That is why she appeared to you. Otherwise, she wouldn't have done it. Nymphs know how to hide in the woods. They are seen only when they wish so."

"Oh, Cyanea! Since I saw her, I only think of her. How could she ever abandon us? Is the love of nature, then, so much bigger than what she felt for her own children? I will never abandon my family, no matter what it costs me. Never."

"You don't need to decide this now. The gods play strange games with mortals. The paths of your life are made for you only. And no one else can follow them—not your mother, not your father. Only you."

"I'll go back. I'll go to find her and ask her to come back."

55

"It is useless, child. She will not. If she appeared to you, it is because she has a message or because she has a worry. She will let you know."

I ate and dressed quickly and rushed out. Iphthimi asked if she could tell Father that I was all right. I told her to tell him that he was a traitor and I would never talk to him again. I knew, though, that Iphthimi wouldn't tell him, and that was good.

As I ran in the yard toward the stable, I again saw the young man. I had forgotten about him, and I wondered why he was back.

"My lady, I have been waiting for you the whole morning. I was really worried about bringing you back in this condition. Do you feel any better today?" he said as he walked with me into the stable.

"I'm well, my lord. Thank you for your attention, but you had better go back with the others. There is no feast and entertainment for you in Amyclaes," I said caustically.

He noticed my irony but didn't seem irritated. "This is entirely clear to me," he said. "I didn't come to Lacedaemon for celebrating—rather, to see the beauty of its women."

"Well, for sure you are missing even that, since the most beautiful is sitting in Sparta right now."

"There are many types of beauty, and they are definitely not all to be found with one woman."

I looked at him incredulously, and I prodded the horse, which started galloping to the exit.

"At least allow me to come with you and be your guard today," he shouted.

"You cannot come where I go," I said.

I rode fast because I wanted only to see my mother again. I entered the woods, left the horse, and moved carefully among the branches of the trees. I had so many things to tell her. She had to come back. We had to make up for all the time we had been separated. I rode to the creek. I waited, but nothing. I started moving up the creek, but the path was too narrow for the horse. So I left it and moved on my own.

"Mother!" I called. "Mother, please, I want to see you. I want to talk to you." And I went farther up the mountain, in places I had never been before.

Suddenly, three men appeared. They were dirty and horrible and started coming closer. "What does the little princess have to do in the woods?" they asked and started touching my hair and my clothes.

"Haven't you heard that little girls should not go around unguarded?" said one.

"Does your father know you are here? I bet he will be very worried if you don't go back this evening," the next one said.

Now they had circled me and were ogling me. I was in a trap, and I knew it could go badly. I found courage and said, "The guards are behind me. They will kill you all if you dare to touch me. Who are you, anyway?"

They grinned. "No one is behind you, my lady. We have been following you for some time now," one of them said, and he took off my coat.

"Don't you dare. I am a princess."

"Yes, we know who you are, and for sure the king will pay a lot to have you back. This is all we want."

I realized I had to escape, so I pushed the one who looked the weakest, and I tried to run, but the others managed to get me and throw me down. They were both over me now, and I was scared.

Then I heard his voice. I was never so happy to hear his voice. "Let her go if you want to live," he shouted.

They pulled me up and used me as a shield. "Not sure who you are, but you surely don't want to harm the princess. Go to Icarius and tell him that we want her weight in gold in a ship in Gythion. We shall let her go once we have sailed out of the gulf."

"You have nothing to order me, you thief. I am Odysseus, son of Laertes and future king of Ithaka. Let this lady go."

They were starting to move backward when I heard the sound of an arrow. The man who was holding me gasped and fell. Odysseus—at least now I knew his name—immediately killed another one with an arrow, and before I realized it, he shot a second arrow to the last one, directly in his throat.

I fell on the trunk of a tree and looked in the direction the first arrow had come from. "Mother," I murmured.

Odysseus had come close to me and was putting my cloak back on my shoulders. "Wait here," he told me. "Do you know how to use the bow?"

I nodded.

"Then use it. I have to check around for others of the sort."

I nodded again. He disappeared into the woods. I pulled the arrow out of the body of one of the dead men. It was a silver arrow, very strong, with blue and white feathers at the end. I knew that only the followers of Artemis had such arrows. I looked around but didn't see her, though I knew she was there.

After a while, Odysseus reappeared. "There is another one dead higher up the river. Probably he was guarding the path. You seem to have friends in this forest."

I was still in shock and was gasping for air. "Yes. My mother. She is a nymph. She was looking after me."

"Well! I'm glad she did. It would have been difficult to deal with all of them on my own."

"Thank you for following me, Odysseus," I managed to say.

"My pleasure, Penelope," he said with a smile. "Let's leave this place."

η′

Odysseus! He was not tall and not short. Not handsome and not ugly. Not famous and not an unknown. Not a vicious fighter and not a coward. He was just perfect…always in measure and always just him. And something more—he had the sparkling eyes of a god and an eternal smile. He kept his hair to his shoulders and the beard well trimmed. His eyes were brown and quick, and it was obvious that he was fully aware of any circumstance he was in.

On the way back to Amyclaes, he told me about the funny events of Sparta, where so many kings and nobles were bidding for Helen. We laughed about how the tall and broad-shouldered Ajax would lose his words and become red when Helen crossed the yard. Or how Leonteus claimed to know everything about how to satisfy a woman in bed due to his grandpa's double life, first as a woman and later as a man. He told me that Machaon had been checking on Aunt Leda's healing practices, making her mad, and that Eumelus had helplessly fallen in love with Iphthimi. The latter gave me shivers, and then I realized suddenly that not only might Helen soon be married and gone, but my sister as well. I didn't let him understand it, though. He made me laugh, and I appreciated his efforts to make me feel at ease.

As we arrived at the palace, he told me that he would inform Icarius about what had happened in the mountains and that he would come to visit me again as soon as possible.

"You know that if you talk, Icarius will start a big expedition to clean the mountains of the thieves," I said, "which would mean I won't be able to stay in Amyclaes on my own any longer."

"I know," he replied. "But this is serious. It is risky for you to stay here if the mountains are not cleared. It's better if you go to Sparta with me now."

"No, I'm safe with Cyanea and the guards," I said and dismounted the horse. "Thank you, and good night." I turned toward Cyanea, who had arrived with a cloak.

"My lady, you should not stay out so late on your own," she said, giving Odysseus examining looks.

"She had a difficult day. Give her a warm bath, and double the guards," he told her. "There are thieves in the mountains." He immediately turned the horse and dashed toward Sparta.

Cyanea did as she was told. Once in the hot water, I started crying.

"Calm down, my child," said Cyanea, "and tell me everything. But let me first go and get you a calming tea to warm your heart and restore your mind."

She left, and I was wondering why was I feeling so sad. Was it that I had missed another opportunity to meet my mother, that I was embarrassed to have put myself in such danger, or simply that I was for the first time in my life realizing that love does exist and it was not the imagination of young girls like Iphthimi and Clytemnestra? I hit the water with both arms, as if it were to blame for the silly thoughts, but the water splashed back in my face, as if to slap me for my cheekiness. So I started crying even more.

Cyanea came in with the tea, which she gave me, and I started drinking in small sips. She then started singing one of her lullabies and massaging my head and neck. I told her slowly and calmly everything that had happened in the forest. But I kept for myself the feelings that overwhelmed me about young Odysseus with the hope that they would bring me a warm dream of him during my sleep.

Icarius woke me up at dawn. I felt his warm hand on my forehead, as if he were checking me for temperature. "Collect your things. You are going to Sparta," he said. "Aunt Leda is waiting for you. It was stupid of me to allow you to stay here on your own."

I was just too weak and unwilling to have any discussion with him. Cyanea had already collected most of my stuff. She made sure I got my warm clothes on, since the morning was chilly, and we went out the main door to the yard.

I was struck by the sight. A full army had gathered there. All Achaean leaders were going to follow Icarius on a thief hunt in the mountains. All in their shiny armor, they were keen to show their capabilities in pursuing and tracking the prey.

I swallowed awkwardly. "Mother has the situation under control," I told my father as he helped me get in the chariot.

"This is what she thinks. But I will not allow these beasts to harm any of us or any of her kind," he said quietly.

I swallowed a sob, and my eyes crossed those of Odysseus. He smiled, and I turned my face toward Sparta, which was awaiting me.

Upon my arrival, Aunt Leda and the girls were waiting for me. She immediately took me in her arms and consoled me. "Poor thing; you had to go through that. What a terrible experience."

"She cried during the whole trip," said Cyanea. "I couldn't manage to calm her down."

"Don't worry. I'll do it," Aunt Leda said. She took me straight to her room and gave me some salts to smell. "Tell me what bothers you," she said when I felt better.

"Oh, Auntie, he doesn't want the thieves. It is for my mother that he goes there. He wants to get her back with the excuse of the thieves. I hate him." And I started sobbing again.

But Leda was not shaken by my claims. "Penelope," she said, "you are now all grown up, and you'll be married soon. Although I understand your anger at growing up without your mother, I think you are accusing your father unfairly. He would never oblige her to come back. He also suffered from her absence. Believe me. I spent many hours with him, trying to comfort him for her loss during the first years. He fully respected her position and need for freedom. He is not going to take her back. He only wants the mountains to be cleared. We have had some complaints about the thieves recently. It was not only your case."

"But Aunty, did you see the army that he has taken with him? If they find the nymphs, they will kill them all," I said, terrified.

"You silly little girl. These men can never find the nymphs. The nymphs can become one with the earth, the leaves of the trees, and the pebbles of the creeks. An army of a thousand men may pass next to them, and they will still be unable to detect them. The nymphs are found only if they wish so. They are very clever, and your mother is one of the cleverest of all," she said.

I looked at her hopefully. Her face was beautiful but rarely sweet. But as she talked about my mother, she became candid.

"Have you met her?" I asked.

"Your mother is the cleverest of us. She is the most beautiful, though she managed to escape the attention of Zeus. She knew how to hide, how to use each corner of the forest to her benefit. All animals are her friends. They protect her and help her. She knows all the healing plants, and she has often given me advice about what to use."

"Have you seen her since she left us?" I asked hopefully.

"Yes. I know how to find her if I need her. But only if she wants me to."

"Can you arrange for me to see her, Auntie? Please, Auntie! I need to see her. I need to talk to her," I begged.

"I'll see what I can do, but first we have to finish with this circus here. Be a good girl and have patience. It will require a great deal of my force."

I nodded. She stroked my hair and sent me to find Helen to do our homework.

After two days my father and the suitors came back with five bandits they had managed to capture in the mountains. Apparently, their leaders had been killed as they were defending themselves, and the rest surrendered. The next morning, they arranged for their trial. They had to go into the service of Apollo and live as servants of the temple or die. If they tried to escape, they would die.

All visitors seemed satisfied with their achievements that day, and Tyndareus organized a big feast the same evening. We—Helen, Iphthimi, and me—were thrilled. We made ourselves really beautiful for our appearance. Helen and Iphthimi were stunned at my sudden interest in makeup and nice dresses. I tried to be cool and not to give them room for questions. But I was really happy when Helen offered me one of her fine dresses for the evening. My cousin was wise and a good friend.

Suddenly Aethra came in and told us to stay in our rooms. An argument between Alcmaeon and Polypoetes had evolved into fighting among more of the suitors. Indeed, we could hear plates smashing and clamor from the megaron and the yard. We went toward the door to look outside, but Cyanea and Aethra stopped us. "No, my ladies, you stay here. Let men boast. This is what they know how to do best anyway. You stay here," said Cyanea.

We were disappointed, but I was the first to recover. "Let us put on our pajamas and play pillow wars."

We started laughing and did exactly that. Later, when all was quiet and everybody was asleep, I could see the warm light of the moon entering my room, and the stars were so calling that I decided to go to the veranda and take a bit of fresh air. Outside, I wondered what the megaron would look like, so I started moving toward it carefully.

Then I heard people talking in low voices. I moved closer. They were beneath me, but I couldn't see them. I took the stairs of the servants, and I approached the megaron from a different angle, and then I saw them. It was Tyndareus and Odysseus. In the moonlight, Odysseus seemed different. More enigmatic and obscure, more dangerous.

"I have the solution to your problem," he said to Tyndareus. Tyndareus seemed very concerned, and he looked at Odysseus with hope. "I'll tell you my plan, but only if you help me."

"Let me know the plan. If it is feasible, I'll help you. If not, I'll never use your plan, and I am not bound by you."

"That's fair," said Odysseus, "and I trust your word. The plan is the following. Tomorrow morning, you gather them all in a sacred place, and you make them swear in front of the statue of Zeus and in the waters of Styx that they will all abide with the selected, and they will punish whoever will go against the decision or do anything to harm the couple."

Tyndareus thought for a bit, and then he said, "That's possible. I'm sure Leda will think of something; we have to tell her."

He tried to go out to call her, but Odysseus took him by the hand and said, "First my condition." He put his arm around the shoulder of Tyndareus and started moving toward the other end of the megaron, so I couldn't hear him anymore. I saw Tyndareus give him his hand, and they separated.

I ran up the stairs like a hunted deer, and I closed the door, gasping for air. I threw myself on the bed, and the warm

69

moonlight embraced my body. I looked at the moon. It was a golden disc—not silver, as usual—and it seemed to smile at me. I thought, "Are you his friend or mine, or maybe of both?"

The next day, Iphthimi woke me up. "Aunt Leda made them swear to not fight whomever Helen chooses," she told me happily.

The sun blinded me, and I thought of the discrete light of the moon. The discussion of yesterday evening came to my mind. "So," I said, "and whom is she going to choose?"

"Get dressed, and we'll go to find her. She is at the shrine." She was already throwing clothes at me.

I got dressed quickly, still wondering why the sun was so forceful, so intolerant of secrets and undercover arrangements.

Helen was not in the best mood. Tyndareus had announced his preference for Menelaus. She liked Menelaus, but her free spirit was rebelling against the command. We were so happy for her, and we were all chatting happily on the way back with all the guards behind us.

Icarius asked to see Iphthimi in the little megaron. When she came back, she was glowing and absentminded. "Father asked me if I want to marry Eumelus," she said.

I looked away. I hated the happiness in her voice. I knew she wanted Eumelus and he wanted her, much more than he wanted Helen. I was angry with both of them, Iphthimi and Helen, and at the same time envious because they both had someone who wanted them.

During the evening feast, Tyndareus and Icarius announced the selections. Menelaus for Helen, and Eumelus for Iphthimi. Everybody cheered. I once again wondered about the sanity of men. Just the day before, they had been ready to kill each other. An oath, a silly little oath to nobody and nothing, but a suspicion of afterlife had changed them inside out. There was no logic to that, but maybe people were not logical after all. Maybe it was just me who was expecting too much, or maybe it was Helen's beauty that was driving them all irrational.

I turned and looked at her. She was radiant like a goddess. Menelaus was melting away next to her. I couldn't see what these two had in common. I looked at Iphthimi and Eumelus. They were just happy, and their smiling and relaxed faces made me feel warm. I knew this would be a happy couple. I looked at Leda, who was caring for her guests, and then at Father. His face was bothered. He didn't smile at me. He seemed darkened. I searched for the face of Odysseus, and he as well seemed darkened.

Icarius stood up again and said, as if reading my thoughts, "I announce the bidding for my last daughter and the last princess of the house of Sparta to take place exactly two years from now."

"In two years?" I thought, and I looked again at Odysseus. He seemed hit by lightning. Everybody cheered again, as if they had a renewed chance to enter the Elysium.

θ′

The next day, they started departing. I thought of young Odysseus. It was clear that he had invented the oath, but what had he asked Tyndareus as exchange? It was disturbing that he was leaving also; on the other hand, I couldn't wait to go with Aunt Leda into the mountains to meet my mother.

Helen's and Iphthimi's weddings would be celebrated in a week's time—enough time for Clytemnestra and Timandra to join the family for the event. The palace was getting dressed in beautiful colors with a myriad of flowers. Both girls were excited and were finishing their dresses and trying out makeup.

They were hardly paying any attention to me, so I was spending more time doing Iphthimi's work, keeping the books of the palace. I was in the small room where all accounting was carried out. Father was busy with the salutations and the exchange of presents with those departing. I was trying to concentrate on the numbers when I saw a shadow entering. The sun was falling in my eyes, and I didn't recognize him immediately.

"So here is where you hide when you are not running around in the mountains," he said.

It was him. I felt warm inside and happy. "I'm helping Daddy with the finances," I whispered.

"So you know writing as well!" he said with admiration. "Maybe you could give me a hand back in Ithaka."

I shuddered. "Ithaka?" I said.

He came close. "I'll come back in two years for you," he said, looking at me straight in the eyes.

I realized he was determined, and I felt paralyzed. It was as if I was overwhelmed by a force that I hadn't realized existed. I stood up and said, with trembling voice, "Be prepared, because no oath will help you then. You'll have to compete and win."

His smile disappeared for a moment, but he recovered quickly. "You are worth every competition." He turned to leave, but he stopped and looked back. "In two years, then."

So I had a promise, a dedication by someone I hardly knew. He seemed convinced, but my rationalism prohibited any kind of excitement. I knew two years was a long time, and I knew that relationships between men and women were a fluid question. My parents' marriage had been like that. My need to find Mother was becoming greater every day. I needed to ask her about Father. Why had she left him? Why had she left me?

Aunt Leda was a wise woman, and despite all the work she did in the temple and in the palace, she came into my room early in the morning the day before the wedding. "Wake up," she said. "Now it's the time."

"Why now?" I asked. "What do you mean?"

"Wear something dark," she said. "And leave your hair free. Take a dress to offer."

We departed with the horses. Two guards and a maid with the offerings were following. She rode fast, and we were soon into the woods. It was all uphill until we found the stream. The horses couldn't go any farther, so we left them with the guards and moved on our own.

"Shouldn't the guards follow us, Aunty?"

"They cannot go where we are heading," she said.

"But how are we going to let them know if we are in danger?"

"From now on, we are not in danger. They follow us."

I looked around. "Follow us? Who…" I couldn't see anything.

Aunty seemed to know what she was doing, so I didn't dare to ask any questions. It didn't take long, and we were in front of a cave. Aunty stopped and murmured some prayers. We left our coats and shoes at the entrance, and we entered. It was dark and scary, and Aunt Leda continued murmuring and asking the goddess to grant her permission.

A light appeared at some edge. My feet were cold, and they hurt from the stony ground. The little light became more intense, and the ground was becoming softer. We stooped to go through a narrow and low passage. I felt a heat coming from inside the earth. My feet were suddenly warm, and I thought I saw daylight at the other end of the tunnel.

We entered a beautiful room illuminated with torches. In the middle, a pool of yellowish clear water was steaming. Stalactites and stalagmites were all around. The torches had been placed in a way to illuminate the strangest formations of the stalactites. On the walls, there were scenes of nymphs hunting and playing, with Artemis in the middle. A wooden statue of the goddess stood in the middle of the pool.

"Come closer, my sister," said a voice from deeper in the cave.

Leda smiled and moved with determination. I couldn't help thinking that I knew the place. I had been there before. Then we saw them. There were about thirty of them, all young and beautiful, dressed the same. A short white chiton, a golden belt, and a blue ribbon around the head at the forehead to keep the hair in place.

One of them moved forward. "It is so nice to see you again, Periboia," said Aunt Leda.

"What! That was my mother!" I thought, and I felt my limbs weakening. She didn't seem much older than I was.

"I see you all the time, my dear," she said, "and you know I am very pleased with you. You are a worthy messenger and bearer of the word of the goddess."

"I am happy you are pleased, my sister. Men are getting more and more difficult nowadays. It is not easy to lead them to the right way. They think they can command by power, these fools."

Periboia turned and looked at me with satisfaction. "My daughter," she said, and then she stopped. "I'm pleased with your progress," she said as if worried not to show any feelings. She took my hands. She was standing in front of me. So beautiful and desirable, so tall and magical, so happy and fulfilled. In front of that sight, all questions that I had come prepared to ask vanished.

I wondered if I had ever meant anything to her. "Mother, why did you abandon Iphthimi and me?" I managed to murmur.

"I never abandoned you, my child. The physical world is not the only world that exists. I have always been in you, in your thoughts. When you think rationally, it's me. When you are satisfied with your deeds, it's me. When you help others, it's me. We women, we never abandon our children. We only abandon our physical appearance in order to increase our possibilities to support you."

"But Mother, you made Father suffer—"

"Your father suffered from his own decisions and choices. He should not blame the goddess for that. Come, my daughter. I'll show you my comrades. We are women dedicated to serving the people wherever they need us. We live in the woods to be protected from men who want to subdue us. We are free here from any thought bad or good, any desire, any pride and display. We are pure, and that's why we are more able to help."

Leda said, "You know that tomorrow Helen will wed Menelaus."

"Yes, I know—another display of power. Helen's destiny will soon unfold. She will bring huge challenges to the rule of man."

"How can I protect her, Periboia?" asked Leda.

"She is not the one who needs protection. It is, rather, all Achaeans who will suffer. But you have to lead her when her time comes."

Leda nodded.

"Mother, in two years I'll also marry," I said, worried. "I don't want to, Mother. I want to come here with you."

She said, "Your path is not here. You have also an important role to play. You belong with the women. You'll show them how to recognize their capabilities and live according to them. You'll be the first to show the way."

"Don't make me go back, Mother," I asked with a sob.

She took me into the pool. I could feel the warm water on my feet. I felt the need to go fully into the water to warm me up. She led me in front of the statue and took water that was coming out of the mouth of the goddess and washed my head. "You are forever blessed by the goddess. You'll face difficulties insurmountable for others that you'll overcome with ease. You'll lead, withstand, and forgive. In the name of the huntress Artemis and of the wisdom goddess Metis." She took me back out of the pool. I didn't feel cold or warm. I only felt well, calm, and illuminated.

Leda embraced my mother and then took my hand. "Come. We have to leave now," she said.

We started moving toward the small opening, and already, when I looked back, the nymphs had disappeared, the lighting was fading, my dress was drying quickly, and my feet again felt the stony ground. When we went out and the sunlight blinded us, I wondered again, What was the sun trying to avoid? Was it the lies, or maybe the truth? "Aunt," I asked, "was this real or only a dream?"

"My dear, it was more real than everything you see under the sunlight. Come, my sweet. Let's hurry back, since the dangers are many when we are not there."

ι'

Iphthimi had left, and Helen had a lot to do with her new responsibilities as a wife. Although busy, she stayed close to me. We were still spending many hours together, to my satisfaction. Her need for freedom had increased with the marriage. So she was doing everything to feel free. Sometimes I even had the feeling that she was annoyed by the presence of Menelaus, although she never talked bad about him.

She had her little girl when the suitors came back for me. There were not as many, and the presents were not as beautiful. The palace was also much quieter now. I was prepared. I had organized the games together with Father—archery, riding, wrestling, and spear throwing. The five best also had to compete in running. First, fast running, and then long-distance running. The idea was to send them all back home empty handed. I wanted to stay as close to Mother as possible, and Father wanted to keep me there.

Odysseus came as promised, and he looked good—much better than two years ago. His body was sculpted by training, his black beard was well trimmed, and his hair was long and rich. I was satisfied, but at the same time, I hated him for that. He brought me a beautiful belt as a present. It was made of leather and gold. On the gold there was Artemis with the bow and her sacred deer. It closed with two rubies also engraved with the head of the deer. He knelt in front of me, and with two arms raised, he offered me the belt. "I asked the best goldsmith to prepare a present befitting a proud princess. This is what he came up with. I hope it meets with your approval," he said, keeping his eyes low.

It was by far the most beautiful present, and he knew it. He behaved impeccably the whole time and was a good friend to everybody. The five who remained for the last bit of the competition were Patroclus, Antilochus, Diomedes, Ajax the Lesser, and him. Ajax came in last in speed running, so he retired. The last contest was a run from Gythion to Sparta. It measured around forty kilometers of partly rough terrain. Odysseus came in first.

During the feast in the evening, Icarius announced Odysseus as the winner of the games and as his successor as king of Amycles, through his marriage with me. But Odysseus replied quickly that his intention was not to stay in Amycles but to go back to Ithaka with his new wife and title as prince. Icarius's face darkened. He had been hoping that announcing him king would keep him there, just like Menelaus when he married Helen. But Odysseus had different plans.

Icarius stood up again and said, "Then, sir, you have to win an additional contest. You'll have to face me in a running contest up to the top of Taygetus and back. If you win you may take Penelope with you, if she agrees to follow you."

That was a surprise move. I felt the eyes of Odysseus on me, but I didn't dare to look back. Helen held my hand. I didn't agree with the methods of my father. I knew he wanted to keep me, since I was entitled to become queen. But I also sympathized with Odysseus. After all, he had always been nice and had helped me when I needed help most.

After two days, the race started. We all rode to Amycles, and they entered the forest there. Odysseus was disadvantaged, since he didn't know the paths on the top and back, but this was not a race that he should win. It would take the full day up and the next day down. Anything could happen during the run. They could slip and get killed on some of Taygetus's numerous cliffs. They could encounter thieves or just a nasty wild boar.

Cyanea and I stayed overnight in the palace while the other suitors went back to Sparta with Tyndareus, and the next day after lunch, we made our way to the arrival point.

Some of the guards had followed them the day before up to a certain point. Others had stayed in various parts of the path and were shooting arrows every time one of the two passed. The news was that yesterday Odysseus had had difficulty following Icarius. On the way back, Icarius was flying. He passed the first guard post and then the second, but Odysseus had still not appeared at the second.

The third post was the last one, and Icarius passed it. It was not long from there, and he would soon appear from among the trees. Instead we saw Odysseus running like mad. He was coming toward us with all the power of his legs. He threw himself on the guards, asking if Icarius had beaten him. It was then when we saw my father also coming from among the trees. As he saw Odysseus waiting for him, he slowed and looked with suspicion. He hadn't expected that, and neither had I. Icarius passed in front of Odysseus without asking anything. He came to me and whispered, "Don't go with him. He doesn't deserve you."

I was angry, and I turned my horse and rode all the way back to Sparta without looking back. I went to Aunt Leda and told her everything, including my anger over Father's defeat.

84

"There is only one explanation," she said. "Your mother showed him the fast way from the caves. Only through the caves could he do it faster."

"But why didn't Daddy take the cave way?" I asked.

"The cave way is sacred to the nymphs, and only they know how to find their way in the caves. Any of us would be lost forever in the dark paths and steep corridors," she said, and our eyes locked.

Was it possible, then? My mother had helped him? She wanted me to go with him? Why? She didn't want to see me again? I was having these thoughts walking from the temple to the palace. Then I saw him coming the opposite way. I got agitated. I didn't want to reveal my feelings. I liked him, but I wouldn't follow him. Or maybe I would follow him, but I didn't love him. His pace became slower, the same as mine. As we arrived at talking distance, we stopped.

"I won, but not because of my own effort. I was helped, but I wouldn't know how to tell you by whom," he said.

I nodded and lowered my eyes.

"You don't need to marry me if you think I don't deserve it," he said.

"They helped you, so you must deserve it," I said. "I'll marry you as soon as it is allowed." I lowered my eyes and moved forward.

He stepped aside to let me go by. He seemed puzzled, but he was probably scared that any word from him could change my mind.

That same evening, Icarius accepted his defeat and announced our wedding in a week's time. "Penelope has until the day before to cancel the wedding if she wishes so." He looked at me, hoping I would confirm what he was saying.

But I didn't say anything. Helen, who was sitting next to me, took my hand and squashed it. "He's not so bad after all. Ugly as Menelaus…at least more intelligent, but…not more than you cousin," she whispered in my ear and laughed. I couldn't help but smile.

Everything happened as planned. Two days after the wedding, the mules and carts were loaded with my dowry and my things. I was ready to follow Odysseus to a new place and a new life. My heart was aching at leaving Sparta and Lacedaemon. I was part of this place; I was a child of it, similar to its trees and its rivers. Why did I have to go? What was life about to teach me? Why was I needed in Ithaka? What did my mother know that I didn't? Why with this man? The man who bound all Achaeans with the oath? "Oh, Mother and all the nymphs and the goddesses that lead you…I hope you know what you're doing."

I kissed Helen and Leda goodbye. I kissed Uncle Tyndareus.

"I shall come to see you, child," he said. "Believe me, I shall come to take you back if he doesn't treat you right." He said the last bit looking into my eyes as if delivering a promise.

Castor and Pollux added, as they were kissing me, "Anyway, he won't have a long life if he dares to mistreat you, Paps."

"He won't," I said, feeling bad for the mistrust expressed by my relatives. Daddy was not there. I knew he wouldn't come to say goodbye.

Odysseus helped me onto the cart, where I took my place next to him. Behind us were the carts with Cyanea and Odysseus's guards. We departed. When we arrived at Gythion, the soldiers started loading the carts onto the ships. I stayed on land until everything was finished because Cyanea was scared to go on the ship.

I was trying to calm her down when a hand grabbed me. I turned. My father looked at me with eyes full of sorrow. His face was tired, and he suddenly looked much older. His hair seemed to have become white overnight, and his straight and strong body seemed like that of an old, broken man. "Please don't go," he whispered.

Odysseus had noticed and was coming toward us. "Cyanea, come. I'll help you," he shouted, but mostly for me to hear him.

"Oh boy, what a terrible thing to do at my age," I heard her saying.

I took his arm and pushed it down. "Come to see me whenever you want," I told him, and I pulled my veil in front of my face.

"At least take Dolius with you. He is my best servant, and he has known you since you were a baby. He will look after you as if he were me." He showed me Dolius, who was waiting a bit farther behind, holding his baggage.

I nodded, and Dolius went on board. I breathed deeply and went up the ladder to the ship. Odysseus raised me by my waist, saying "Welcome on board, my lady" as he let me down again.

The soldiers pulled the ladder, and the ship started moving. I felt one chapter of my life was closing and a new one was opening.

ια'

In those days, traveling by sea was much faster than by land. The ships, though, were narrow, and there was not much room for privacy. Fresh water was rationed. Walks on deck were allowed only at certain hours so as not to interfere with the rowers. So Odysseus had planned a number of stops to refill our barrels with fresh water and to allow for walks and stretching.

I wanted to visit my cousins in Messene, since they hadn't managed to come to my wedding, and Odysseus agreed. "Of course, the king and I have some open issues anyway," he said.

We entered the Gulf of Messina late afternoon. Gorgophone, my grandmother, talked often of Messene and the basket mountain Ithomi. She was first married to Perieres, king of Messina, and when he died, she married Oebalus and moved to Sparta. With Perieres she had two sons, Leucippus and Aphareus. Leucippus first had twin daughters, Phoebe and Hilaira, and later a third daughter, Arsinoe, was the most beautiful of all. Aphareus had two sons, Lynceus and Idas, who followed Castor and Pollux on the expedition with Heracles. All these cousins of mine, whom I knew existed but had met only occasionally and only some of them, were now so close.

My heart fluttered as I looked at the bay. The sea was calm, and there was a thin, inviting light over the mountains. As the boat got closer to the beach, the color of the sea changed to bright blue and greenish and in the end transparent, as I could see the sandy bottom with its glittering sunray plays.

We disembarked, and a coast guard of five men came to talk to Odysseus, who told them who we were and why we were visiting the place. Immediately after that, a rider launched himself toward the mountains. We took the carts out of the ships and loaded some of the presents that we had gotten from Sparta, but we were not allowed to move before approval had come back from the palace. Indeed, the same rider came back after some time to ask us to follow him to the palace.

The road was wide, and there was a lot of movement. The region was fertile from the waters of Pamisos River. It was getting dark, and we could see the farmers going back home from their fields and traders moving their goods in the villages and soldiers patrolling for security. It was a much different setting from Gythion, which was more rocky and isolated.

We started ascending toward the basket mountain, and the views of the Gulf of Messene were breathtaking. We passed through some small villages mainly of shepherds and some beautiful water fountains. I thought of the nymphs. Here the mountains were not as steep and dangerous as Taygetus, so the nymphs had a tough time staying hidden. We entered the basin from the Laconian gate, and we could only distinguish the city wall. The city was sitting right in middle of that natural basket created by the mountains, as if someone had placed his eggs there. The guards had lit their torches, but the road was well paved, so we could easily follow. When we got close, we could distinguish the lights of the palace torches. Entering the small city, we saw the temples and shrines—that of Demeter; of Zeus, which Queen Messene herself had built; and Artemis. Next to the marketplace, there was a small marketplace and a small theater.

Lynceus came to greet us. "Welcome, Cousin and honorable Odysseus, lord of Ithaka" he said. "Allow us to host you in our city for as long as you wish. You'll find all you need here, and, more than everything, you'll be allowed to participate in the Andania mysteries, due to start in a week's time."

Odysseus said, "We are honored by your hospitality. This place looks as if it were made by the hands of the gods—so nice and protected. I'm glad that my wife has asked to meet this part of her family. Otherwise, I would have never had the opportunity to see it."

Lynceus smiled and moved his horse along the road. Arriving at the palace, we realized it was extended but very simple. The very few frescos on the walls mainly depicted Demeter looking for her daughter Persephone. Servants unloaded the carts, and Odysseus offered the presents.

"Come, cousin. Arsinoe is waiting for you," Lynceus said after accepting the offers, and we made our way toward the temples.

We found Arsinoe dressed as a priestess among some people. She was healing, similar to Leda back in Sparta. She waved when she saw us and came close. "Thanks, Lynceus," she said. "You can go now."

I tried to get close to greet her, but she made a sign. "Let's go back to the palace," she said. I knew from Leda that priestesses when working with the sick didn't want to be touched by the healthy for fear they would spread the disease.

Back at the palace, she sent for someone to call for her sisters, Thebe and Hilaira, who were in the grove preparing the mysteries. "We start in a week's time, and it goes on for another two weeks. There is a lot to do, and we all work until late in the evening."

We were both very happy to meet each other. I started telling her the news from Sparta and the greetings from everybody. She showed us our rooms and let us get washed. Dinner would be served soon, and we would have more time to talk with each other.

The servants lit the fireplace in our room, and it was the first time that Odysseus and I had been on firm land since our wedding. We were not sure what to do. The servants washed our hands and feet and left the room. We watched each other silently for some time. His lips were full of desire, and I felt a need to kiss them, but I didn't dare. I was scared by my feelings. I was terrified by my own urges. We were sitting on either side of the bed looking at each other's eyes as if trying to decipher each other's thoughts. He put his hand on my arm and slowly stroked my shoulder, neck, and hair. We were moving closer to each other when someone knocked on our door to announce that dinner was served.

We entered the megaron. All my cousins were gathered now. We greeted each one separately. Lynceus and Idas had a great similarity to Castor and Pollux. All four of them had fought together in the past and knew one another well. The girls were merry and cute. Arsinoe was, however, the undisputable boss of the place. She was bright and fast thinking, and sometimes I felt Odysseus's surprise at her spirit. I felt challenged but not jealous. In fact, I was curious to see how far she could lead him with her wit.

It was a simple meal consisting mainly of bread, wine, and cooked vegetables. There were also some fruits and honey. They explained that this was the fasting period for the mysteries, and no animal killing was allowed in the whole region. The fasting was the week before the mysteries and included the complete refusal of any animal products, so even milk was ruled out. We followed the custom without any complaint.

Back in our room, our minds were confused. We still hadn't consummated our wedding. We were trying to understand how to do it. On the other hand, we were experiencing a new place and new customs, and these upcoming mysteries were making everything even more weird. The girls had made an effort to make a wedding bed, and Odysseus told me stories from his travels. I listened carefully, hoping to understand better the man I had married.

We lay next to each other, still dressed, and he pulled my head onto his shoulder, gently stroking my cheek. I followed the move, and I was also willing when he kissed my lips, my face, and my neck. His hands were quick to undress us both. He put his lips on my nipples, and a sweet feeling of love overwhelmed me. His lips continued to my belly and then to my vulva. He looked at me as if to assure himself that I was comfortable. He directed his kissing back to toward my face and then tried to penetrate me, and for some reason I felt uncomfortable, as if this were not part of the agreement, as if he were trying to cheat me.

I told him to wait, not to rush me, but he was unstoppable. He started loving me, but I was feeling only pain and discomfort. It didn't last long. He kissed me tenderly on the lips again and asked if he could continue the story the following day. I nodded, and he put back on his nightgown and just turned to sleep. I stood up and went to wash myself. When I was back in bed, he was sleeping deeply.

I didn't know what to think. Was that love? Should I be happy or sad? Was that what all of us were expecting with such eagerness? He was so peacefully asleep and in complete repose. Should I love him more or less, or maybe try to escape?

But no, there was no way back for me. I turned to the opposite side of the bed and thought that I should give us more time before judging. And with this comforting thought, I fell asleep.

The next day, Thebe and Hilaira took us to the grove. It was a half-day walk on a beautiful path among the hills and lush vegetation. We passed a bridge that apparently Heracles had helped to build, and we descended toward a valley. It was the greenest place I had ever seen. Hilaira explained that this was one of the places where Pan would come to get a rest. It was full of springs and beautiful trees. It was called Andania, and Queen Messene many years ago had introduced the mysteries of Demeter, similar to those in Eleusis. In fact, Adania was the second-most important festival to Demeter and her daughter Persephone, after the Eleusenian Mysteries. People had already started gathering from all around the region.

We entered the grove and understood what she meant. It was beautiful. The smell of the trees—cypress, pines, and sycamores—and moist earth was all over. There was a sweet scent from incense burning outside the tents. Water was flowing here and there from little springs, but the most beautiful place was the spring of Hagnes, where everybody was gathering. The water was sacred and none could take it except the priests, but all were welcome to sit around and meditate. It was enough to close the eyes and be transferred to another dimension. The sound of the water flowing calmly and freely and birds chirping happily even during the heat of midday; the incense burning; and a soft, warm wind embracing the body as if to steal it from its soul. I understood why the mysteries were celebrated in there. It was peaceful and beautiful.

We stayed in the tent that was set for the palace. We were asked to honor the place, and that meant abstinence from all carnal pleasures. Somehow this period helped me overcome the first not-so-nice love experience. He was falling more and more in love, and I was gaining time. The mysteries were an important experience for all those who had done them, and we couldn't wait to experience them.

People were gathering daily. They were making tents in the place allocated to them by the priests. Male priests were responsible for organization and keeping order. No one could contaminate the grove, leave rubbish, or destroy anything. There was no speaking or laughing loud, so as not to disturb the wildlife. No one could kill any animals of the grove, even scorpions, or take any branch of the trees even if it was on the ground. However, people could eat the fruits of the trees or collect herbs and greens to eat right there during the mysteries but by no means take them away. There was no showing off with expensive clothes or jewelry. We each had on a simple white chiton.

The temples were arranged surrounding a big area, next to the spring of Hagnes, in which we spent most of the day. On the first day, all the initiates, several hundred, were sitting around, and in the middle of the place, the priests were calling Demeter and her daughter Persephone to stand by the ceremony and illuminate the initiates and guide them in their travel in the underworld, soon to follow.

In this gathering I met Iole. She was sitting next to me. She asked me if I was the wife of Odysseus, grandchild of Autolycus, and I replied positively. Then she fell on her knees in front of Odysseus, asking him to lead her to his grandfather.

"But he is already dead," Odysseus replied.

"I came here to find relief in this world by finding the dead who caused my life to be so miserable," she said. "Many years ago, cattle from the big herds of my father, Eurytus, were stolen, and he was quick to blame Heracles for that. Heracles denied it and asked my father to withdraw the accusations, but my father refused and insulted him even more, saying that not only was he a thief, but a liar as well. Heracles killed all of Eurytus's sons and took me as his concubine for revenge. However, he never touched me, and he even promised me to set me free.

"But his wife, Deianeira, was very jealous of me. She couldn't harm me because Heracles was protecting me, but she asked the centaur Nessus, who hated Heracles for the death of all centaurs, to help her win him back. He gave her this cloak and told her to cover him with it while sleeping, and he would go back to her.

"Oh! What terrible cries filled the night air that night. The cloak was poisoned, and Heracles had terrible pains. Pains that lasted for days. His beautiful body started turning black, and the skin was coming off. He was soon covered with terrible wounds, and pus and blood were coming out of some of them. I tried to help him as I could, but the poison was entering deeper into his skin every day. Any other mortal man would have died after some hours, but his torture lasted for days, and he would probably still be here today if Philoctetes hadn't helped him die.

"Since his death, Deianeira, this horrible woman who never felt pity for him or for me, has held me slave, saying that I was the reason for his death."

She looked at Odysseus with imploring eyes. "I need to oblige my father and ask Heracles for exoneration, but this will only happen if Autolycus admits his wrongdoing. Then I'll be free and I can leave the house of Heracles and his horrible wife," she said with expectation.

Odysseus felt awkward. He lowered his head and said, "You are not the only one who has suffered from the atrocities of my grandfather. But I'm not sure I can help you."

I felt an immense pity for Iole. I couldn't understand why this woman had to go through so much distress for an old affair of stolen cattle. She looked so desperate and exhausted, and I prompted Odysseus to promise her that he'd do all possible to help her through their way in the underworld. He didn't want to contradict me, so he told her to stay close to him in the underworld, and she agreed.

It was a warm August, and we didn't feel much hunger during the ceremonies. We could fill our bellies with the delicious water of the springs, which had some body-cleansing function. Afterward, each spelled out the oath. The oath that we shall never disclose the details of, not even when dead. The next days were very intense. We looked for our lost dreams for our dead relatives in the realm of Hades and in the depths of Tartarus. It was a spiritual travel in an unknown world. The shadows of the dead scared us, and their cries drove us crazy. Darkness filled our souls, and cold paralyzed our limbs. Some were crying, some were hollering, some were cursing their miserable lives, and some wanted to take their lives for all time.

But then we all found what we were looking for. We met our dead part, and we accepted it back; we became one with it. We took it back to life, and we were happy about it. Similar to how Demeter had gotten back her daughter from the underworld, our joy made us blossom like Demeter's joy at seeing her daughter again when almighty Zeus brought her back from Hades and made the trees blossom and the soil green again. Our minds relaxed, our fears and grief subsided. It was a wonderful feeling of fulfillment of meaning and happiness. At a single blow, our lives on earth made sense, and we knew nothing could go wrong because the gods were on our side. We sacrificed a hecatomb, which kept us all fed in abundance for two days. During the festivities we exchanged presents with each other, similar to how Demeter and Persephone did when they met again.

It was then that Iole, daughter of Eurytus and granddaughter of Apollo, gave us the bow of her father. The beautiful bow was very tall and was made from a very tough bone instead of wood. Apollo himself had given Eurytus the bow, which had followed him everywhere until he died. Iole had found what she was looking for in her way through the underworld, and she gave us the bow as a sign of gratitude for the support of Odysseus. "May the bow find its target when you most need it," she said as she handed it to Odysseus. I gave her one of my rings as a sign of friendship, and I told her that she could earn a lot of money if she were to sell it.

ιβ'

Upon our return to Messene, and when we found a bit of privacy, I thanked Odysseus for helping Iole and asked him what he was looking for in the underworld. His face darkened. I felt his hesitation to entrust me with his deepest thoughts, but in the end he decided to do so. "Some years ago, at the age of sixteen, I went to visit my grandfather Autolycus on Mount Parnassus. I was an innocent boy, growing up as a single kid in the palace of Ithaka. My father, Laertes, and his father, Acrisius, were simple and straightforward people who never lied or cheated anybody. Their word was trusted by all lords in the region, and although they had never been kings, they were and still are respected and reliable.

"Autolycus, my grandfather from my mother's side, was exactly the opposite. A man of trickery. He was cheeky and deceitful even to his best friends. Whenever someone showed him sympathy or generosity, he paid that person with dishonesty and deception. He could never be caught, since he was the son of Hermes, but people hated him forever.

"I was just like my father when I entered my grandfather's house on Mount Parnassus. He immediately tried his tricks on me, making things disappear in front of my eyes and asking me to steal the property of some of his sons so that he could laugh his head off when he saw me failing or becoming ridiculous. I was highly frustrated, and I wanted to go back home.

"He agreed to send me back, but first he organized this big hunt in which I had to participate. I was happy, because, after all, I could show my capabilities as a hunter, so I agreed. Mount Parnassus is of such a beauty that the muses rightly made it their home. The sounds of the spring water and the singing of the birds accompanied by the rustle of the leaves when the wind delicately touches them are magical.

"It was at such a moment that I lowered my attention and my spear to listen more carefully, and a boar appeared in front of me. It was huge, and I knew I had not enough time to shoot with the bow. The boar charged, and I knew the only thing that could save me was my spear if I could manage to hit him. I knew I had to let him come as close as possible. When the time came, I leaned to the side and shot, and I hit exactly where I wanted—in the heart. But he was strong, and he still caught my leg before he fell dead. I lost consciousness.

"When I woke up, it was a week after the incident. I had fought for my life with a high fever and unthinkable pain. My grandfather was always next to me, sure to capture my soul from Hermes's hands if he would come to claim it. I could hear his singing, my grandfather's singing, as he was exorcising the bad spirits. Whenever I opened my eyes, I could see his worried face, and he was singing even louder. He had a wonderful voice, since the muses themselves had taught him to sing. His song was in a language incomprehensible to me, but it made me feel light as a feather. It made me fly around and see all the beauty of earth from the eyes of an eagle. After a week it looked as if I would recover. He was happy. In fact, I had never seen a happier person than him when he realized I was out of danger.

"But I was not the same person anymore. It was as if the little naïve Odysseus had died from the boar and a different Odysseus, much more similar to Autolycus, had taken his place. I had never accepted the death of young Odysseus until I met him in the underworld."

His story gave me the chills. I knew he was persistent, and I had discovered he was also profound. "I don't think you are deceitful," I said. "You fought for me as much as you could."

He looked at me deep in the eyes. "I didn't win with my powers only. The nymphs helped me."

"But if the nymphs like you, they must have a reason," I said.

I saw his eyes sparkling before his lips touched mine. We kissed and undressed quickly. I felt his warm body on me, and it smelled nice. Empowered from my endorsement, he kissed me tenderly on the lips and on the cheeks. With his hand he touched my breasts, and he took my nipple in his fingers. I don't know why a discomfort filled me. As if someone had entered my room without my permission. I wanted to give permission to him because I liked him and he was my husband, after all, but I was not there yet.

I turned to free myself, and he got the message. He stayed quiet, though, and he limited himself to stroking my back.

"So, what were you looking for in the underworld?" he asked in an attempt to take my attention away from the act of love.

"My grandmother Gorgophone," I said. "She died when I was small. My grandfather Oebalus always claimed she was the best wife ever, and she knew how to make a man happy. She could have told me how to become a better wife for you…" I stopped and looked at him apologetically. "I would need her advice now."

"Oh, Penelope," he said. "I cannot imagine a better wife for me, my love. You are all I want. Your free spirit, your independence, your unconventional thinking and positive attitude. I love it. You are the only one who can contrast Autolycus in me. If you cannot do it, I don't think anyone can do it."

Still another time he had managed to capture me. I threw myself in his arms now, and suddenly I was convinced. He had obtained the license to enter the room. I gave myself to him, and it was wonderful. We became husband and wife that night and all other nights of our stay in Messene, although by the light of the day, I couldn't help but think that in the end, maybe it was Autolycus's cunning that had defeated Penelope's ingenuity.

During our stay in Messene, Arsinoe took me to the shrine of Neda, another nymph of Messene and one of the most famous. We went to offer libations to the nymphs that had helped Rhea, the titan goddess, mother of the gods, to give birth and save Zeus from the avidity of her husband, Cronos. During the long, dusty ride, I confessed to her my original distrust toward Odysseus and that we had become husband and wife only after our participation in the mysteries.

"This is typical of the mysteries," she said. "They help one connect to one's inner values and to find the courage to pursue them. Bonds you make during the mysteries hold forever, and nothing can ever break them."

Neda had hidden Rhea in a cave in the forests of Arcadia's Mount Lykaion, and, together with her sisters Theisoa and Hagno, helped her give birth, washed her and little Zeus, and gave a stone wrapped in baby clothes to Cronos to devour. Then they took the baby to Crete and hid it there until he grew and freed his brothers and sisters and led the battle against his father and the titans. The place was so special, all under the leaves of huge oak and sycamore trees. A river flowed calmly among the cliffs. The cicadas were singing loudly, as if to cover Rhea's screams of childbirth.

"In these waters Rhea washed herself after the birth," said Arsinoe. "The waters are sacred. Neda is the only river with a female name in Greece. She will protect the birth of your child," she told me and took me in her arms.

"I am really happy I met you," I replied, returning the embrace.

We spent all evening talking about our lives and our ancestors. The next day, we went to the sanctuary of Zeus and offered sacrifice. It was on the top of the mountain, and I could even see the top of Taygetus. I knew my previous life was behind that mountain, and I became emotional. I wiped a tear, thinking that I might never see my birthplace again.

I turned to the statue of Zeus and asked silently for his support to withstand and weather the challenges ahead. A gray-eyed girl came to me and told me with a smile that the table was prepared, and I should join Zeus in the feast of my sacrifice. I thought, what a strange way to be asked to go for lunch. "Join Zeus." I smiled back and turned to go to the tables that had been prepared for the feast, and I wondered why the girl was not following. I looked around, and I didn't see her anymore. An eagle passed with a great shriek, and for a moment, I thought that the girl was the goddess Athena. "Strange—all these mysteries and sacred tours that I've experienced the last few days have definitely had an impact on my rationality," I thought, and I moved toward the table. Was I followed by the gods? Was I under their protection or persecution? Better not to think of it. I joined the feast.

Upon our return to Messene, Odysseus, who had also come back from a hunting trip with Idas and Lynceus, gave the order to prepare for our departure. Cyanea and Dolius were not too happy to go back to the boat, but they complied. It had already been three months, and we wanted to avoid traveling in the winter. It was tough to say goodbye to my cousins, but I had really enjoyed the time in the basket mountain, and we had stayed with the promise that they would come to pay us a visit in Ithaka as soon as possible.

ιγ′

Odysseus's ships exited the gulf with pride, and we turned around the horn to enter the Ionian Sea. However, the weather changed, and big waves awaited us. I noticed he got worried, and he led the little fleet to the protected port of Pylos. The guard of King Nestor spotted us from afar and came to greet us. Odysseus told them who we were and that we would only wait for the sea to calm and depart again soon. But not much later, an officer of King Nestor showed up and prompted us to follow him to the palace, since the king wanted to offer us his hospitality. There was not much we could do to avoid the invitation, and although Odysseus wanted to go back as soon as possible, we disembarked and followed the officer.

Odysseus showed me the palace of Nestor gleaming on the top of a hill. Soldiers came to greet us and to guide us to the palace. We took along some presents, since we knew the hospitality of King Nestor and his wife was legendary. It was a beautiful road going up, with a view to the sea and the little port. People were working the fields and were stopping to watch the royal convoy passing. Kids were running behind us, offering fruit.

I was glad to be on firm land again, but Cyanea was the happiest of all. "I will stay here," she said. "The sea has too much motion for my taste."

We entered the walls of the citadel. In front of us were the stairs to enter the palace. The king was waiting for us at the top of the stairs. To the left and right were stables and workshops. The palace arrangement was similar to that of Sparta, but somehow it had more light around it. Behind it I could see the glimmering sea again and a beautiful view of the marshes and the bay of Pylos. I realized the glimmering sea was the source of the light that illuminated the palace. Somehow it was entering the palace and was reflected by the walls. Sparta was surrounded by mountains with dark forests that absorbed light rather than reflect it.

"Odysseus, my boy," said Nestor, taking him in his arms. "I heard about your wedding." He greeted me in a royal manner, while his wife, Euridice, hugged me. "Come, my children, the servants have prepared your bath. After that, let the gods be pleased with the smell of the burned fat of the lamb and our offers. We have loads to talk about."

Nestor was a very aware king. He had followed Heracles in many of his adventures. He had fought many wars with the

Arcadians and the Eleans. He knew all that was happening in the surrounding seas, since his fleet was active in trade and in military operations almost everywhere. He traveled often to Mycenae, and Achaean kings were often his guests. Messene was his ally, so he never led war against them. Besides, it was my uncle Aphareus who had given Neleus, the father of Nestor, the land at the coast of Ionian Sea to govern and reign over.

After almost a week of festivities for our arrival, Nestor and Euridice took us to Polylimnio, many lakes. It was a beautiful setting in a gorge. The river arrived in the gorge by forming a waterfall and a lake of turquoise water. Then it moved down the gorge, forming small lakes. The water flew from lake to lake. Every little lake had more or less turquoise water, depending from the amount of light it was exposed to. It was simply graceful, taking a walk along the little lakes. The vegetation was thick in the little space between the gorge walls, but there was a nice path that Nestor was keeping clear for those who wanted to offer libations and sacrifice to the nymphs. Yes, this was a typical nymph retreat, I thought, wondering if my mother knew this place.

We arrived at the shrine, where we sacrificed two lambs. The men stayed there to grill the meat, and Euridice took me with her daughters for a bath in the waterfall lake. We undressed and entered the cold water, giggling and chatting. The girls wanted to know about my cousin Helen and if she was as beautiful as they were saying. Then they asked about Pollux, Helen's handsome twin. As I was explaining how perfect a rider and how smart he was, the girls became quiet and were listening carefully. I felt embarrassed as I realized that I was talking about my first love, and some of the girls were of age to get married.

"But," I added to dump their ambitions, "he and his brother, Castor, have their minds only on adventures. They neither want to marry nor reign over Sparta. So I think the kingdom will remain with Helen and Menelaus."

I felt a bitterness coming up to my throat as I was talking about my hometown of Sparta. My eyes filled with tears that I kept back from running on my cheeks. And I couldn't stop thinking, "Oh, Mother, why did you let me go? When am I going to see you again?"

The men sent a servant girl to call us for lunch, and I turned around with relief to hide my watery eyes and red face. We put on our clothes and ran to them. We must all have looked very beautiful with our cheeks rosy from the sun, our hair half-wet, and our clothes stuck to our wet bodies. Odysseus welcomed me with a kiss. He took me in his arms and started feeding me by hand. For the first time, I felt he wanted to show everybody that he owned me.

There are two feelings when you realize someone is trying to own you. First, you are flattered. You think there must be something special and desirable in you if someone wants to own you. Then it becomes frightening. You start thinking—and this was my case—that one only belongs to oneself, and no one can own another person. However, I didn't worry much, and for a moment I thought that maybe that was the sense of marriage—to own each other.

We slept in the gorge that night, but in a high-up place to avoid surprises from a sudden flood. The night was so calm, the sky starry, the crickets even louder than the river water. The others were asleep, and I was admiring nature when I saw a dim light coming out of one of the little lakes. Attracted by the light, I stood up to see it better and started walking toward it. It looked as if a female figure was coming out of the water.

As I got closer, I could hear a song—yes, a nymph song. I knew this type of singing. I had experienced it in Taygetus when Aunt Leda took me to my mother.

"Come closer, my child," a voice said. There she was. Not my mother, but the local nymph, all naked and beautiful. "I'm Earine, the nymph of these lakes. Welcome to my domain. Your mother sends me to let you know that she will be waiting for you in Ithaka," she said, and then she started disappearing.

"Wait a moment. Where is Mother now? How can I talk to her?" I asked.

"You look lovely, my child, and I wish you all the best luck for your wedding. Your mother will find you," she said, and then she disappeared along with the song and the light.

I stood there trying to interpret this message. Had I seen it, or was it only a dream?

"Come back to the camp. You risk being kidnapped by the nymphs here all alone." I heard the voice of Odysseus behind me. He put his hand on my shoulder and pulled me back.

I only then realized that I was standing at the edge of the cliff. He pulled me back gently. Had he seen her also? I didn't dare to ask, maybe for fear he would laugh at me or for fear I would have to share my mother with him. I wasn't sure which was stronger. He put his arms around me and started kissing me. The moonlight, the sound of the water, the song of the crickets, the smooth terrain—we loved each other there, and I

117

was sure all the nymphs of these lakes were watching our pleasure, sharing it and amplifying it, giving me my first orgasm ever. My relation with Odysseus was becoming ever more intimate.

We had a nice time in Pylos, but the weather was deteriorating quickly. The sea was rougher every day, and it was almost impossible to depart. Nestor was an excellent host and involved Odysseus in his decision-making. He was receiving news from all around the country and news from his guards and his fleet, which was moving in the Aegean and Ionian Seas. Odysseus had never felt more involved or proud, and he was already making big plans for how to expand Ithaka's small fleet.

He enjoyed hunting with Nestor and his sons, and I was happy to stay with his daughters. I was teaching them the odes to the nymphs, to Artemis and Apollo, that we had back in Sparta, and they were teaching me to embroider griffins on my loom work.

We spent the whole winter there, and still there was no sign of my pregnancy. "Don't worry," Euridice told me. "It took me four years to get the first child, and fifteen others followed after him."

I was impressed and scared at the same time. "Fifteen are too many," I dared say disapprovingly.

"They are the gods' will," she said. "What can you do? I'm happy about them, and Nestor even more."

We left at the end of March. We filled our ships with even more presents, and we headed north toward Zakynthos. I knew Zakynthos was a very fertile island, and its lords were noble men and women. Odysseus insisted on stopping and greeting Lord Adamas, a good friend of his father.

ιδ′

We entered the Gulf of Laganas and headed toward one end of it. The countryside seemed flat in the middle. I couldn't see mountains, and the beach was all sandy. "It seems a nice place to live," I said to Odysseus.

"It is," he replied. "They are lucky people. But it is important they pay their part for the expenses of the army and navy," he added in a decisive tone.

I didn't understand what he meant, but I decided not to ask any questions. When we arrived at the beach, a small guard of soldiers came to greet us. "Our lord Adamas greets you, Odysseus, and asks you and your wife to become his guests."

Odysseus smiled with satisfaction. "We start well," he whispered in my ear.

The soldiers pulled the vessels and moored them. We selected presents and followed the guards along with our escort. We arrived at a big house surrounded by other smaller buildings, and beyond the big house were the stables and fields and beyond those the dark forests.

Lord Adamas was expecting us at the entrance. "Welcome to Zakynthos," said the old man with a smirk.

Odysseus jumped down from the horse, obviously feeling at home. "Is that how you welcome your lord?" said Odysseus, also with a smirk, as he gave him the arm. I realized there was some kind of rivalry between the two.

Adamas turned to me, already standing next to Odysseus. "So, after all the Perseides returned to our country, we are honored to greet you, daughter of Icarius and granddaughter of Oebalus and Gorgophone and great-granddaughter of the great king Perseus."

Then he turned to Odysseus again. "It is a pleasure and an honor to have you, my lord. We knew you were guests of Nestor for the winter, and we were hoping to see you stop also at our place. Your father and friend of mine, Laertes, has advised you well, my son. Tell me, how is he? I haven't seen him lately."

"My father is well, as far as I know. He is tired of governing and has passed all the displeasing duties to me now," Odysseus said, as if to reaffirm his supremacy. Then he greeted the sons of Adamas one by one with gestures that showed endorsement.

They took us into the palace, where Adamas's wife and daughters were waiting. They had us sit. They washed our hands and feet and invited us to lunch. I was very hungry, so I enjoyed it.

Odysseus came straight to the point. "We need to build up our fleet. Pirates from Libya attack our coasts and our traders. Nestor says we can never have enough galleys these days."

"We do have ten of our boats that always travel with the fleet of Nestor," said Adamas. "It is better for us to have strong allies, and your father has always agreed with that."

"And I agree, Adamas," Odysseus said. "Sparta and therefore Mycenae are our allies now. We can move our trade also with the Mycenaean fleet now if we wish."

"That's great news, Odysseus," exclaimed Adamas. Then his face darkened. "But I would be careful with King Agamemnon. He is very ambitious, they say. And he is quick to request resources for little in exchange."

"Don't worry about him. I can manage him well. Menelaus, his brother, owes his nice and peaceful kingdom in Sparta to me. He will follow my advice. But we need to organize our forces better, because many of our men are on the boats as rowers, soldiers, and traders, and our cities remain unprotected from pirate attacks. Nestor has complained about pirates from the land of the Hittites, who seem to steal and attack trade and cities on the coast of Asia Minor. We should make sure they don't come over here."

Adamas stayed silent for a while, and I noticed he was looking at Odysseus intently. "I agree to help you, Odysseus," he said, "but then you'll need to represent me worthily to Agamemnon and Nestor. None of us lords from Zakynthos wants to pay two masters. Tomorrow we shall convene a meeting with the other lords of the island, if you allow me to discuss this in more detail."

Odysseus couldn't hide his satisfaction, and secretly he pressed my hand.

I only then understood his plan. He hadn't told me anything of it, but now it was unfolding in front of my eyes, like a nice carpet that a virgin unrolls in front of the eyes of her mother to show her capabilities in weaving. All the mastery is in how well one succeeds, and Odysseus had made a good work toward his goal. During the week all the lords of Zakynthos gathered and agreed to make Odysseus their administrative and military leader, at the price that he would represent them in front of the great Achaean leader Agamemnon. They would break this agreement if they deemed Odysseus unworthy to represent them. I was an important piece of the motive of

Odysseus. Without me as legitimate descendant of Perseus, they would be reluctant. I was the connecting piece to his supremacy.

He was satisfied when we departed for Ithaka after two weeks. He kissed my ear gently as I was watching the sandy beach of Laganas disappear. "Now we have to do the same in Sami and Doulichion," he whispered in my ear.

So he knew I had discovered his plan, and he was considering me on his side. I smiled stiffly, my eyes lost on the beach. Someone called him, and he left me, telling me to cover my shoulders so as not to get cold. I nodded, and a million thoughts came to my mind. Why hadn't he asked my opinion of the plan? Why had he assumed I'd play his game? I felt again my individual freedom being constrained by his actions. He was assuming my consent; he was not asking for it. Should I be honored? After all, I was his wife. This was why marriages were arranged. Helen's wedding was the same, and she knew it. She was not even in love with Menelaus, but I was with Odysseus. He had inspired me from the first moment. Why wasn't he trusting me with his plans in advance? I was confused. I wanted to be happy for him. I wanted to be honored, but some thought about a lack of respect was obscuring my mind. "You are exaggerating," I thought, and I turned to go to the tent.

It didn't take long to arrive in Ithaka. The wind was good, and we soon saw the land he considered home. The boat moved between two islands, Ithaka and Sami. Both islands had smooth but rocky slopes of low vegetation. I couldn't see any settlements, but that was normal. People preferred to live farther inland, away from the dangers of the sea. Some sandy beaches with their turquoise waters were appearing and disappearing again behind the rocks.

We arrived at a beach where the land was flat, and we moored. People had gathered at the shore, and there was some sort of convoy behind some people standing patiently. "Now you'll meet your parents-in-law," he whispered in my ear, and he laid his arm around my shoulder. He had put on all his armor and helmet and looked much bigger than he actually was. I had put on my blue dress with a golden rim that combined perfectly with the colors of the sea and the bright blue of the sail. I noticed that the woman who was waiting was also dressed in blue, in a different tone.

We disembarked carefully, so as not to wet our clothes, and Odysseus carried me in his arms until the ground was completely dry. We moved closer to the convoy, and people started cheering. "Welcome back, Odysseus, our king."

He firmly stopped in front of his parents and took his mother in his arms. She was silently crying from happiness. Then he did the same with his father. Then he put his hands on my shoulders and said, "Mother, Father, I present to you my wife, Penelope, daughter of King Icarius of Sparta and great-granddaughter of our lord Perseus."

Laertes moved toward me and said, "You are most welcome, our daughter. Our house is also yours from now and onward, and there is nothing that we shall not share with you. You can count on our full support as wife of our son and queen of Ithaka." He took my hand and put a golden ring with a blue stone on my finger.

Then his mother came to me and said, "My daughter, this is our only child, and we fully entrust him to you. May the gods give you a long and prosperous life." And she put on the same arm a beautiful golden armband with the same blue stones.

Then we moved toward home. Anticlea—that was the name of his mother—and I rode the carriage. Odysseus and Laertes rode their horses held by a guard.

ιε′

Odysseus showed me our new house as we turned the first bend. It didn't look big. As we got closer, it was a large house rather than a palace. The stables were very close, and the smell of dung overwhelmed my nostrils. Odysseus understood that I was disturbed and took my hand. "It is rarely that smelly," he said and smiled at me.

There was a small guardhouse and almost no workshops. Once we arrived in the palace and walked in the megaron, I felt even more disappointed. There were no paintings on the walls except some meanders around the top part. A big armchair made of wood was in the middle of the room.

"I'll make sure another one is put there as soon as possible, my daughter," Laertes said. "But, you see, Anticlea and I don't live here. We have a little house in the mountains, and we stay there. Odysseus is now the king and you his queen. We never liked to govern anyway. Anticlea and I, we thought you should choose how your throne should be."

Odysseus intervened. "I'm afraid you shall have a lot to do, darling," he said. "Even our bedroom is not ready yet. But it has a beautiful view. Come; I'll show you." He pulled my hand.

I threw a quick look to Laertes, as if to excuse myself for the bad manners of my husband, and ran behind him. He took me to the second floor, to a long room with a veranda and a fireplace in one of the walls. The view from the veranda was breathtaking. I could see the mountains on the left, the narrow passage that separated Sami from Ithaki on the right, and the immense big blue of the sea as far as my eyes could reach in front of me. On the right side of the veranda, the branches of an olive tree were making their way around the edge. The sun was setting and becoming orange.

"We shall watch the sunset every day from here," he whispered in my ear as he embraced me and kissed my neck. We stood for a while watching the sun as it became more and more red. A sweet feeling of family and love overwhelmed me, and I realized I'd like him to hold me like that forever. I breathed the spring air, and I felt love filling every part of my body. I turned and kissed him, and he carried me inside. We undressed quickly and made love. Only when we were finished did I notice a small detail. There was no bed in the room. We had loved each other next to the trunk of an olive tree on an improvised mattress.

He anticipated my question. "I'll make our bed on this trunk. I'll carve it directly into the tree. I've slept on this olive tree since I was small. When I saw you the first time in Sparta and came back here, I decided to build our room in a way that the tree would host our marital bed."

I looked at him in amazement. He had cut the branches of a huge olive tree, leaving only the central trunk, and he had rounded it off and had put wax all around to prevent new branches from growing. "How did you do that?" I asked him.

"It was easy. Wait to see our bed. You'll love it."

I looked at him lovingly. "Odysseus," I whispered.

"Now, my lady, you have lots to do. I have asked the best families to send you their daughters to become your court ladies, and I asked the families of the villages to send us their girls to become your servants, maids, and cooks. They shall all wait to be inspected by you in the next days. Until our bed is ready, we can use the room next door to sleep in a normal bed. I hope our things are all here in between, and we'll enjoy a hot bath and some dinner."

Our things had been unloaded and put in the megaron. No one knew what their position should be, and me even less. I asked for the chests with my clothes and dowry to be taken upstairs. Odysseus made sure someone warmed water, and we were given fresh bread, goat cheese, honey, and nuts for dinner. I was feeling good for the first time since I had met him. I was feeling home, although there was nothing there that could remind me of a home. But I knew he was all mine, and I knew he was on my side. I knew he had sides he had not revealed and things he was keeping to himself. He was like that. Nevertheless, he had no other to lean on, and sooner or later, he would trust me entirely.

The next day when I woke up, he had already left our bed. I dressed and went downstairs to find something for breakfast. In the yard there were some ladies watching me, and I realized these were the girls to be my court ladies. As I crossed the yard, Dolion approached me. "My lady, I don't know where to put the nice piece of furniture you brought along. Your bedroom is still a workshop, and the megaron is poorly decorated. Soon the ships from Sparta with your bigger pieces of furniture will arrive, and I don't think there is sufficient room for them here."

I didn't know what to say. As we entered the kitchen, we saw Cyanea. She was already up and had made sure the cooks made breakfast. She was happy to see me. "My lady," she said, almost crying. "There is nothing here. The kitchen is a mess, the storeroom is tiny, and it smells of animal dung everywhere. No one knows how to cook properly. There is no place to put your nice dishes. What are we going to do?"

I looked at her with patience. "I know," I said, and I put the cup with the fresh milk to my mouth. "We have a lot of work. Have you seen Odysseus?"

"He rode off, my lady, with one of his guard. I told him that you'd like to know where he is in case you need him. But he didn't reply, my lady."

"It doesn't matter. This is our home now. We shouldn't need him for anything. Where is the shrine here? Is there a temple around? I'd like to make an offering to the gods for helping me arrive here and to ask their blessing for the future."

"Not even a temple, my lady. There is nothing here…not even a shrine for our lady Artemis…"

"Don't be so negative, woman." I heard his voice as he entered the room. He took me in his arms and raised me from the floor. "We have everything here. Come; I'll show you."

He put me down and took my arm. Whatever he had done in the morning had obviously made him happy. It felt nice. He made a sign to the three ladies who were chatting in the yard to follow. We climbed the little hill next to the palace. And there they were—small shrines for almost all the gods. "They are all here, except for Poseidon, who is at the beach. You can offer whatever you like and admire the view and let the sunrays warm you," he said.

"I'd like to make a small temple for Hera and Zeus together," I whispered.

"We shall do whatever you want," he said, and he kissed me on the lips.

"And why can't they be next to the palace, as they are at all palaces?" asked Cyanea, who had just arrived, breathing heavily.

"Oh, it will do you well, going up and down the little hill," Odysseus said, laughing.

"Wait until my lady is pregnant and heavier than me. Then you'll sympathize with me," said Cyanea.

We all laughed and started on our way back.

"Odysseus, I need some of your rowers and soldiers to make the storage room bigger and build a wardrobe for my things," I told him.

"You can have that, and I'll ask my friend Polydorus, who's an architect, to help you design it," he replied.

When we arrived, he left again, and I went through the whole palace, opening each room and checking the spaces. "I also need to make the yard bigger," I thought, and, as my nostrils got annoyed with the smell, "and I need to get these stables out of here."

Odysseus came back with Polydorus. We sat all together, and I explained to him the changes I wanted. He had good ideas as to how to do it, and by the end of the day, we had a plan that I liked. Instead of the storage room, the plan suggested a complete overhaul of the whole palace. The only thing that remained the same was our bedroom with our bed carved in the centenary olive tree. Polydorus discussed something with Odysseus, and then he left.

"He's going to find the best builders in Same, and he'll start as soon as he gets back. I promised him one hundred of my best sheep and twenty gold coins for the work," he said, smiling at me.

Since our bedroom didn't need to change, I started decorating it. I hung my beautiful white curtains and started painting the walls. I was making gold and red meanders on a blue background on the part of the walls near the ceiling. I did this myself, since I was good in geometrical design. Next to the bedroom were two smaller rooms. I took one as my wardrobe, and in the other I put the sink and the bathtub. There was a small fireplace, where I would keep the water warm. The room was our secret. No one was allowed to enter the room, and we were filling the work pauses with lots of young and carefree love.

During that period, I was feeling inebriated by Eros. I was familiarizing myself with the male and was fully immersed in Aphrodite's practices. When I woke up in the morning and he was not next to me, I was worried. Often, I would stop my work to just watch him. He was having such an impact on me. I would watch his hands working the wood, and I had a need to kiss them; his face concentrated on his work, and I needed to stroke him…he was making me feel so different. He was strong and delicate at the same time. Rough while talking to his compatriots and gentle when he was lying down with me. And most of all, I enjoyed the stories of his travels and the way he described the character of his fellows. In the evenings, next to Hestia's fire, we would discuss all the problems and issues he had faced throughout the day. His parents were often with us. He would speak openly and take advice from whoever was offering it, and most of all from me. All my initial worries vanished.

I decided to keep all three ladies who had been sent to me by the best families of Ithaka. It would have been an offense to send them back. The girls' names were Thekla, daughter of Aigyptius from Ithaka; Autonoe, daughter of Adamas from Zakynthos; and Hippodamia, daughter of Polytherses from Same. They were all at the age of fourteen. This was the typical age at which girls could become followers of the queen. The queen, then, was responsible for their further education, dowry, and eventual marriage. I gave them rooms in the eastern wing of the palace. Cyanea and Dolius took rooms downstairs. Euriclea, the nanny of Odysseus, was sleeping there also. He wanted her with him much more than he wanted his own parents. She was hardworking and obedient, and she immediately became friends with Cyanea, so I had nothing against her staying with us.

ις'

Life in Ithaka was quite different from that in Sparta. Sparta was by far more sophisticated and the people much more cultivated and polite. I was struck by the difference in female attitudes, but I could hardly change them. Also, the men who were often coming to see Odysseus were definitely less cultivated than Spartan men. They were more mountain men with just essential education and manners. Their concerns were more about how to divide land and game and fend off pirates than governance, discipline, and culture. Odysseus had known from the beginning that a Spartan wife would be very sophisticated for the rough people of Ithaka, but he knew this could also bring benefits to the people while supporting him in decision-making. Indeed, I was the inspiration for some new things in Ithaka.

A week after our arrival, he invited all nobles of Ithaka to a feast, first to introduce me, and also to establish his supremacy over the lords of all surrounding islands acquired through his wedding with me. There were Eupithes and his wife; Aigyptius and his wife; Polybus; Mestor; Meges, lord of Dulichium; Mentes, a captain and lord of the Echinae Islands; and Polites, a man of Odysseus's age who had come to live in Ithaka from

Phthia and to whom Odysseus had ceded land for his herds. The chief of Odysseus's herd, Eumaeus, was also there.

The dinner was simple, far from the luxury and abundance one could find in Sparta. The tables were simple wooden tables without lacquering or any elaborations. The plates and glasses were simple ceramic without paintings. There were no musicians, dancers, or poetry. It was plainly a sad dinner where I only managed to introduce the thanking hymn to Hestia just before the meat was served. The lamb was cooked excellently, though, and I wondered how they had done it so soft. I stayed quiet during most of the dinner, since all faces were new to me. Anyway, it was in my nature not to talk before I understood how the others were thinking.

Not more, not less, Odysseus asked to represent them in the big gathering of the Achaeans in Mycenae. He also asked them to contribute to create an Ithakan fleet by building ships, and he promised to invite important shipbuilders from Pylos to help. They were all skeptical and said that ships would take time and money and would need rowers not available in the region—most of the young men were busy with agriculture and farming.

Then Mentes stood up and said, "I don't know, fellows, why you are suddenly such cowards. The Taphians have always been pirates. We have no intention of withdrawing from ruling the seas to do farming. On our islands, when men retreat from sailing because of old age, they become farmers, but before that they rule the seas. All our young are on the boats. We have five ships of thirty rowers each. They are fast and flexible, and we do know how to make our living from them. I am sure we can find the resources to make the fleet Odysseus wants."

The Taphians were sea people who moved from island to island, and it was difficult to pin them down and negotiate with them. Many years ago, Amphitryon, one of my uncles from Argos, together with Cephalus, the great-grandfather of Odysseus, suppressed their uprising and brought peace in the Ionian islands, where Cephalus established himself as lord. Cephalus brought up his son, Arcesius, and reigned until the end of his days. He was a fair lord, giving them a great deal of autonomy. They could continue their sea adventures so long as they were not attacking his or other Mycenaean cities and were paying one-third of their booty to him and his son. The tax ensured that Ithaka would protect the islands against invasion when the Taphian fleet was traveling.

Odysseus stood up and said, "Mentes is right. We have done it before, and we can do it again. The coastal Egyptian and Lybian cities have a great deal of booty for us. Remember when we kidnapped the daughter of the Lybian king as she was bathing with her maids? The king paid a large ransom, among which was the beautiful belt that my wife has on now, which became a symbol of our bond. We were young adventurers then and we only had fun, but more money can be brought in by doing this systematically."

Mentes took the floor again. "The Phoenicians trade through the sea the timber, and the Sidonians the fabrics for the sails. Egyptian vessels are often full of gold for paying their soldiers, and—"

Odysseus interrupted him. "Our islands don't produce much, but they do produce clever and capable men."

Eupithes then asked, "Can you, Odysseus, lead such entrepreneurship, or do you want to stay in the warm arms of your wife now that you're married?"

Odysseus looked at him as if he had slapped him and responded with vigor and a dose of scorn. "Piracy needs speed, impeccable organization, and intuitive flexibility. My leadership is indispensable, Eupithes."

Aigyptius stood up and said, "Son of Laertes, your father never engaged in piracy and lived a good and long life. Why do you think this needs to change now?"

"Because everything has changed. There are folks who come from the east and sack Mycenaean cities in Asia Minor. Agamemnon, the new king of Mycenae, has promised to protect the trade routes, similar to how Minos did in the past for the Cretans. The expeditions of Heracles have opened new routes up to the land of Scythians or others from the Black Sea. Agamemnon wants to negotiate with Egyptians new passages to Ethiopia, and Miletus is important for our trade routes with the Hittites. Our kingdom will be asked, together with that of Nestor's, to take part in such operation and be in charge of the Ionian Sea and the sea of Libya. Nestor has built a big fleet and can escort Achaean merchant ships everywhere. We have to be able to join these activities and build up our own capabilities. And for that we need big ships that we don't have."

Everybody stayed quiet for a while. Odysseus invited everybody to drink and eat. Most young people came over to talk with him and offer their help. Most elders kept their distance and left the meeting with mixed feelings. But they all made themselves or their sons available for the first operation that Odysseus organized, whenever it would be.

Back in our room, as I was brushing my hair, I asked, "So the belt was stolen from a Lybian princess?"

He turned to me, surprised. "Does it make any difference to you?"

"You lied to me when you said you had asked the most famous goldsmith to prepare the belt," I said, locking eyes with him.

"Only partly," he replied. "The belt is made by a famous goldsmith. And I did ask him to prepare this for you." He pulled a small box from his pocket and opened it. Inside was a golden ring with a ruby with the same engraving as on the belt rubies—the deer head.

I looked at him and then at the ring. "I'd have preferred you hadn't lied to me. I'd have preferred the ring as a present," I said.

He put the ring on my finger. "It will never happen again," he murmured in my ear as he kissed me. "Besides, the ring was not ready when I came to Sparta. My good friend Polydorus brought it to me from Mycenae. On these islands no one knows how to do this work."

That evening I realized how poor the islands were. They had hardly any resources, no copper or other metals, no precious stones to be exported. There were some olive trees and many fig trees, but that production covered only the needs of its people. The sea was bringing fish, but fish is not good for trade. There were some wool and leather workshops and one for weapons made of wood and bronze. There was a shipbuilding workshop in a protected harbor, but it built mainly small boats, as big boats required other capabilities, such as those seen in Pylos.

Odysseus had a dream. He wanted to be important to the Achaeans and offer them protection for their sea trade, and he could achieve that only if he stole and sacked. I watched him as he was undressing. His moves were fast and determined. He hadn't told me that he was a pirate. This was another new thing I was now learning about him.

ιζ'

Odysseus prepared everything for his first trip since our wedding. He told me he was not expecting to be gone more than a couple of months. Mentes and his Taphian fleet of two small vessels appeared. Odysseus and his men from Ithaka added another two of these vessels and left. The two big vessels that had brought him to Sparta stayed anchored in the shipyard.

I was on my own suddenly. The palace was all mine. The ceremonies all mine. The kingdom's problems all mine. "You can do it," he whispered in my ear as he kissed my cheek to leave. "My father will help if there is a problem."

I had not much time to think, to discuss, to object. I threw myself into work. The palace was a mess due to the rebuilding. But I had made important progress. The stables had moved behind the hill, so no smell anymore. The storeroom was bigger, and I could start storing larger quantities of food. Cyanea was happy with this. I made the wool workshop bigger, and I put more ladies to work, but I realized there were not enough hands on the islands. Infant mortality was great, so families had fewer children than on the mainland. Women were suffering from high postnatal mortality.

We needed more hands to boost the economy, so the issue of mortality had to be tackled. I shared my thoughts with Polydorus, who was now spending all his time in the palace due to the many jobs he had. "I am sure Odysseus will bring back some war prisoners," he replied quickly.

"But that's not the point," I said. "Back in Sparta, women rarely die after birth. Why should it be different here?"

"Back in Sparta, you have your aunt Leda and her priestesses to look after the sick. Here there is no one," he said.

"Oh, great goddess," I thought. "There is nothing here. Where have I ended up? That's the end of the world."

Indeed, after two months Odysseus was back with a huge ship full of timber. He said they intercepted it as it was bringing the timber to Egypt from Ugarit along with its slaves. He was happy. He spent two days sleeping and celebrating. Then he ordered the construction of another big ship, the fourth. During the night, after our love, he recited the happenings on the sea. It was nice to hear to his voice. My imagination was all excited by his stories. I was really happy he was back, but before long he told me that he would leave again within three days. He had to bring some gold for the shipyard's needs and to pay the engineers. "This time it will take longer," he said.

"How much longer?" I asked.

"Not sure. Maybe a month. I have to make sure no one follows me."

I hadn't expected this, and I was upset. "I need you here," I said. "There are not enough hands for everything. And in two weeks we have the thanksgiving ceremony. The king has to be here."

"I'll bring you hands," he said, and he put his arms around me. "Laertes will give you a hand with the ceremony."

"But I want you here," I said, crying now.

He wiped my tears and said, "I have to go. I know of a gold expedition in Byblos. I have to be there before they are."

Two days later, he left. I threw myself again into the work. I decided to send some of my ladies to Aunt Leda to learn her healing methods. But first I had to talk to their families to receive endorsement. Most were against it, except the mother of Thekla, who not only agreed but also offered herself and her youngest son to accompany her. I was thrilled, and I prepared the expedition, which would depart in a month.

145

The thanksgiving ceremony was very different from what I knew. The offerings to the gods and therefore to the palace were marginal. I asked Laertes why, and he replied that there was not much arable land on Ithaka. Ithaka was dependent on Zakynthos for its bread.

"Good job Zakynthos is an ally, then," I whispered. "And what do we do when Zakynthos's production goes bad?"

"Well, in that case, I go over to Aetolia, where the blond fields are. I used to pay with our tasty lambs, but last time, they wanted gold. That's why Odysseus had to go out to get it."

"You mean to steal it," I said.

"Well, some have more than they need, but they share it only if they are obliged," he said, lowering his head. "I am not proud of it either, but we don't have much choice."

During the next few days, I caught myself taking a more positive attitude toward piracy, but the events that followed made me reconsider it. One day a ship appeared at our coast. It was a big ship with high sails; it didn't seem Achaean. Perimedes, Odysseus's friend who had stayed behind to look after the island, came to report this to me. I asked him to monitor the ship and to tell me immediately if it made any attempt to land. Then I gathered Ithaka's small army to be ready for an attack.

The ship cruised around the island for the next two days. The third day, they disembarked. They asked to see the king and said they had brought presents, so the guards brought an Egyptian officer and his guard to me. The officer asked me to give him back his stolen boat with the timber. He said that this material belonged to his lord.

I was shocked. I certainly hadn't expected that, and I was not sure what answer to give to him. "With all respect, it is an audacity to enter my kingdom and accuse me of having stolen a ship. My husband is in Pylos for business, and he will be very offended to hear these accusations. I expect your apologies and your immediate departure, sir," I said with a tone that made even me believe my false words.

"You may expect what you want, but you cannot expect me to leave this ship in your shipyard, lady," he said, and he bent himself with false respect.

I knew the man was my enemy, and I was relieved when I saw his little fleet disappearing straight after our discussion. I was at the edge of the cliff watching them depart when

Perimedes came next to me and said, "They may come back with more ships. We had better call Odysseus back."

"Yes," I murmured with uncertainty. "But how? I have no idea where he is."

"I may be able to find him," he said. "I'll depart tomorrow."

I turned and looked at him with thankful eyes. He bowed and left. I knew I was not safe. Ithaka was not safe, and that was only because Odysseus had challenged someone bigger than he was. I had to have a fleet to fight such invasions, but very few people in Ithaka and Same knew how to fight a naval battle. Those who knew how to do it were already occupied by the piracy activities of my husband.

Perimedes didn't manage to go because things changed the same night. The foreign vessel came back. They attempted to set the shipyard, including their own ship and the timber, on fire. Perimedes intercepted me as I was ready to go to bed. "We have to stop them, my lady," he said. "But I need you to order the men to follow me."

"All right," I said. "But how?"

"Put something warm on and follow me."

I followed him to the seashore. Toward the north I could see the fire that was coming from the shipyard.

"There are men fighting the fire," he said, "but we need to sink their boats. There isn't much time. This way."

I went the way he indicated, and my guards followed us. We arrived at a hole in the ground. People were waiting at the brink. Some rafts were around, but no one was doing anything.

"This is the cave of the nymphs, my lady. Men are scared to go down, for the nymphs might kill them or enchant them. But the cave has a secret opening to the sea. I know because I entered once to escape from my persecutors. The opening is just behind the foreign vessels. We shall approach them in the darkness, kill the guards, and set them on fire."

I nodded that it sounded like a good plan, although it was unclear how to implement it.

"If you go down with us, the men will follow, my lady. You are our priestess, and your mother was a nymph. She will protect you."

I nodded again, unsure whether my mother would know anything about this ever. But somehow I felt valued, and I made a sign to start moving. I was emotionally loaded, but I knew he was right. I had no guarantee that I could offer any special protection to these men. But that was not the point.

Soon we arrived at the bottom, and yes, I was enchanted myself. The pool was beautiful. There was no moon, and that was excellent for the operation. But then, where was the light coming from? There were millions of fireflies creating a soft light that as a whole was reflecting on the water, giving a very special green glow to the surface of the motionless lake. When the fireflies came too close to the surface, fish would jump out to get them. The movement of the fish was so fast that the only thing I could manage to see were the ripples their dives were leaving on the water.

I was looking around, and I was completely absorbed by the suggestive atmosphere of the place when Perimedes touched my shoulder. "The men are bringing the rafts down, my lady. You have to move."

They pushed the two rafts into the pool, and we went on. Perimedes let them row around the pool close to the walls of the cave to find the opening. It was a small fissure in the wall that could let only one boat pass at a time. We navigated for a while in the darkness of the cave toward the opening, and then

I heard the waves of the sea crashing. It was obvious that the sea was behind that wall.

"Hold yourself tight, and row with all your power, my queen. Get in the middle of the raft and hold tight," he said.

I did as he asked. We arrived at the mouth of the cave at the sea. At the beginning it was protected, but then the waves battered us. Men started rowing with all their power to avoid being thrown on the rocky walls of the mountain where they disappeared to the sea bottom. The waves splashed on the boat, breaking up into droplets that penetrated our clothes. For a moment I felt our end was close, but soon we were far off the coast, and there was no danger. I looked up toward the stars and breathed out.

"My lady, some of us will go on the ship now. The boats will go to the external part of the formation to set the ship ablaze from a position less visible. Once this operation is finished, one raft will take you to the shipyard, and the other one will wait to collect us."

He looked at me as if waiting for something.

"May the power of Zeus and the cunning of Athena be with you," I murmured, trying to sound convincing. I was scared and didn't believe the operation would be successful, but he seemed happy and pushed through.

They dropped the ropes, and, fast like acrobats, they climbed the ship and disappeared. I understood why they were good pirates. They seemed very agile doing such operations.

The other raft did the same toward the external side of the left ship. They drilled little holes in the hull and put in cloth soaked in oil, which they lit up with a flame that they had kept alive but hidden with care throughout the short journey. Then we moved toward the shore. Turning around the mountain slope, I saw the shipyard still burning.

We arrived, and they put me on land. "We have to go back and get the others, my lady," they told me.

I nodded and moved with my two guards to reach the small group that was trying to stop the fire. We started pulling water and throwing it on the fire. At some point, I got an idea. "Let the ship burn," I shouted. "Pull the others out and soak the timber. At least we shall save the timber."

This was what they did. The effort lasted the whole night. At some point, someone showed me behind the mountain slope. There was a big blaze to be seen, and it was obvious the open-sea operation had succeeded. With the first light of the sun, we understood the amount of damage. The foreign ship in the shipyard was still burning, but the three Ithakan ships and the new one were saved. Some of the shipyard construction had been damaged.

We decided to pull the foreign vessel into the open sea to let it burn there. Someone took me to a place with some forty tied-up men. "These survived, my lady. We fished them out of the sea. What are we supposed to do with them?"

"They shall work in the workshops of the palace," I said, realizing that I had now some gratis hands. "Have you seen Perimedes and those who boarded the foreign ship?"

No one replied. I started running in the direction of the other foreign ship. Then I heard voices. "They are here, my lady."

I saw some hands waving. They were all back safe, their clothes covered with blood. Their bodies had the marks of hard fighting.

"They are all dead, my lady, and those who didn't die from the fires died from the waves, thrown on the rocky coast. Those who may still have survived, we shall capture and bring to you."

I looked at them approvingly. "You did a great job tonight. You saved us all and saved our island. You shall be greatly rewarded when my man is back."

I left and asked to be taken back to the palace. Someone brought a horse, which I mounted. My clothes were torn apart and my hair undone. My hands were black from soot, and my face was probably the same. I was exhausted and thirsty. I wished my man were there.

When I arrived at the palace, I saw it: a beautiful royal chariot from Sparta. My father's chariot. He was there. I ran into the megaron, and I fell into his arms, crying from happiness. I only managed to whisper "Father, thank the gods you are here" before I lost my senses.

I woke up late in the afternoon. My father and Cyanea were next to my bed. Cyanea was crying, murmuring, "My poor lady, what a horrible night."

"Stop it, Cyanea," I said. "I am not dead yet."

She started crying even louder and left to bring me something to eat.

"Daughter, what great acts of valor have you accomplished. Everybody here is talking about your courage."

"I had to cover for the audacity of my husband, Father. He goes around and steals," I said angrily.

"A man has to do what he must do, but he should not leave you in your condition alone fighting enemies. You are pregnant, aren't you."

I nodded.

"I am not moving from here until he is back. Your uncle has already taken over governing."

"Is Uncle Tyndareus also here?"

"Of course. Now that Menelaus and Helen have taken over, we decided to come see you. And not only him—your cousin Arsinoe is also here."

Cyanea entered with a bowl of soup, which I ate avidly.

After a week, Odysseus arrived. He brought a great deal of gold, and he managed to start his little fleet. He organized a ceremony to thank the gods and the nymphs for protecting us both and the islands. I cut the throat of the first of a hecatomb, which officially established me as the high priestess of Zeus and whisperer of the nymphs. I had now the same position Aunt Leda had back in Sparta, and that was much higher than anybody else in the islands, even the king himself. After six months, our son was born.

ιη′

My father waited to take him in his arms and bless him first of all. My cousin Arsinoe was a great help during birth and the first days. Then they departed. Odysseus was the happiest man ever, and I was a proud mother. I had so much to do during that time. The little baby was absorbing me completely. He was filling my life with so much joy and devotion. I could hardly find any time for work in the palace and the extension of the workshops. Most of the prisoners Odysseus had brought from his trips were working there. Although some of the prisoners found accommodations in the palace, which had to be extended with new dormitories, a little village was established close to the palace to give shelter for the newcomers. I put a lot of attention toward the services of the place because I wanted the prisoners to stay and not go at the first opportunity. There were two wells for fresh water, and they could make altars for their deities.

Among these people were some women, and one of them, Armeria, became the wife of Dolius. Dolius was keeping the palace's gardens and plants and was looking after the olive grove that my father had planted at the south part of the palace during his stay. Armeria had her first baby, a little girl, some months after me, so she made an excellent nanny for my son.

I could really say *palace* by now, because Polydorus had done an excellent job of creating a palace out of what we had moved into originally. The megaron was much bigger now, but I still needed a master painter for the decorations. I had hands enough for the clothing and the ceramic workshop and some good carpenters as well. I had ordered all new furniture for the megaron and the big dining room as well as the room of my son. Odysseus made sure some of the timber he had gotten for his ships was diverted for new furniture.

The shipyard had produced two big ships by now and had the next two under construction. Odysseus felt honored to be invited by Agamemnon to the big gathering of the Achaeans to talk about the future of trade. He took the two new ships and the three older ones, and armed with confidence from his alliance with the other lords of the islands and reassured as to the continuation of his reign by his newborn son, he went to meet the others.

He came back more worried than when he had left. He didn't tell me anything of his worries, but I sensed them. I was too busy and had little spare time to hear his theories. He ordered the shipyard to hurry up with the construction, and he brought along from Mycenae more tin and copper to make bronze armature. He ordered the bronze workshop to double their production in the next year. They said that this was possible only if they had at least one more engineer and another set of workers for a new shift. So he left again for a while, and upon his return, we had even more new shelters and a new engineer from Thebes. The engineer settled with his family in the nearby village.

During my father's presence on the islands, we had started work to create more arable land and to teach Ithakans the cultivation of the olive tree. Olive trees existed, but the islanders didn't know how to properly take care of them, prune them, and harvest the valuable fruit. Both Odysseus and I were busy with these activities. I was looking after the olive oil production, and he was cleaning the fields of stones to create arable land. We were both working hard, but we were enjoying it because we had a common dream to make Ithaka and Same food self-sufficient. Zakyhthos was already, but the lords of Zakynthos were often hostile to one another, and Odysseus had to intervene to ensure peace. He often traveled to Zakynthos for this purpose.

I advised him to create a military academy for young men on Ithaka so he could have the new generation properly trained and instructed. At first he didn't understand what I meant. He said that these people had no intelligence whatsoever. My husband was clever but not a visionary.

I started the discussion again during a dinner with some of the other lords. Everybody complained that there was not enough war experience on the islands. Acrisius and Laertes had both avoided conflicts, and that had worked well so far. Some were saying that Odysseus should continue in this way, and some were saying that times had changed and the islands should develop their own war capabilities before it was too late.

When the discussion started getting hot, I decided to intervene. "My lords and ladies," I said, "even without a concrete threat, young men need to receive proper training for war. It makes them more respectful and more willing to accept authority, which they don't learn when they lead lives of freedom up on the mountains as shepherds. Training for battle gives their bodies strength and an upright posture, which is not the case when they have to cultivate the land bent over all day."

"And who's going to teach them how to fight? We don't have anybody like Centaur Chiron here," said Aigyptius, who often liked to contradict me.

"Surely not." I turned to him. "But yourself, Aigyptius—you are an excellent spear thrower. You can teach them that. My husband knows sea battle well and can teach them that. Also—"

Odysseus felt I had talked enough, and he intervened. "Maybe your cousins Pollux and Castor could come to give us a hand."

"I'll send them a message asking them to join us and help us construct the academy," I said, and then I stayed quiet.

I did send for them, and they came. It was a short visit, but they helped me design a military academy for boys from ten to fourteen years old. After that age, boys could, in theory, go to war. They selected the old stable close to the palace as the place, and they put down a study plan that included all major battle techniques, such as spear throwing, sword training, wrestling, endurance training, and so on. My husband added naval techniques and naval battles to the program. I added music and poetry, and I took this up myself.

In the end we only needed to find the right teachers. My brothers organized sessions to test the capacities of the most experienced in war on the islands, and indeed we found someone for each discipline. During these tests, two of the people we had captured from the Phoenician ships came forward. One was a trained language teacher and the other a charioteer. My brothers were glad to include them in the training program, and they were glad they didn't need to work in the workshops anymore. It took some half a year to prepare the whole study program, and then they left.

Odysseus was left with the job of materializing the plan, and I made sure he did it. We started building the academy next to the palace—the gymnasium, the baths, the classroom, and the shrine to Zeus. We wanted to start hosting about thirty, and we left plenty of room for expansion.

ιθ′

One day bad news arrived: Helen's abduction by Paris. Telemachus was almost two and a half years old. Nestor, with two of his sons, paid us a visit to ask Odysseus to participate in an expedition to fetch her back. Helen was next after Leda to become the high priestess of Zeus in Sparta. The daughter of Zeus was a sacred person whom no one could touch without her consent; elsewise they risked the wrath of Zeus. Theseus had abducted her before, but Theseus was the son of Poseidon and a hero himself. Who was this Paris, anyway?

Against any common sense, Greek men decided to go to fetch her back.

Odysseus agreed that they should form an expedition to go and ask for her back, and he consented to be part of such an expedition. Soon after Nestor departed, a messenger arrived from Menelaus with a request to go to Mycenae, from where the expedition to request Helen back would depart. Odysseus left with two of his ships.

And he came back only a month later. He was very concerned, and he told me that war was inevitable because the Trojans had pretended they didn't know anything about Helen's abduction. Agamemnon had started gathering the armies in Aulis on the basis of the oath given in Sparta. "I don't want to go to war, Penelope," he told me one night as he was holding me, "but they will soon come for me. I don't want to leave all this that we've created together—the palace, the academy, the workshops, the making of more arable land. What will happen if I go?"

"Maybe you could go away. I could tell them you're away for business in Egypt," I said.

"They will wait for me to come back," he said. "I could pretend I went mad."

"You mad?" I said. "Do you think it will sell? You—"

He kissed me to stop me from talking. The shadow of war was hanging over the olive tree that served as our wedding bed like a black rain cloud.

A week later, Palamedes and his men arrived. Odysseus knew and was waiting for him. He started playing his role, that of a madman. He had persuaded his friends to help him, and all pretended that Odysseus was really not a man who could bear any responsibilities. During dinner, after Palamedes explained the reasons why he should join the war for Helen, Odysseus pretended he didn't know who Helen was and spoke about Menelaus as if he were his friend from youth and was now dead. He was also saying things that had no connection to what was discussed. I was once again surprised by his capability to pretend, and I often had to apologize on his behalf for disrupting the discussion.

The next day, he took all the fresh milk that his shepherds had brought to the palace, went to the shore, and threw it in the water in order to "feed the fish." Cyanea was all upset and went around the palace saying that she had no milk to give to anybody for breakfast because her lord Odysseus had fed the fish with it.

When Odysseus came back, I led a loud discussion, urging him to stay in his room in order to avoid any other mischief while I took Palamedes to show him our military academy. Odysseus then insisted that he felt well, and he would take the foreigners to the academy and I should go on preparing a worthy dinner for our guests.

So I agreed, and Odysseus took the foreigners to the stables instead of the military academy. The funniest thing was that he was trying to explain how the sheep were good at fighting. Odysseus's show continued during the evening, and Palamedes was already convinced and ready to go back to declare Odysseus's madness to the Achaeans.

On the day of the departure, Odysseus was out in the fields that he had cleared of stones. He was sowing them with salt, which was making me nervous because we didn't have much of it. I was standing there with our son in my arms because he was crying and wanted his father, who had been neglecting him during Palamedes's stay. The oxen were pulling the plow, and Odysseus was leading with broken lines and throwing salt. Palamedes had been skeptical at first, but then he grabbed the crying boy from my arms and put him, at the last moment, in front of the oxen and then moved away. I let out a cry because it looked sure that the oxen and the plow would go over the boy. Palamedes observed with a grin. Odysseus had to use all his mastery to turn the oxen and stop them in time. I ran and collected the child.

Palamedes, satisfied, went to Odysseus, who stood all withered. "We are expecting you in Aulis," he said.

Odysseus lowered his head and didn't say anything. He had lost this game.

A month later, he was ready to depart. Most men of Ithaka, as well as the new ships except one, with their rowers and many of the servants, departed with him. Before he left, he called all men destined to stay, either because they were too old or too young, and told them that it was I, Penelope, who should reign over the island during his absence, and his father would be my adviser. Such was his trust in my capabilities and wit.

I saw his fleet leaving—twelve of our best ships from our own shipyard, the three long ones with seventy men on each of them, built similar to the Phoenician ship we had captured. These ships could take horses on board, and there was storage room for tents and all the equipment the army would need for a longer stay, such as kitchen equipment, blankets, food and water containers, armaments, and, of course, servants. The rest were penteconters, fast and versatile ships that Odysseus had been using for his piracy expeditions. He took nine of them and left me the last two to defend the island if needed.

I watched them become smaller and smaller on the blue morning horizon as they headed south to go around Peloponnese and then north, past Aegina and Athens, to Aulis to meet the others. Telemachus—we had given this name to our boy, in the arms of his nanny—was also watching. Odysseus had said six months maximum, but I knew this was optimistic. Inside my mind I was preparing for a long period of absence.

As the sea swallowed the sight of them, I took a deep breath and went back to the palace.

κ'

I started feeling the weight of ruling and reigning. I was now holding the audiences all on my own. There were not any because most adult men had followed Odysseus, but still I would have preferred to spend my time with my little son. Odysseus had dissolved the military academy before his departure. He had told the boys that they should help their mothers with all the work they had now that their fathers had to go to war. I wanted to keep the academy running with all my heart, but it seemed impossible without adult men with war experience to teach.

More than the academy, though, were the households suffering. Sooner rather than later, I understood that there were not enough hands for all the jobs on the island. Women would have to replace their husbands and work twice as hard.

Women! I thought of all the houses of Ithaka that were without men. What were these women thinking now? I guessed the same as me—they would be back soon. "Let's hope!" I whispered during my loom work on one of the late afternoons.

And Cyanea, who was close to me, turned and looked at me. "Are you talking to yourself, my queen?" She laughed.

My maids, who were also working the wool, looked at me, worried.

"I guess this is the tiniest of my problems," I said.

"I know," she said. "You have to find some people to reap the fields. Odysseus did a good job plowing as much as possible during spring, but now, who's going to reap them?"

"I don't know, Cyanea," I whispered, and my hands worked harder as I thought about the problem.

"We have to get more work from the women, my lady, and maybe we could get the Taphians to help. Only a few of them followed our lord, your husband."

"I know. I have to go to talk to them," I said.

Everything seemed so difficult. "How am I going to do it?" I thought. Little Telemachus was sleeping in his cradle. Next to him, Armeria was breastfeeding her second child. I gazed at his lovely face—the smooth skin, the little lips. I had to make it for him.

I left my seat and went closer to the boy. He was giving me power. Autonoe immediately took my post at the loom, since the work had to be done.

Hippodamia, who was spinning, said in a low voice, "The purple is running out, my lady. And in the storage room, there

169

is no more of this purple that you like so much. We have to get some more."

Thekla looked at her with disapproval and said, "Well, if there is no more purple, we shall use more red. That's also a nice color, my lady, and we can do it ourselves."

I looked at her with love. "We shall buy some purple when the trader passes by again. But for sure we shall have to use more red in the future."

"I say we should use more undyed with more colorful embroidering," said Autonoe, who was very good at it.

"Yes, for sure we can do that," said Thekla. "I want so much to experiment with the golden swallows that you did last time on your dress. They look so beautiful."

"Oh, yes, but even the golden thread will soon run out," said Hippodamia nastily.

"We shall buy some more of it also," I said quietly. I left the side of my son and went to the statue of goddess Athena that was in the room. I felt the need to implore the goddess for help, but I limited myself to saying "We need to make a new head cover for our goddess. It has to be the best head cover we've ever made, and it should be all with material we can produce ourselves." I turned and looked at the maids. "Who of you will take this challenge upon herself?" I asked with eyes full of new hope.

"Me, my lady," they said all together, and Cyanea looked at me with admiration for how quickly I had changed their mood.

We stayed together, talking about the new peplos of Athena until late in the evening, even when there was no light to weave any longer.

The first harvest arrived. All autumn there was harvest. The grapes, the cereals, the olives, the production of wine, flour, olive oil. I was unprepared. Most of the production rotted on the plants. There were simply not enough hands to do everything. The year was good; we had a lot of everything, but most was falling from the plants, overripe. I was not sure if we had enough food to get through the winter.

During the thanksgiving fest, we thanked the gods for the good year, but I couldn't avoid thinking of the irony with which they treated us. For years, this or that harvest would go bad due to too much rain or too much heat or a sudden hail. And men were sitting around with nothing to do. This year all was perfect. Rain, as much as needed, when it was needed. No prolonged heat, no hail, nor storms. But when the moment came, no men were around to collect the fruits of nature. "At least we have the animals," said Autonoe, who was sitting next to me, as if reading my thoughts. "And anyway, fewer men means spare food."

I smiled with some bitterness.

The days were short now, and the long evenings were making me even more unhappy. It was the first winter without Odysseus, and I was already overwhelmed. Many fears were filling my brain and were obscuring my otherwise impeccable capability to reason. Laertes, who was coming every day to the palace, either for the audiences or to bring me meat or just to tell me the news, noticed my agitation. "You could ask your father to come again, my daughter," he said. "He is a wise man and can give you a hand with ruling."

I didn't want to call my father. I wanted to make it myself, exactly as all other women on Ithaka had to make it themselves. What would they think of me if I started bringing in help for myself and not for them? So I discarded the idea.

"In the spring we shall need hands for the preparation of the fields, my lady," he said.

"I know," I whispered. "Let us go through the winter without problems first. In March I'll go to the mainland to pay for people to come."

"They have their own land to take care of first," he said.

"In the mountains they start later," I said.

"Still, they will need persuasion."

I knew I was in trouble, but what was the gain of thinking about it now? Now I needed to think of the winter. "Do you think they have enough wood for heating?" I asked him.

"Well, this is also a job carried out by the men. We pruned the olive trees after the harvest, and that is usually enough. With the help of the gods, the winter will be light."

I looked at him warily.

The next day I went to the temple and made libations, asking the gods to protect us. But the gods didn't do so. The winter was tough. Probably the toughest I had ever experienced. It snowed for many days in a row, and the available wood was quickly used. Some people left their houses and went to live in caves, since they were warmer inside. There was not enough food, and some older people died from the combination of cold and hunger. The elders came to me to tell me to send a delegation to Delphi to ask the gods what we were doing wrong, so we did. The delegation took three weeks to go and come back, and in between, the cold subsided. They said that all Greece had suffered the cold.

People were saying that the gods had sent a warning to our men to come back to their homes and stop thinking about Troy. Agamemnon's fleet was sitting in Aulis waiting for the proper wind to sail. But it was not coming. Men were stuck there, not allowed to go back to their homes and unable to sail to Troy.

The oracle's message was even stranger. "The problems of Ithaka will recede when the lake waters recede and the queen embraces her mother." My mother? My mother was a free soul. I hadn't seen her since Aunt Leda had taken me to her. I knew she had joined Artemis and her huntresses, but they never stood still. They were always in the woods, bringing order and the rule of gods. How could I ever embrace her? And then…what lake? There were no lakes on the islands.

When the elders heard the oracle, they were worried. "The only lakes we have on the islands, my lady, are in the caves. We don't dare to go close to the caves. They are dangerous and mystical, and the nymphs who live there are unpredictable and not the friends of man."

"I've been in one of those," I said, remembering the operation to get rid of the Egyptian vessel. "It didn't seem so dangerous."

"Maybe you should go back to Sparta, my lady, and find your mother there," someone said.

I turned, surprised. "I'm not leaving the palace. If I have to embrace my mother, then she should come here to me," I said.

The next day, I took the horse and rode to the cliff with the cave. The place looked weird in the daylight. It was still winter, and nature seemed naked. I looked down the cliff, and the animal bones of the sacrifices, whitened by the sun, made me shiver. I knew there was a lake down there, but I couldn't see it from here above.

I looked around but couldn't find the little road that I had taken with Perimedes. I raised my head and looked at the sea. It was swollen. The waves were crashing on each other, making foam. The roar was scary.

I walked to the edge to find the little path to go down, and it didn't take me long to find it. It was narrow, and I wondered how I had managed to go down this little path during the night. Arriving down, I saw again the beach with the bones, and the lake was now opening in front of me with crystal-clear waters, calm and beautiful. The passing sunrays were coloring it emerald green. It reminded me of the colors and lights that were coming out of the water back in Polylimnio of Pylos.

The beach was confined by the cave walls. I knew this cave had an opening to the sea, but I could not see it from the beach. It was becoming darker and darker toward the deep part of the cave. It was mystical; they were right, and I didn't see how these waters would ever recede.

I went closer and put my fingers on the calm water surface, which rippled. The first ripple made a second one and then a third, and instead of getting smaller and disappearing, they amplified and moved decisively toward the dark part of the cave. I pulled my hand away when I noticed the unnatural phenomenon, as if not to get burned.

I felt unease and was turning to leave when I felt a murmur, as if the wind had gotten entangled in my hair and was trying to escape. I looked around suspiciously and ran up the path. I wanted to reach the top as soon as possible. I rode the horse hastily, and in my imagination, angry nymph spirits were hunting me.

I arrived home, went straight to the kitchen, opened the wine jar, and a filled a cup, which I drank in one draw. The cook looked at me, surprised. I looked back to discourage him from making any comments. I spent the rest of the day with Telemachus trying to dispel the spirits in my head and the fears in my heart. But during night, thoughts of guilt overwhelmed me. The queendom was in bad shape. Soon, work for the preparation of the fields would start, and there were no hands. How would we ensure food for next winter? This winter had been tough, and I didn't see how to stop the next one from being the same. I knew I had to go around the country and see what the needs were, but I felt scared to face my subjects, scared they thought their queen was not up to the challenge. Maybe they were right. Maybe I should call Icarius to give me a hand or go back to Sparta altogether.

Laertes came to see me. He was a wise man. He offered me his help. He said that he was ready to support me in all these jobs and to be next to me whenever I needed him. I was relieved. I, the queen of Ithaka, twenty-three years old and mother of a little boy, surely needed any help I could find. At the beginning of spring, Laertes, Telemachus, and I took the carriage around our island—Zakynthos, Dulichium, Same, and Taphos. I couldn't solve the problems, but it was good to look the people in the eyes. Nobody complained, nobody criticized. I could see appreciation for my visit in their eyes. They only expressed the wish to see their men return quickly.

But the contrary happened. One morning I felt a nice, fresh wind that I had not felt for years. It was coming from the south, and I knew this was the wind that the ships had been awaiting. The wind that swept over all Greece brought along the consent of Artemis to the expedition. It blew the sails of the Achaean ships, and they departed for Troy, and it was another blow to my expectation for a quick return of Odysseus.

When the plowing and pruning started, I closed the palace workshops and the shipyard, and I sent the workers to help with the field work. I also sent my people to the mainland to find paid workers, but it was impossible to compete with the salaries my cousin Clytemnestra was offering. The few workers available had moved to Argos and Mycenae. I sent a message asking for help to Icarius, and he sent me a small team of fifty people. I worked hard myself in the fields, and even my maids and the palace servants helped. It was a difficult time. The sheep and goat herds, decimated by the winter hunger, started giving birth. I ordered a limit on sacrifice, to keep the animals for the winter, but some thought that was an offense to the gods and ignored my order.

Summer arrived and passed without any problems. Harvest and winter came again, and no sign of the men returning. This winter was milder, but another sad event happened. Pirates attacked Zakynthos. We saw the fires signaling attack overnight and we sailed there, but it was already too late. A full village was ravaged. Dead everywhere, and all women and children taken to be sold as slaves. I was crying from anger, and I decided not to accept that. I created a small team of men with Aigyptius as their leader to go and find them. I gave all the palace's treasure to bring back the people. And indeed, some we managed to recover, but most we lost forever. Some months later another calamity occurred. Odysseus sent us some of his loot from the war in Troy, but the ship that was bringing it was attacked by pirates past Pylos, and all the gold was stolen. So I was left now even without any gold to pay for hands. My problems had multiplied, and I had to find a way out of it.

κα′

The night of the news of the lost gold mission, I didn't manage to sleep. I was angry and desperate. I was watching Athena's statue, and I couldn't help thinking that she was making fun of me. The next day, the sun was shining with all its strength, and the air was thin and perfumed of spring and sea. Everything seemed so light and beautiful, and I was suddenly filled with a power that was not mine. I had to find a way out of the trouble. I had to become stronger and beat the odds. I felt my rationality was limiting me in seeing the difficulty of the situation instead of envisioning a bright future. I started walking around talking to myself. "Think of how you want your future to be, of how you want the people of Ithaka to be: fed and happy."

My steps took me back to the cave lake. This time I was determined to stay and face the spirits of the lake. I also knew what I wanted to ask. They should put me in contact with my mother. I went down and looked at the gray water with some fear and distress. I looked up to check the color of the sky, and it looked the same. I wondered what I was doing there, and I embraced myself as if to protect myself from the cold of the day—but more to dispel my bad thoughts.

There was no movement. Nothing at all. "I want to talk to Mum," I shouted toward the dark part of the lake.

"What an idiot you are," my rational part was saying to me. No reaction, no change in the waters, no movement.

I looked around. My discomfort was getting bigger. "Look, I don't want to scare you, but if you could help me find my mum, it'd be great. I am in great difficulty, and she is the only one who can help me. I am Penelope, queen of this place, and I shall offer you great sacrifices for your help. My mum is Periboia, a follower—"

"I know who you are and who your mother is," a female voice said.

I couldn't see her, but the waters started changing colors. "And can you help me?" I asked with agony.

"I don't know. I have to see. Artemis does not always respond to the requests of the nymphs."

The water was changing colors with the tone of her voice. It turned from gray to blue to green to blue again. It was as if I were talking to the water. It remained blue, and then it began getting gray again.

I got scared that she had lost interest and that she was about to leave. So I added quickly, "Will you try it for me?"

"Why should I? I don't have anything to gain from helping humans. You are not reliable, and you never stop asking for things."

"Oh, I'm sorry for any bad experience humans have given you, but I'm the daughter of a nymph myself, and I need to find Mum. Do you have any children yourself?"

The water became red. "I'd never allow myself to fall in love with a mortal man," her voice thundered.

I got scared and turned to leave.

"Put your hand on the water, and let it mirror your face," she asked. "I'll make sure your image is sent through all waters until your mother sees you. We shall let you know when to come back." She was calmer now.

I did as she asked, and I left. On the way back, I was thinking of what had happened. The more I thought about it, the less I believed it. The next day, it was only a remote memory, a visit to a lake, and nothing could foretell what was to follow.

One day as I was holding my audience in the palace, an old lady, so old and bent that I asked the guards to give her a chair, entered the room. There was nothing unusual about ladies coming to the royal audiences, since there were hardly any adult men left on the islands. But this one seemed so old and broken that all other speakers put her first in the queue.

"Speak, old lady, and let us know what bothers you so much to make you come here and requires the queen's attention. But first, tell us who you are and where your home is, since I don't remember seeing you before, either in the palace or during my round trips," I said.

She was now sitting in front of me on the chair brought by the guards. "Queen of Ithaka, you are distinguished among women to rule us all. Great-grandchild of our king Theseus, you carry all the wisdom of the house in which you were born. Difficult days await our people, and the thoughts of all elder women are with you. In nine days we shall have the spring solstice, and all our ladies will meet in the great cave to honor the daughter of Demeter. You are also expected, my lady."

"Me?" I asked. "Who are the ladies? Where is the great cave? Who are you?"

She continued as if I had not talked at all. "Be there at dawn, and be modestly dressed. Bring fresh bread and wine with you as an offering to those who expect you. Your mother-in-law knows the way to the great cave." She stood up and left swiftly with moves that didn't correspond to her looks anymore.

A murmur rose upon her disappearance. "This was a goddess. Athena herself."

"My lady, the goddesses themselves speak to you. They have granted you access to their council. This is a great honor, my lady," Anticlea, who was sitting farther back, said.

All were looking at me with admiration. "Ithaka has the blessing of the goddess," one of them said.

"Nothing can go wrong anymore," another one shouted.

And then they all started singing the hymn to the mother goddess, an ancient hymn that went like this:

> Stand up, you beauty of my heart, and
> move your body through the rays of the sun.
>
> Green fields reflect your eyes, and the
> rain of your lashes, wealthy nourishment they give.
>
> With your lips so full of love, Eros flies all over us.
>
> Sheep and horses and yellow bees all so long for your sweet, lovely kiss.

> Hair so blond as ripe wheat sweeps the
> leaves of the tall trees. The wind shies from
> any touch of it for fear he may not ever again
> be free.

They continued, each singing one stanza like the above, blessing the goddess.

"Come, my lady. We shall go to offer libations," Cyanea whispered and helped me up.

I was feeling confused and at the same time touched by the spontaneity of the women. They had suddenly seen a ray of hope in their desperation. And it was I who had brought it to them. I wanted so much to make it better for them. I didn't want to fail them.

Anticlea prepared everything for me. She gave me one white chiton made of the finest lamb's wool, undyed and worn for the first time. She prepared the bread first thing the same morning, and she took me to the entrance of the cave. After she had seen me disappear into the entrance, she drove back while two guards stayed and waited for me.

Although it was still dark outside, I could see quite well. The cave, though, was stygian. I stayed there, waiting for my eyes to get used to it or for someone to come and get me. I was holding the bread in one hand and the wine jar in the other. I dared to move forward. A sudden wind blew, and I stopped. I took another step, and I felt the wind stronger.

"This way," said the wind, and it pushed me from behind.

I was not scared but was a bit annoyed. Someone could have come to welcome me and show me the way. I took some steps and then realized my feet were wet. I stopped when, suddenly, the water started illuminating with a soft yellow light that slowly turned the cave golden. Only then I realized I was in an open space of the cavern with tall walls and beautiful stalactites and stalagmites. The water retracted from my feet and started swelling at the back wall, opposite me.

The swells turned to faces and hair and female bodies, and each of them was a goddess or a nymph. At the moment of their appearance, they were extremely tall, so tall that I thought they would break the roof of the cavern. But then immediately they came down to my size. They were all beautiful and perfect in proportions and dressed in rays more than clothes. I felt my mind being blown away from the sight, and my knees became weak.

One of the stalagmites started changing shape in the same way as the water, and following the same process, a goddess with a long chiton appeared with a helmet on her head. I blanched, since I knew who she was.

"Excuse me for the delay," she said, immediately turning to me, "but I hate this watery thing. Let us introduce ourselves. I'm Athena, and she over there is your mother, Periboia."

I turned. She was more beautiful than I could remember from the last time I had seen her, with Aunt Leda. She sent me back a thin smile, thinner than the air of the cave but still present.

"I know her looks have improved, but she is an immortal now and lives among us. Next to her is Thetis—you remember her from her wedding in Pelion, maybe. She is the absolute lady of the Mediterranean Sea. Next is Calypso, the nymph of the invisible island. She has powers that we may need. Leukothea is the fastest swimmer and messenger, and she will quickly be at your side when needed. And last but not least, Melissanthe, the nymph of the cave whom you implored for help. We are here to help you after your request for the approval of Zeus, the giver of life.

"None of the gods resisted helping you, which means you are a worthy human. Stay so and dare to go for your dreams, because we trust your judgment, and we shall help whenever you invoke us. If you need to meet with us again, Melissanthe knows where to find us. As a symbol of our bond, each will eat a piece of the ambrosia and drink from the nectar that you brought."

I wanted to correct her and say it was only bread and wine, but no voice came out, and when I looked in my hands, the bread and wine were different. Thetis appeared first in front of me, although she hadn't moved at all. She took a piece of the ambrosia, soaked it with nectar, and ate it. She did this looking into my eyes so intensely that I felt she was sucking my brain.

Then the others came, one after the other—Athena, and last, my mother. Once she had eaten her bit, she took the last bit, which had remained exactly as big as what the others had eaten. She wetted it with the last drop of nectar without letting anything be spilled and gave it to me to eat. I chewed and swallowed instinctively without thinking and without feeling the taste of it. Then she embraced me with love and stepped back.

The will of the oracle of Delphi had been materialized, and she had embraced me. They all disappeared again, in the same way they had appeared, and I was suddenly next to the guards outside the cave. The guards were asleep, and at that exact moment, the first rays of the sun hit their eyes, awakening them. They noticed me and stood up, bowing and asking my pardon. They asked if we could go back.

I was numbed, and I only nodded to their requests, still unable to speak. It took me a week to elaborate this experience. In fact, at some stage I was wondering if it was only my imagination. But then I accepted that this was my way of becoming stronger and envisioning my future. Female goddesses were key in my empowerment. They had practically given me a promise of help for whatever I decided to do. This was more powerful than whatever I had expected. Moreover, my mother had embraced me, meaning Ithaka would not suffer disasters anymore, and I had eaten ambrosia wetted in nectar, which was making me personally invulnerable. In this way I had armed myself for overcoming my future challenges. Still, it was not clear to me how or if I would be up to the task, but a first step had been taken.

κβ′

Armed with a new power, I decided to take the initiative. I wanted to protect, by all means, the new mission of gold Odysseus had sent me from Thrace. This time the gold had to arrive at Ithaka, at any price. I knew when Odysseus had sent the boat, and together with Polydorus, we calculated the time it would need under normal conditions to arrive at Cape Tenaron.

This time I'd take care of this personally. I prepared the two boats Odysseus had left me and took with me all older men who could still hold a sword and some of the older young boys I knew from the academy. Some had just started getting beards but were keen to fight. I talked to them with warm words. I explained how important it was for the survival of the kingdom to protect the gold mission. It would pay for workers and for food that we needed to survive next winter. They were so young, and they would have to carry out their first mission under the command of a woman. They didn't seem to worry. They trusted me more than I was trusting myself.

The evening before, I went to Melissanthe's cave. I mirrored my face in the water, and she emerged on the surface as if in a fountain. She walked on the water, which filled me with awe, and she said, "Tell me, daughter of Periboia, how can I help you?"

"I'm departing tomorrow with the boys of the island to protect the gold mission of my husband. The country has no money. I'm in difficulty to feed the people. I would like to ask for your blessing."

"You have it, my queen. Be aware, though, that your husband destroys and loots the villages of Thrace. This is how this gold is obtained. You'll be asked to pay it back, and you shall do that when the time comes," she said and disappeared.

So my husband was doing what he knew well—looting and killing. I felt ashamed, but I had no time to think about it. I realized I was being given a loan that I'd need to pay back later, but my first worry was to obtain it.

The next day at dawn, I left my son with the maids and Mentor—a man Odysseus had entrusted him with his education before he'd left—and sailed away. We had time to stop at Zakynthos. We met Adamas and explained our plan. He was too old to follow Odysseus, but his bigger sons had done so. He laughed. "You don't expect to defeat experienced sea people with a handful of schoolboys and some old folk," he started saying, but then he felt ashamed and diminished his voice, looking away. "I wish you good luck. We have no people to contribute to it except my younger son, who is already under your command. I only beg to the gods for his life," he said bitterly. I could understand his feelings, and I didn't want to discuss it or my decision to protect the mission.

I left, and his son followed me, although Adamas tried secretly to persuade him to remain behind later in the night. We passed by Pylos, but we didn't stop. We knew Pylos had fewer problems than we did, since their missions were much better protected by the army of Nestor.

We arrived in the Messenian Gulf and waited. The mission arrived after two days. We recognized the boat of Ithaka, with our colors of bright blue. As we saw them, we started moving toward them. They slowed down their rowing, and, as we approached, I recognized Perimedes with happiness. Odysseus had entrusted the gold to him to increase the chances of arrival.

He came on board my ship happy, but his face darkened when he saw how young most of the sailors were and how old the officers were. "This is the best I could do." I smiled. "But the goddesses are with us."

He nodded and said, "I can't imagine any better choice the godesses could make." He paused. "Odysseus told me to give the gold only to you. But most likely he didn't think of handing it over in the middle of the sea. If you wish so, my lady, I can accompany you all the way to Ithaka, although my heart longs to go back to my companions as soon as possible."

"No, no need to accompany me, Perimedes. How is Odysseus?" I asked.

"Well, as war allows it. Sometimes we are lucky, and we obtain good loot, such as this. Sometimes we count only our wounds. But our lord Odysseus is a cunning man and knows how to spare his people."

"Tell him that his wife and son long to see him back home again," I said.

He nodded and went back on his boat and gave the order to unload the heavy chests on the beach and then to load them on our boat. Once done, they immediately turned around and sailed back.

We found refuge for the night on the same beach of the gulf before rounding the cape toward Zakynthos. The next morning, we hadn't sailed far when we saw them. Two boats with black sails were following us. They were rowing with full power, and they were closing the gap quickly. They were longer than us and were approaching at high speed. It was obvious to me we couldn't escape. I started thinking of possible ways. The old men were watching, alarmed, but they didn't say anything. The boys couldn't wait to fight. I didn't wish to fight. I didn't want to lose any of my crew. I had to be cleverer than they were. But how?

"They have bronze at the sides," I heard the voice of Aigyptius say.

Indeed, the two pirate boats had kind of wings with sharp ends made of bronze. It was clear that by passing close to our ship, they would cut our wooden hull like butter. "This is their method. They will try to pierce us at the sides and loot the boats while we're trying to save ourselves from drowning." They all looked worried now.

I looked at the sea and thought, "Let's see if you'll remember your promise, Thetis."

"Separate," I shouted. "One boat toward the left, one toward the right. Don't let them come close to you. Row with all your power."

They seemed unsure and hesitant, and I then shouted with all my power, as if to wake them up. "This is an order."

They started rowing as I had asked. A sign was made to the other boat that they had to row to the left while we were rowing to the right. The pirate boats started following. The race had started, and it was close.

"Faster, faster," I shouted, and I took the drumsticks to create a faster beat.

When we had them well behind us, I turned our boats toward each other, so our two vessels were rowing against each other, with the pirate boats behind them and decreasing the distance. The pirate boat behind us was almost touching ours now, and I could almost see their faces. I noticed they were already throwing the hooks to pull our vessel toward their bronze sides. Some of the rowers were cutting the ropes to escape. But now our two vessels were almost passing side by side in opposite directions.

"Pull the oars," I shouted, and they did.

The sea seemed to separate into two lanes, and the two boats slid so close to each other that it seemed a miracle they didn't touch. It took only a minute, and we all looked to one another as if we didn't believe to our own eyes.

The disaster came right after. The two pirate vessels, in their excitement to get us, didn't notice that they were too close to avoid each other's bronze sides. They pierced each other with terrible noise, shouting, and cursing. I made a sign to continue without looking back. I noticed the looks of my sailors—full of amazement at a plan that had been spontaneous and worked only due to a miracle. So Thetis did help when needed, I thought, and I thanked her silently for her intervention.

The sea remained calm for the rest of the journey, and we reached Ithaka without any problems.

Odysseus had sent a load of gold, armor, jewels, tin, clothes, and jars full of wine, cotton, barley, and honey. "I'm not sure how I'll pay all this back," I thought, worried, watching the full chests. "But let's don't think about it now."

I made sure everything was stored properly, and I organized a sacrifice to thank the nymphs and goddesses for their help. All the islands were invited, and they all came. It was a great feast during which I made sure all the young men who had followed me were rewarded with extra portions of food and each with a new spear from Odysseus's mission. The gold allowed me to pay for workers and buy extra food so that no one would get hungry in the winters to come. Armed with confidence, I went out on the sea again and again to protect further gold missions from Troy, which always worked fine with the help of the great goddess. Only rarely did we have to fight, and even so, none of my boys were killed, which added to my fame. More people were coming to work for me, to be my rowers or soldiers. So I decided to reopen the military academy to accommodate all the boys who were coming to my help. I realized I had no young and strong teachers, but some of the prisoners and palace servants came to our help, as well as some of the elders who could still hold weapons. And the older ones would pass by to give their advice every now and then. I was very happy with this development and proud that the academy now had a life of its own.

κγ'

More boys were coming to join my military academy. And suddenly my classes on language and history were full. The boys were coming with much more lust, and some even with passion. I was an established leader now in their eyes, in an Achaean world starved for males. Moreover, they hoped I would take them along on my next journey and adventure. I had always loved teaching, but now, with all the young blood in it, all the questions and attempts to draw my attention, it was really great. The lesson was, for me, intellectually stimulating and rewarding. I could improvise and push my thinking, logic, and instinct in order to search for answers and propose explanations. Even some of the elders were coming to listen to me, and they were happy to give a hand with teaching or other tasks, such as preparing lunch and dinner and keeping the rooms clean and fixing all that needed fixing.

Telemachus, my son, was growing fast and wanted to join the academy as soon as possible. I had promised him he would be able to do so on his eighth birthday, and so it was. He was a clever boy and was learning fast, but he started developing a sort of jealousy of the other students, particularly my best students. His mother was his, and no other boy had the right to receive her attention. It looked for a while as if this would be my biggest challenge—how to make my son feel part of the group and take his bond with me to a level where jealousy had no chance.

"But why should you, for heaven's name, want this?" Thekla, my maid, asked when I explained my worries to my weaving team, my maids, and Cyanea. "The beauty of having boys is exactly this strong bond they have with their mothers."

"No, Thekla," I said. "Don't you see that I need my independence? And so does he. We cannot behave like lovers. We have a country to rule, and each citizen should have a bond with his or her ruler. If my son gets jealous about this and tries to break it, he only risks his own succession on the throne."

Cyanea jumped into the discussion. "Which bond with citizens are you talking about, my lady? No man ever does this. Most of them rule by fear and the exercise of power. Even your uncle Tyndareus and your father, Icarius, who were the best kings I knew, were established by Heracles, who was highly respected, even feared. Men don't make bonds." She concluded as she rocked her chair and did her sewing, looking wise. "They do give an expectation of power, though, to those who support them. This is also a way of ruling. They raise the expectation to some, promise more power to others, or even give small portions of it to their followers, who slowly become dependent on them and blinded to their atrocities."

I looked at her in surprise. What she was saying was true. I had never thought of it. Was it a difference between a man's and a woman's way of ruling? Why did I need to create a bond? After all, I didn't need it—I was the great-granddaughter of Perseus, and they should accept me for that.

But somehow, this thought was not satisfactory. "I believe power is a necessary but not sufficient condition of ruling," I heard myself saying. And I continued as if someone else were using my lips to speak through my mouth, not so much for the others to listen but more for me. "Through the bond, each individual may see in you what inspires her. Power does not inspire everybody, and mostly not the ladies, whom I need to run the business of the country. Some men may feel challenged more than subdued by my power, or they may even be scared away."

"Not if the power comes from the gods, my lady," said Thekla, who was very pious. "Gods rectify everything, even pathological hierarchies. This is what Heracles did when he reestablished your father and uncles in power. And you do the same, my lady. You are the legitimate ruler of this place. Everybody thinks it."

I looked at the statue of Athena. Was she giving me power to rule? Sure she was, but it was a power to resolve the conflicts, find solutions to problems, and foresee the future. It was not raw power over my subjects. It was not suppression. I was definitely not using the power of the gods to intimidate my subjects, and I knew many rulers were doing exactly that. "Ruling under the power of the gods, Thekla, is even more dangerous. It may lead to the complete overthrow of the gods themselves. A kingdom that overthrows its rulers is a rebelling society, and a society that overthrows its gods has lost its set of values and is bound to be vanish." I was again struck by my own words. I felt they were too profound for me, not to say for poor Thekla.

"But then, my lady, your bond with the citizens must be in parallel with and part of the bond of the citizens with the gods. Then these underpin the values of the society," she said, as if for a moment illuminated.

I smiled and stroked her hair. "Yes, my child. You said it correctly," I said and looked again at the statue of the virgin with gratitude. I had explained my instinct. I knew I was doing the right thing, but now I also had the logical explanation for it. Mine would be a reign based on values, not on power.

But the same evening, I saw Thekla leaving the palace hastily, holding libations. I asked her where was she going, and she turned to me, scared, with tears in her eyes. "The discussion we had this morning, my lady, made me worry who was first. Do values make gods, or gods values? And I got so ashamed, my lady, and now I'll go to all altars to offer libations with the hope that the gods will have pity on me and will not punish me for thinking such things." She tried to leave.

"But the gods want us to think. Athena wants us to use our minds."

"But not for things that question their power, my lady. I'll ask pardon also for you, my lady," she said and left.

And I stayed back, watching her going. If the gods were only personifications of societal values, then challenging them undermined the fabric of our own existence, the source of our regenerative forces, the same forces that were helping me win over my fears. In this respect the gods had a reason for being and therefore their own presence.

For a moment I got scared myself—I might get punished for too much thinking the wrong things. I decided to go back to the original problem of how to manage my son, of how to show him that instead of watching out for me, he should make bonds with his future subjects.

κδ'

It was not only the academy that was receiving many recruits. Also, the palace was now full of children. Autonoe had married Polydorus, and they had two kids already. Hippodamia had married one of the older soldiers of the academy and already had one child, while Dolius and Armeria had three kids.

Thekla, to the surprise of all, had married one of the officers of the captured Egyptian ship, and he was now working in the bronze workshop and teaching sword fighting at the academy. He was amazing, and he quickly adapted to the new situation. He fell in love with Thekla almost at first sight, but it took him more than five years to conquer her. I guess this was the reason why he never tried to escape. I had noticed his interest but kept quiet, initially because I wanted to know him better and judge his character. Then it became clear to me that he was a noble person with excellent manners and a hardworking mentality. He asked to help me at the academy, and I agreed, although many disapproved of my decision to give him the sword. Slowly he became one of my best advisers on national interests and defense. Thekla was encouraged by my trust in him, and one day she came to me to ask my opinion about him. I was happy she had done so. I had long since understood their feelings, and I knew they belonged together. So I released her from her doubts, promising her that I would announce him a free man on the day of their wedding and that I would give him a parcel of land and help him build their house, so as to persuade her family to agree with the wedding and hand over Thekla's dowry. It was a beautiful wedding, and I was proud for their union. Moreover, he never left Ithaka, even when he could have.

So all my maids now had their own families, and their kids were growing quickly. But I was feeling more alone, and I was praying to the gods to end the war and let my husband come back. I didn't care if he was wounded or broken, didn't mind his craftiness and cunning. I just wanted him back. I would straighten his mischief, and I would never let him go on any piracy mission or war anymore. I was dreaming of a quiet life—yes, a boring life, similar to those my maids had with their husbands.

I was already collecting gold to pay back my debts, exactly as Melissani had advised me. No one should suffer for a strong and wealthy Ithaka. I was wise enough to know that injustice brings more injustice, and in one way or another, injustice comes back to those who inflict it in the first place. So gold should go from Ithaka back to those from whom it had been stolen so they wouldn't feel unjustly treated by the king and queen of Ithaka and they wouldn't implore the gods to distribute justice against us. Telemachus wouldn't have to pay for the mistakes of his parents.

Telemachus was growing, together with so many other kids in the palace, playing, learning, and being happy. And I found the formula to free him from his jealousy. Despite Mentor's opposition, I took him for a month's trip to visit all our guard posts on the island. Just him and me. We went up mountains and down the rocky beaches and on windy capes, and we stood on foggy cliffs where only the eagle could reach. It was a great experience for both. We talked a lot and brought presents to the frontiersmen, and they appreciated the visit of their future king.

Their conditions were harsh. Some of them had their families with them. Some of them were on their own. We promised to fix their houses and send them more supplies. This became a project for Telemachus, who now felt in charge of the people who were safeguarding us. Now he knew what I meant about creating bonds with the people. These people depended on him, and they expected his care and attention. This filled him with a feeling of responsibility that took him out of his childish jealousy and gave him a new, more fulfilled life.

After a year he returned to the posts, now on his own with his own guard. And when he became twelve, I officially gave him the title of chief of the frontier guard, with new armor and a new sword. Ithakans cheered for their future king, and he started taking ownership of his future kingdom.

κε'

It was during this time that my cousin Clytemnestra, queen of Mycenae and therefore of all Achaeans, asked all the rulers to meet in Mycenae during the first full moon of the summer. Eight winters had already passed from when Agamemnon's army had gathered. Clytemnestra had had a difficult time, I knew. Her daughter had been sacrificed for the war. She was the price that Agamemnon had to pay for taking leadership of the expedition to Troy. I was sure Clytemnestra still hated Agamemnon for that. She had been left alone to govern the city, the kingdom, and all Achaeans. I knew her father, Tyndareus, was often there to help her, and I also knew that her task was much bigger than mine.

Along with me, other wives joined the meeting. Egialea, the wife of Diomedes and queen of Argos; Clytemnestra's sister Timandra from Pisa; Meda, wife of Idomeneus and queen in Crete; Glauca, wife of Ajax the Great of Salamis; Polyxo, wife of Tlepolemus on Rhodes; Euridice, wife of Nestor from Pylos; and, last but not least, my sister Iphthimi, as queen of Pheraes.

We all arrived on the same evening, right before the day of the full moon of September, as Clytemnestra wished. The trip took us a week. I had with me a guard of twenty of my best soldiers from the academy.

I hadn't been in Mycenae since the wedding of Clytemnestra. The palace there was impressive. The walls were massive. A huge paved road led chariots from Argos and Tiryns up to the hill where the palace was situated. One had a wonderful view of all the surrounding valley. The guard took me to the megaron and told me to wait there for the great queen. An officer came to greet me officially, and again I was asked to wait for the great queen. They were all very formal, much more than my guard at my palace back in Ithaka. The megaron was beautifully decorated, but more than that, there was armor exhibited around and double axes, spears, swords, and other weapons hanging from the walls. It was a warriors' place, and it made me feel awkward.

My attention was drawn by the exhibits and their shining glory, and then a young girl, probably the same age as Telemachus, came close to me. "This is the sword with which Perseus killed Medusa," she said. "Come; I'll show you the lion-skin armor of Uncle Heracles."

She took me to a huge suit of armor partly made of bronze and partly made of lion skin. It was breathtaking. "And here is his club as well." She tried to take it, but it was too heavy for her. "Here, try yourself. Impossible to hold for a normal human," she said, full of pride.

I tried to take the club myself, and I realized she was right. "And who are you?" I asked.

"I'm Electra. Mummy will be here soon. She got important news from Troy. That is why she's late to meet you. When Daddy comes back, we shall put his armor here also. He is an important warrior himself, you know."

We heard a door opening and realized Clytemnestra had arrived.

When I saw her, tall and thin, standing in front of the main door, I was awestruck. She was a real queen, standing majestic and sober. "Cousin," she said. "I'm honored you are my guest and glad to see you are well."

I embraced her. "You can't imagine my happiness at seeing you, cousin, and in such good health. It has been many years since your wedding. How is your family? And most of all, how are you coming along with all the difficulties of the kingdom?"

"Come, cousin; let me show you your apartments first, and there is time to discuss everything later. I have put you together with your sister Iphthimi. I hope you'll enjoy it."

"My sister is here?" I whispered, and my heart fluttered.

Clytemnestra made a sign to one of her maids and told her, "Accompany my cousin to the double room." She moved back to the main gate, since another set of chariots had just arrived.

I ran up the stairs, and when the maid opened the door, I saw her in front of me. My sister. I was moved and she the same. We cried each other's names and fell into each other's arms. We had eyes full of tears when we looked at each other. "I'm so glad you are well, little sister," she told me.

We sat on the bed and started recounting our lives, first with our husbands and then without them. I was amazed to hear that she had problems similar to mine in running the country without adult men. She was astonished to hear my story about the help of the goddesses, though. "You must be a special person, Penelope, if gods talk to you," she said, looking at me with awe.

"No, only goddesses," I said.

"They are even more difficult for humans to come into direct contact with," she said.

I tried to downplay it. "I only wanted to talk to Mother."

"No, Penelope. Mother never appeared to me. Only to you," she said, and I suddenly realized she was right. In all my encounters with Mother, I had been on my own, except for the first time, with Aunt Leda.

"But Aunt Leda took me to her the first time."

"Aunt Leda never offered me the possibility of meeting Mother, Penelope. Only you. There must be a reason."

I didn't know what to say. I felt bad. I thought Iphthimi would help me explain all these appearances of goddesses. But she was more lost than I was. Maybe I shouldn't have mentioned it. I had behaved stupidly.

"But, sister, it is good that the goddesses help you. It is fantastic that you can talk to them," she said, as if she could read my thoughts.

"I'm sure they also help you, Iphthimi. I'm sure Mother is close to you always. It is only that you don't see her because you are so busy with your daily jobs."

"Yes, that must be it," she said skeptically. "Let's see what Clytemnestra wants from us. Do you have any idea?"

"No," I said, "but I hope she wants to announce the return of our husbands."

Clytemnestra let us rest the next day, which I appreciated. I met her kids, little Chrysothemis, Orestes, and Electra, whom I had met in the megaron. They were nice, but they seemed to dislike their uncle Aegisthus, who was always around Clytemnestra, making sure the servants were following commands but himself talking very little.

On the second day, Clytemnestra asked all wives to the megaron. The maids were offering fruit water with honey and water with wine. As the last lady appeared, the guards closed the doors, and Clytemnestra, who was sitting on her throne, stood up. "Sit down, my ladies," she said. "I hope you enjoy our hospitality. It is my pleasure to have you here, and now I realize I should have done it earlier. But it took me a long time to overcome the violent death of my daughter Iphigenia, killed by the hand of her own father to soothe the gods for this unhallowed war."

Her voice became rough, and one could notice the hate overwhelming her. The room was dead silent, all eyes turned to her. She regained control of herself, calmed her voice, came down from her throne base, and started moving around us, often putting her hand on someone's shoulder. "But we are not here to talk about that. Our husbands have left us all alone, to reign and master the difficulties and problems of the kingdoms, left mainly with women, old men, and babies. And we all know how horrible that was. No hands to harvest, no food in the winter. Cold and disease. Pirates on our coasts destroying the villages, and no army left behind to protect us. We all went through this. And even when gold and war prisoners were arriving, theft and murder was thriving. We all went through thick and thin. We worked with our own bare hands to carry out the jobs to be done. We went through any challenge to save the kingdom."

She stopped in front of me. "My dear cousin Penelope became a pirate herself to save her boats." She turned to Meda. "Meda dressed as a male priest to carry out the ceremonies as the protocol prescribes." Then she touched the hands of Egialea. "And you, my dear friend, had to work in the fields yourself, together with me, with our bare hands, to harvest the barley for the kids to have enough bread during the winter. All of us opened up the palace storehouses to give everybody food."

"We only do what our duty is as queens, Clytemnestra," Iphthimi said.

"Yes, we were all wonderful doing our duty and following the rules that our men had put in place but were unable to follow themselves." Again her voice was rough and full of hate.

"What do you mean, Clytemnestra? They also did their duty, by going to war," said Glauca.

"Did they?" shouted Egialea. "Was this war their duty? The Trojans never attacked any of our cities. Never took any of us as slaves. Never stole or destroyed any of our property. Was this war necessary?"

"They did steal Helen, queen of Sparta and high priestess of the Achaeans," Euridice said.

"Euridice, you know Helen. She is not someone who can be stolen. You know as well as I do that she left Menelaus on her own will, and probably for good reason. And probably she never expected this reaction from our men. Even the gods themselves were against this expedition. They were refusing to fill the sails with air for months, not allowing them to depart—until my wicked husband killed his firstborn to show to the Olympians and all Achaeans that he knew what he was doing," said Clytemnestra. "No, my dears, this was not a necessary war. This was only an adventure trip, a shared looting exercise, a group expression of male egocentrism. They left us behind to do the hard job, and they went off for their fun.

"And you know what is even worse? They will come back with loads of spoils and new wives. Young girls they will steal from the beds of their freshly married husbands by killing them. They will claim back their kingdoms, full of themselves and proud as peacocks at the time of love, and they will push us aside as if we were nothing, as if we were nonexistent. And you know what happens to the kids of the older wives? In the best case, they are thrown in prison. In the worst, they are killed."

"Tlepolemus would never do that," Polyxo whispered, worried and skeptical.

Clytemnestra looked around at the darkened faces. She knew she had made a point.

"And what do you suggest?" Euridice said.

"I suggest we send them a letter asking them to respect the sacredness of their families, to fear the goddesses Hestia and Hera, to acknowledge the people of their city and the rules, and not to bring any new wives from the conquered lands into their cities. And if they do it despite our requests, then entrance to the cities has to be forbidden."

A whisper rose, and women looked at one another and talked to one another.

"But they are the legitimate kings. We cannot refuse them entrance to their cities! Besides, they will come back with their armies, used to war and siege. They will attack us," Timandra said.

"From what I hear, the army is exhausted. They don't have the courage for further war. The idea is to make them wait only until they have given the wives to the temple of Aphrodite and then enter the city without them, acknowledging only us as the legitimate wives."

The idea resonated in the ears of the wives, and they all agreed with this plan. Clytemnestra seemed satisfied. She then opened the gates of the megaron and asked the guards to bring food and drinks and to have the shows start. We had a nice evening chatting with one another, joyful like kids who play relaxed in the garden after Mother has dispelled their worst worries from their minds.

I thought of Odysseus. Would he bring back new wives from Troy? I didn't see that. Women were not his worry. Rather, riches and power. But maybe I was wrong. Maybe long-term war and spoils had changed him. Maybe he would bring a new wife. "If he does, I'll go back to Sparta," I thought, "rather than not let him enter his island."

I discussed this thought with Iphthimi. To my surprise, she had a different view. "I have ruled the city for all these years now. People love me and trust me. I will not go back to Sparta. I wish to continue my work there. Eumelus will never bring another wife, I'm sure. He loves me, and we shall rule together until our death from old age," she said.

I embraced her and kissed her. "This is my sister," I said. "I'm sure this is what will be."

As I was going to my room that night, I heard a voice calling me. "Penelope, Penelope, could I talk to you for a moment?"

I saw Meda calling me. I went to her, and she pulled me quickly into her room. "I'm in trouble, Penelope, and I need your advice," she said.

"Go ahead," I told her.

"For some time now, I have had to be careful of some young man who wants to claim the kingdom for himself. I speak about Leukos, who believes that we should not wait for Idomeneus any longer. He goes around and says to the people that the king has betrayed them, that he has abandoned them in misery and poverty to go for adventures, girls, and spoils and that he deserves to be thrown into prison when he comes back. He has managed to turn the palace guards against me.

"Now I'm obliged to do as he requests in order to save my life and that of my daughter. I'd like to talk to Clytemnestra and ask her for help, but I'm afraid of Aegisthus, who seems to be a good friend of Leukos. Did you also notice he is always around her and always talks into her ear before she answers any questions?"

"Yes, I did," I said.

"Do you think this meeting was his idea?" she asked.

"I think these are genuine worries of Clytemnestra and probably others. But he does seem to have her respect. You are right. But what do you want to ask her to do?" I asked.

"My daughter and I need to escape from Leukos, Penelope. If Idomeneus dies, this man has no scruples. He will kill us also, without fear of punishment."

"Oh dear! I'm sure Idomeneus will come back without a new wife and will make sure Leukos is punished. If not, I'll come to get you out myself."

"You! I heard you have won many battles with pirates, but would you do this for me?"

"Of course! Me or Odysseus, when he is back," I said, suddenly feeling uncomfortable making a promise in the name of Odysseus.

219

"But how will I know you are there?" she asked.

I was wearing a pair of golden earrings that my cousins from Messene had given me as a present when I was with them. They showed two pigeons kissing each other. I gave her one. "When you receive the other one, it will mean I am there, and you should search the beaches for our boats."

"OK," she said, and she looked at me with awe and happiness at the same time.

I left her and went to my bedroom. Lying in bed, I wondered what I was doing. How would I ever do what I had promised? I wanted to give her hope and make her feel better, but how would I ever be able to run such a job? "Oh, goddess," I whispered, "you let me know when time comes." And with this thought, I went to sleep.

κς'

On the way back, I stopped at Delphi for offerings to Gaia and Athena and to ask the advice of Sibylla on the return of my husband. During those years, Sibylla was still active in Delphi. Women would go to her, while men would ask Pythia, the oracle of Apollo. We had to leave our carts at the bottom of the mountain and take the path up to the temples. The boy who came to take our carts said he would also feed and give water to the horses. He then asked us if we needed a goat or a buck to offer to the gods up there. It was custom to offer a buck to Gaia so Sibylla would speak or a goat to Apollo for Pythia's oracle. Many were coming without the sacrifice, and if you got it from the priests, it would cost twice as much. We agreed to take one from the boy. He also told us to look out for thieves, since often people would arrive at the top without their offerings.

There were many visitors, some richer, some poorer, but we all had to take the path up together. The path was not very wide, and there were those who were going up and those who were going down. The first group had with them their goats and other offerings, some quite voluminous. At the path's rand there were vendors and dealers of all sorts. It was difficult to walk up, and at times it was so packed that we had to push our way through the crowd that was stopping to buy things. The air was sweet from the appetizing honey pies that were sold by the local people, and those who were thirsty could have a bowl of fresh milk or a mug of wine mixed with water.

As we went higher, the sound of running water became stronger, and we noticed people were amassing to fill pitchers to take with them. The water was the holy water of the Castalian spring. A part of the water from the spring was going into a pool, and the rest was flowing through the river to the sea. People believed in its forces and were taking it for a variety of reasons—to make mud to build their houses, as they believed that houses that contained mud made with such water withstood all natural hazards; or to give to their animals to drink, so they would give birth to good-quality offspring.

From there onward, we had only to follow the stream until we saw the temples. People were sitting, sleeping, talking in groups, or praying as they were waiting for the seventh of the month to consult the oracle. Priests were everywhere. Some talking to the people, and some trying to help those in need.

We headed straight into the temple of Athena. The priests checked our dresses and gave my maids, who were wearing short chitons, long white cloaks, since the goddess was seemly and modest. They asked us who we were and told us to keep the cloaks for all our stay and give them back on the way out.

We made the libations, and as we were going out, one priest dressed in a long brown chiton came to greet us. "I see you have a buck with you. However, Sibyl only talks when she wants. On the other hand, if you wait for the seventh of the month, three days from now, you may ask the oracle of Apollo," he said as if favoring the latter option. "You are lucky there are not so many people currently. On other occasions, waiting times may be more than a week. There are people who have been waiting here since last month." He looked at me again and continued. "Being a queen, though, you have the right to a monk's cell with your maids, and you may even consult the oracle early at dawn."

I smiled and followed him; we passed in front of the rock of the sibyl, which was standing empty. "The sibyl doesn't follow any rules. She only talks when she wants. She may not talk for months. She is strange. She disappears and comes back when she wants, saying crazy things that no one can follow."

He took us to Hestia's temple to sacrifice the goat, and they told us to also sacrifice a sheep after my cleansing, which should take place in the morning. As we walked toward the cloister, I observed an old woman standing next to the sibyl's stone. She was tall, unusually tall for an old lady, and had her arms long along her sides and her hands crossed. She was wearing a hood, so I couldn't see her face well. Her long gray hair was coming out of the hood uncombed. I was sure her eyes were on me. I asked the priest who she was, but as he turned to see, she disappeared.

The brown-dressed officiant explained he was not a regular priest, took us to the cloister, and showed me my cell. We fitted another two beds for my maids to sleep with me, and my guards could camp outside. Then he invited me for lunch in the big dining room by sunset. We rested a bit, and as the sun started disappearing, I left my room to go the dining room as requested.

By now all the space around the temples was quiet. The light was dim, and people were sent back down to the valley to sleep. As I entered, one of the priests took me directly to one of the tables, where an older man in white was sitting with some younger ones. I was welcomed and given a bowl of lamb soup. I was not supposed to eat anything else until I was given food again by the priests. They explained this was part of my catharsis. Then they asked me a lot of questions about the purpose of my trip to Mycenae. I explained that most of the Achaean queens were worried that their husbands would come back with young wives and would break up with them. "It would be unfair after what we have gone through to protect the kingdoms so far," I said, looking at the most senior of them, who also looked the most wise. But he didn't reciprocate my worry and even stood up and left. I was now certain that this worry was a real one and that Clytemnestra had been right to warn us.

The next day, I wandered around the temples and watched the activities. New people were arriving to consult the oracle or Sibyl, who was still absent. People were passing in front of her rock, some were leaving their libations, and some were touching the rock in the hope it would tell them what the absence of Sibylla was denying them to know.

That day a numerous representation from the kingdoms of Thrace arrived. They were simple soldiers, and they claimed that their new kings had nothing to offer to the oracle, since the Achaeans had taken everything from their countries and destroyed what they couldn't take along. The Phrygians had come to ask how to make sure the Achaeans would not invade their land once they had finished with Troy. The lord of an

Egyptian city had come to ask how to keep the Lybians away from their cities, while some Tyrians wanted to ask how to protect themselves from the raids of the new people. The Egyptians were offering jewels with beautiful turquoise stones and the Lybians their purple dyed cloaks. The Iliyrians were there to ask the oracle what would be the best present for Agamemnon. Their king wanted to negotiate an agreement with the great king of the Achaeans once the latter came back from Troy.

I used all my language knowledge to talk to these people and understand their background, fears, and hopes. It was amazing. I was there in Delphi, and it felt as if I were in the center of the world. I knew all news. Among the representatives from the various kingdoms and their valuable offerings, there were simple people, those who had come to find out whether their child would recover from a long disease or those couples who wished for a child that was not arriving, or even those who wanted to migrate and wanted to ask where to go—was the east or the west more favorable?

I spent the whole day going around and speaking to people, together with the priests who appreciated my knowledge of languages. Every day the priests were accumulating an enormous amount of information, and they had a good understanding of the situation in and around Greece. From them I understood that Hector and Achilles were dead, the Achaeans had immobilized all activities around Troy, and they were preparing their last attack. A lot of it was in the hands of Odysseus, my husband.

In the evening we gathered to eat in cloister. Everybody was talking about Troy. Some were saying that the Achaeans had to attack one last time, since Troy's defenses were already consumed. Some were saying that Priam should capitulate and make a contract with Agamemnon. Some knew about a movement in Troy to overthrow Priam, who was old and crazy. Some even talked about Helen, who was now the wife of Deiophobus, but she hadn't allowed him to consummate their wedding. This created some giggling among the males, who wondered what the point was of marrying the most beautiful woman in the world if not that. Others wondered what the point was of taking her back to Sparta after all the pain she had caused.

I got fed up hearing all this talk about my best friend ever, so I stood up forcefully and hit my hand on the table. "My cousin Helen is, and will always be, the queen of Sparta and the Achaeans' high priestess." I looked into their eyes and felt their shame. I left the room. My head was full of anger that I couldn't elaborate. It reminded me of the time of her abduction by Theseus. The issues discussed about her hadn't changed much. Men considered her a troublemaker. She was beautiful and at the same time independent. Every single man wanted her for himself, but only she decided with whom and for how long.

Hold on a minute—I had not known why, but this time it became clear. I was defending Helen's independence for fear that they might restrict mine. This would be unacceptable for me; my freedom was for me as important as the air that I breathed. I realized that the years without Odysseus had accenuated this basic need. I decided to go for a walk before I went to bed.

People were mostly in their tents or just sleeping on the steps of the temples, in the various little caves around the rock, or just under the trees. There were fires still lit, and the air still smelled of dinner. I heard the sweet notes of the lyre, and looking in the direction of the music, I noticed many people sitting around a fire, so I went there. A group of people from Magnesia was listening to the songs of a bard. His music was sweet and his voice magical. He was dressed like a man, but his voice was like a woman's.

I sat with them, and someone passed me a piece of grilled bread with olive oil and oregano and a cup of wine. I realized the bard was describing a battle, and soon I knew it was the battle between Achilles and Hector in which the latter died. He was giving details of the battle that I had never heard and never seen. He was glorifying the capabilities of Achilles, and at the same time, he was pining over the loss of a great man, Hector. He presented the death of Hector not as a loss for Troy only but for all of humanity, since he was a great leader and more fair and just than his father, Priam.

As I was sitting there, I saw the old lady again. She was among the crowd listening to the bard and was watching me. I decided to slowly move toward her, but as I got a bit closer, she again disappeared.

I went to bed confused. What was going on? It looked as if the war had implications much greater than I had ever imagined. It was creating homeless people and destroying kingdoms. It was part of a bigger change in the whole region, and there was no way that things could go back to the way they were before. It was becoming clear to me. Nothing would be the same as before. I wanted to go back to Clytemnestra and tell her that. Changes were in the air. But maybe she knew it already, and it was exactly this that she was trying to communicate to us.

The next day, I ran to the sibyl's stone with the hope of finding her there, receiving my pronouncement, and going. But the stone was empty. I sat and waited. I was certain the old lady who had been watching me on those various occasions was her. My intention was to grab her the next time I saw her.

The sun was becoming hot, so I moved under the shadow of the closest tree. I sat on a rock under the oak tree, and I was looking around to detect the presence of the old lady. Suddenly I felt movement toward the rock, and I heard a female voice. "Penelope, daughter of Periboia."

I turned, and there she was. The same clothes. The same hair hanging free and uncombed. She took the hood off, and I could see her face. She was not old; in fact, I thought she was beautiful but somehow distant. I stood up and ran toward her, and she once again shouted, "Be faithful to yourself, no matter what it takes."

A priest in white was crossing, and at the sight of the sibyl, he stopped and lowered his head. It was prohibited to cross the path when she was on her stone.

"What do you mean?" I asked.

"You are accountable only to yourself and not to any man, be it father, husband, son, priest, king, or even the worthiest warrior."

"Will my husband come back alone or with a new wife?" I shouted my question to her, and I felt the emptiness of my false words reflecting back to me and making me feel ashamed. Then, at that moment, I understood that was not the real question.

"After the rule of man, your glory will come."

I don't know what happened then because suddenly the wind blew and made all the bells hanging from the trees ring. Dust rose, and we had to close our eyes to protect them. A swirl appeared above the stone, and things were flying around. Then the wind suddenly subsided, and we could see a bit better again. She had disappeared. The stone was standing empty and full of promises.

The priest saw my confusion and came to me. "Don't worry if you don't understand her crazy sayings. Tomorrow you may consult the oracle of Apollo."

I leaned against the stone. "What was the real question, then?" I murmured.

"The oracle will answer your question, my queen."

I went back to my room, and her words were always there. "Be faithful to yourself." I felt ashamed again. How could I be so superficial and egoistic? Sibyl didn't care about my marital state but about my placement in the world. She wanted me to take my responsibilities instead of asking when my husband would come to free me from them. The real question in my mind, the one to which she was responding, was, What was my role in all that was happening in the world right now? And although the world was governed by men, I had to continue act like a woman.

The next day at dawn, I did all that was requested by the priests in order to consult the oracle. In fact, I was not interested anymore, but the priests insisted, and somehow I didn't want to disappoint them or insult the gods. I bathed in the Castalian pool, and I ate what was given to me.

When I was allowed to ask the oracle about the future of my marriage, the oracle responded, "Achaean blood will continue to be spilled for many years after the war, but because of the duckling and not the swan."

My flesh crawled at her words. The priests took me out. My guards were waiting for me. I was skeptical. I hadn't expected that. I had expected to hear that my husband would be back and that we would live together happily for the rest of our lives on our island, but the oracle sounded like more war was coming. *The duckling must be me, while the swan must be an allusion to my cousin Helen, in which form I'd spill Achaean blood.* The saying of Apollo was not easier to understand than that of Sibyl.

In the span of some hours, I had received two oracles. The one from Sibyl represented the female world and the one from Apollo the male world, and they were both useless to me. Neither could give a straight answer to my question. So I still had no hint of the return of Odysseus and of our future life. I decided not to think about it but to concentrate on my return to Ithaka.

κζ'

It was wonderful to see my son, Telemachus, again. He was almost twelve now, and he looked great. He had my soft characteristics. Long arms and legs, and big maroon eyes. I was so pleased to take him in my arms, and I could see he had also missed me. Cyanea was also happy to have me back, and all my maids the same.

The evenings of the next weeks he passed with me to hear the stories about Mycenae and Prince Orestes and the princesses Electra and Chrysothemis. One day the news arrived that the war was over and that the king would be back soon. The various kings were coming back with their ships full of spoils and Trojan girls, exactly as Clytemnestra had foretold. Every day I thought of him coming back as a winner with all his Trojan concubines.

But the news was faster again. The great king was dead. What? Agamemnon was dead, fallen at the hands of his wife, Clytemnestra, and his cousin Aegisthus. I took the messenger by the shoulders and started moving him back and forth. "No, it can't be," I shouted.

"My queen, it is not worth it, harming the messenger. Aegisthus is now the king of the golden city, and he says that

Odysseus has to submit himself to the new king, or he will be captured and executed as a traitor to the Achaeans."

"I will communicate this to my husband immediately when he is back," I said and sent him out.

More days passed, and the news from Sparta was not nice. Apparently, Menelaus and Helen had found refuge in Egypt. Menelaus was scared for his life now that his brother was dead. Diomedes, king of Argos, was not allowed to enter his city and had to leave. The situation was awkward.

I was worried about Odysseus, so I decided to go and consult my friends. I went down into Melissani's cave with the idea of talking to her and the others. The water was so still, and it mirrored its surroundings and rejected any insight. I touched the water and made sure my face was mirrored. I realized my face had become much more mature than it had been the last time I'd looked at its reflection.

Slowly my face took another form, and the young, beautiful face of Melissani started forming. She appeared out of the water. "Hello, Penelope," she said with a sweet voice.

"I need your advice and help," I said.

"What makes you so worried that you forgot to bring me an offering? Not even milk with honey. Not even the sweet onion pie," she said with a soft, sad voice.

"You are right, my friend. Here. I have a bit of both. I didn't forget. How could I? Yes, I'm worried. Things change quickly up there, and I'm not sure what to do. Odysseus is on his way back, but the great king Agamemnon is dead. The new king requires submission, but I know this is not possible. It will be death if I don't warn him."

"I see," she said, and nibbled on the pie. "This is an excellent pie," she added with enthusiasm. "I'll have to talk to our princess Athena. Let's meet again tonight in the cave." She poured the milk at once down her throat, let the decanter fall, and disappeared quickly.

I did as she asked and went to the cave when it became dark. I disliked doing it, but I entered the cave thinking, "Why do I have to enter in the dark an even darker cave, oh goddess?"

But my thought hadn't finished when I felt the soft, warm wind guiding me through the galleries again until I arrived in the open space with the pool. It was illuminated, and they were all there.

"Here we are, child," Mother told me. "There is no need to worry. Calypso will hide your husband on her island as long as it is needed. None of the mortals has ever managed to find her island, so he will be fully protected there."

Calypso came closer. "Leukothea will take him to me directly. He will not need to disembark to Ithaka or to any other place where danger looms."

"We hope you agree with this solution, child," Mother said.

"It will mean for me not seeing my husband for who knows how long. I'm getting old so quickly. No man has touched me since he left, and now even more sacrifice," I said. "But what other choice do I have?"

"Through my eyes you will see him; through my body you will feel him. Whenever he looks in my eyes, he will see you. Whenever he touches me, all his senses will be filled with you," Calypso said. "I'll keep you united."

I looked at her, dubious. "How, when I grow old and ugly and you remain beautiful and young?"

But she smiled with satisfaction. "From now on, your beauty will increase every day that passes until you see your husband again," Athena said. "It will be up to you to manage it."

Then she and the rest of them disappeared, leaving me in the darkness. I managed to find my way back. Again, the words were confusing. What did it mean to manage my beauty? I had obtained wisdom. Time would show. Indeed, my friends were talking to me in dreams. I knew when Leukothea appeared to Odysseus and led him to the island of Calypso. And I knew that Calypso had taken custody of my husband and his men. Now I was free to go on with my other worries.

κη′

In the following days, I gave the order to prepare the boats for a rescue operation in Crete. "And whom are we going to rescue, my lady?" my faithful friend Polydorus asked carefully.

"Queen Meda," I said.

"But they say that the queen and her lover have denied access in the city to Idomeneus, who is hiding now and fears for his life."

"The queen fears for her life also; trust me."

He bowed and left to prepare.

Once again I departed, and I knew that I had Thetis on my side.

Hiding at Calypso's island, Odysseus was safe, and I was reassured. The sea was calm until we reached Pylos. We stopped to get supplies and to welcome back King Nestor. I needed to know from him what the conditions were in Crete and where to best anchor the ships for safety.

Euridiki welcomed me and took me directly to her throne room. "Penelope, don't go there. You'll put yourself in danger. Leukos is a good ally of Aegisthus. He will kill you if he captures you," she said.

"I know, but I promised to help her. Athena will guide me and help me."

"My daughter, I've never seen a woman like you—so confident and sure about the support of the gods. I wish you good luck. But let's go to find Nestor. He will have a lot to tell you about your husband and your cousin Helen."

She took me to his room, where he was lying awaiting death. He seemed an old, wrecked man. Euridiki whispered in his ear that the daughter of Icarius and wife of Odysseus was there to see him.

He opened his eyes. "Come, my daughter, sit next to me. Your husband won the war. He and Diomedes screwed them all. The two did all tricks necessary, killing the Thracian kings, bringing Neoptolemus into the battle, stealing the palladium, and building the horse. They worked well together. It was their genius that led to the victory after the death of Achilles the great warrior." And then he looked into my eyes. "But this is not what you want to know, is it? No, he didn't take any other wife. He was not interested. His only care was for you and Ithaka, and he sent all his loot to you to make sure you had enough for the palace and the country." His words made me so happy, so light and proud. "But I heard he didn't arrive in Ithaka. Where can he be?" he asked.

"He is safe, sir. The nymphs have granted him protection as long as needed to escape from Aegisthus."

"Ah, daughter, what a terrible fate has awaited the Achaeans after their return. The great king dead, and this sneak in charge. He will never dare to invade Pylos, but he has made sure that the great brotherhood is destroyed. Look, Diomedes has left, and Idomeneus the same. Odysseus and Menelaus are hiding. None knows how this will finish. You know, in Sparta Tyndareus is on his own with the little princess Hermione. Leda died when she heard about Clytemnestra's atrocity, and your father is very frail. With Leda dead and Clytemnestra a murderer, there is no high priestess to guide us. Difficult times for our people. You have to take the lead, my daughter, at least as long Helen is in Egypt," he said.

"What do I have to do, my king?" I asked.

"You have to go to Sparta and take Leda's golden diadem and scepter. She hung them on Hera's statue before she died. Clytemnestra went to take them, but they were not to be detached from the goddess's statue. I'm sure she will give them to you if you go."

"I promise I'll go. But first I have to go to collect Meda and her daughter. I promised some time ago."

He nodded and touched my cheek with love. Then he turned to his wife. "Go and call Nausos, my navigator," he asked nicely.

Euridice disappeared, and he told me, "I'll give you my best navigator to help you with this. You have to keep out of sight of the guards. If Leukos sees you, he will take you prisoner. He doesn't trust anybody. You have to approach Crete in the night and hide the vessel in the beach of the boar. They don't have guards there because the waters are tricky. Nausos knows how to take you there, and he knows how to keep you safe. He'll find the path up from the caves, and once up, he'll take you to Sotirios the herdsman, who knows the secret way to the palace. He was my good friend from childhood here in Pylos. Later he migrated to Crete and became the herdsman of Idomeneus. Tell him I sent you."

In the meantime, Nausos and Euridice had entered the room, and Nestor asked him to help me get to the beach of the boar. He turned to me. "Good luck, my daughter," he said, and he closed his eyes, exhausted.

Euridice took my hand and led me out of the room. "He is so weak. The war took a heavy toll on him. Go and rest now. I'll make sure that your ships have everything they need for the trip from here to Crete and back to Sparta," she said.

"Yes," I whispered thoughtfully and went to bed.

I woke up with the first dawn, and we departed. Nausos took up his role as navigator. There was a light breeze that took us straight to Crete in a day and a half. When we saw the island from afar, Nausos turned west first and headed toward a skerry, behind which he waited until dark. Then he asked the rowers to make as little noise as possible, and we proceeded toward the main island. I couldn't see anything, and I admired Nausos's ability to read the signs by the light of the moon.

We arrived on the beach, and he told me that this was the beach of the boar, and we could sleep until dawn. At dawn, Polydorus, Nausos, and I found the caves and took the path, which we could see in front of us. Soon we were out in a harsh and rocky terrain. Nausos started walking inland, and we followed. We soon heard the sounds of animals at pasture. We had found Idomeneus's herdsman.

He was not surprised to see Nausos. "What brings you here, my friend?"

"Sotirios, it is nice to see you, even if your lord has been pushed away."

"Well, it seems that there are many who can do the work of the king today, but only a few who can be good herdsmen," he replied with a cynical smile. "And who are the noble people you have with you?"

"They come from our lord Nestor, and you are better off if you don't know them. We have to reach the palace to give a message to the queen. Can you help us with this?"

He nodded. "The queen is in captivity because she tried to help Idomeneus. It will be difficult to reach her."

"When can we depart?" asked Nausos.

"I see you are in a hurry to help her. Let me call my son to take over the herd, and we can go." He whistled, and after a while, a young boy appeared. Sotirios talked to him, and the boy went to take his guard position.

We walked until the sun was up in the sky. We passed the rocky part and entered the canyon of a dry river. Then we exited the canyon and entered a forest. After some time, he told us the palace was very near now, although we couldn't see it. He then moved some bushes and then some fallen branches, and there it appeared—the opening of a cave. He made a sign to wait, and he entered. Nausos gathered some branches to make a torch. Sotirios's head appeared at the opening again, and he made a sign to follow him.

It was pitch dark, and I felt the hand of Polydorus taking mine while he was holding the shoulder of Nausos and he the shoulder of Sotirios. After a few steps, there was light again. "This is the labyrinth of Daidalus," Sotirios said.

"Really?" I said, and my skin crawled. Daidalus's labyrinth hosted the monster of Knossos, which was killed by the Athenian king Theseus many years go. Everyone knew this story, and now I was there entering that famous labyrinth myself.

"How can you be sure we won't lose our path?"

"Don't worry, my lady. Even if we lose it, there is no monster in there to eat us anymore. The labyrinth is disintegrating, and nature has found its way into it. So it is not difficult to know where we are," he whispered. "Just keep quiet now, because just above us, there are many guards."

Indeed, there were openings in the roof, and we could hear voices and passing soldiers.

Then he showed us a gate. "This leads to a low and narrow corridor. It was narrow so that the monster couldn't pass even if he managed to break the bars. At the end there is the garden of the palace. After lunch the queen takes a walk there."

"OK, I'll go through. You wait here," I said. But when I saw the dirty corridor, I took a step back.

"It is impossible for you to crawl in this corridor, my lady. I'll go," said Polydorus.

I took the earing and put it in his hand. "Give this to her when you see her," I said.

So he entered the corridor and started crawling. At the other end, he stopped and tried to push the bars open, but it was not possible. He looked around to see the queen. He could hear her well but not see her. A ball arrived at the wall, and a small girl moved to take it. Polydorus threw the earring. The girl collected the ball and the earring and ran back.

After two minutes, Meda appeared at the wall.

"My queen, Penelope is here to take you out of the country," he said.

"It's not easy for me to move," she whispered. "But I can take a walk outside the palace once a month. Where do I find you?"

"We shall wait for you in the beach of the boar."

"I'll be there in two days," she said, and she left when one of the guards started moving toward her.

Polydorus crawled back the corridor and told us everything. We went back to the boat and waited there. Two days passed, and we decided to wait a third day. Then, instead of the queen, the herdsman arrived. "Queen Meda and her daughter are dead. Executed by King Leukos for an attempt to escape and join Idomeneus."

Our mission had failed. I felt sad and miserable. I had failed to save this woman. Maybe if I had been more active in helping her to escape. Heavy tears came down my face.

"Leukos has started a search to find where Idomeneus is hiding, so you had better leave as soon as possible. There is no time to mourn."

"What a terrible fate," I said.

We again waited for dark, and then we departed for Sparta.

We arrived in Gythion around noon, since we had south wind, and headed toward Sparta. There were no soldiers welcoming us, and the country seemed empty. My father's guard appeared only when we were close to the city. The sergeant recognized us, and for some reason, that pleased me. All his soldiers were much younger than he was. I reckoned all of Greece was suffering under the loss of men. Menelaus and his men were not back yet.

All Greece seemed empty. They brought me to the palace. It was a huge happiness to be back in the city where I had grown up, to walk up the palace's stairs to go into the painted megaron and see all the richness of the paintings, the marble statues, and the Krokean columns. It was a relief, a feeling of lightness and happiness that overwhelmed me and made my heart flutter.

Both my father and Uncle Tyndareus were there. I first kissed my uncle's hand, and then I fell into the arms of my father, who held me with love and affection. When I looked at him, I realized he was frail. "Father, what's wrong with you?" I asked.

"Oh, it's not worth asking, girl. He is fine. He only needs to rest," said Tyndareus, who seemed not to want to admit that my father was sick.

"Come, Father, you need to sit down," I said.

He listened to me.

"Go and call my wife, Leda. She knows how to deal with these things. A wise woman, my wife. Oh, yes, a wise woman."

I looked at him and then to Father. He took my hand, and he walked out with me. "Ah, he doesn't want to admit Leda is dead, or that Helen left Sparta, or that Clytemnestra killed her husband, or that Timandra abandoned hers. He lives in his own dream. What can I do? I look after him, but the situation is not good. We are both old. The country was left without men. The younger ones miss the guidance of their fathers. Menelaus and Helen are hiding in Egypt because of the crazy man in Mycenae. Leda died shortly after Clytemnestra's murder. We are without a high priestess to show us the way."

"Was Aunt Leda the high priestess?" I asked.

"Yes! You didn't know? Leda took over the tiara from Gorgophone. After Helen departed, Leda didn't visit the bed of Tyndareus anymore. She became a Parthenos, and the tiara was given to her. Besides her healing powers obtained by the power of Zeus, she also had all chthonic powers attributed to her by Demetra and her daughter Persephone."

A young woman walked into the yard. "Are you talking again about Granny, honored Icarius? Isn't it better to talk about the living than the dead? I see you are in beautiful company. Who is the noble lady of excellent ancestry?"

"Come, my child. You bring us the sun every time you talk to us. You warm our hearts, and you brighten our minds. Come; I'll introduce you to my daughter and your aunt Penelope."

"You are Hermione. Noble daughter of Helen and Menelaus," I said, and I opened my arms.

She came toward me with a smile and embraced me. She was certainly beautiful. Not like her mother, but still a daughter of Lacedaemon, worthy of the best king for husband. And I knew they would fight for her. "You are so beautiful, my child. And your dress is so soft and the colors so vivid."

"I made it myself. It shows my mother carried away by the enemies. I'm so relieved Mummy is again free and can come back." Then her face changed, became darker and worried. "Some tell me that she left me on her own will. But I don't believe them. How can a mother leave her only daughter alone? Would you ever leave your child and go, Aunt Penelope?" she asked.

"No, she didn't leave you. She's coming back for you. I'm sure you are her only thought now," I said to calm her down, and I looked, worried, toward my father. I realized the palace of Sparta was still in shock. Tyndareus was half-mad and

Hermione deeply wounded. Only my father was still keeping his mind, but his body was weak, and it was clear to me his days were numbered.

I stayed with Hermione the rest of the day. She was so eager to show me her dowry and her room and to tell me how she imagined her future husband. She was missing female company and advice, the guidance of a mother, or even an older woman. She was on her own with two old and half-crazy men whose only wish was to keep the kingdom alive until the return of Helen and Menelaus. It was sad. Hermione's mind was also floating in half madness, and I didn't know how to fix it. I kept telling her that her parents would be back soon and that she would get married to the most valiant prince of all Achaeans. That seemed to give her some comfort.

The next day after breakfast, my father came to take me to the temple in which Leda was operating. On the way, we talked.

"The tiara is still here," he said. "Clytemnestra was here to take it after Leda's death, but the tiara didn't come off the head of Hera. Timandra came after her, but it was the same. You are our last hope, child," he said with a voice that was trembling.

"Don't worry, Father. We don't need the tiara if the goddess doesn't want to give it back. We only need to talk to the people to give them a vision of a better future. To support them in recovering from the war. I am not a healer like Leda, but I can organize things well, and I have support from the nymphs and Athena. I'm sure they will help us out."

When I said "nymphs," his face illuminated. "Do you see your mother?" he asked.

I nodded.

"I knew it. I knew she would appear to you. You are so different, so stable and robust. Of course she would come to you. Tell me, how is she? Still as beautiful as when I met her, or old and frail like me?"

It was exactly then that I realized the difference between her and him, and everything suddenly became clear to me. "Father, she is beautiful. She is young, and her body agile and vigorous. Her eyes sparkle, and she has her long black hair free. She goes around with Artemis, and she is free, as she always wanted to be."

"Ah, yes. This was what she wanted—to be always free. You said it correctly, my daughter. And she left us mortals to obtain her objectives. I don't blame her. Do you?"

"There was a time when I was angry with her because I missed her. I wanted her to be around like all other mothers. But not anymore, because now she is more around than I could ever imagine."

"Ah! Maybe you should say this to young Hermione."

He was right. Maybe I should tell her.

We reached the temple. It was completely empty, contrary to how it had been when Leda was still operating there. The huge statue of Zeus on one side was severe and expressionless. The lesser statue of Hera was on the opposite side, on her head the tiara. I imagined the scene when Leda had put the tiara on her head, asking her to protect it and give it to the one who deserved it. I had no healing powers, and I was quite sure the goddess had no intention of passing it on to me.

So I stretched my arm, just to examine it, since I realized that I had never really looked at it before.

With my first touch, the tiara moved, lost its balance, and fell into my arms. I looked at my father, surprised, and then I turned to examine this artifact. It was a simple wooden tiara that used to be decorated with flowers in spring, bird feathers in summer, chrysanthemums and yellow leaves in autumn, and fir branches in the winter. No one knew either who had made it or when. People said that it used to choose the heads of the ladies instead of the ladies choosing it. And now it seemed to have chosen me.

I looked again at Father, who couldn't stop a tear going down his cheek.

"Take it, my daughter. Tomorrow I'll call the assembly to announce the new priestess of the Achaeans."

"But Father, I don't want to be a Parthenos. I want my man back. I can't wait to have him back. I wouldn't know what to do with this tiara."

"Don't worry. It will tell you what it wants from you."

The next day, Icarius organized a celebration with thanksgivings to the gods, sacrifices, libations, singing and dancing, and big banquets. And since I was the first priestess of the Achaeans, I had the privilege to sacrifice—that meant to slaughter the animals of the sacrifice. Usually this was a job strictly reserved for the males of the palace, with the one exception of the first priestess, who was also the chthonic priestess. She could also do it. She was in charge of all communications between the deep of the earth and the people. There were two earth goddesses, Demetra and her daughter, Persephone, and two chthonic gods, Ades and Hermes. And my job was to establish this dialogue between the dead and the alive and to call these gods to guide me.

κθ′

Back in Ithaka, it seemed that everything had changed. People were waiting for me at the harbor. They were waving at me happily. As I disembarked, they started throwing flowers to me, and I noticed that the way was covered with carpets. "Our queen, our priestess," they were crying.

After a few steps on land, they took me in their arms and placed me on my throne, which they carried all the way up to the palace, where they let me down and started dispersing, giving me blessings and kissing my hands and robes.

Telemachus ran to me, and we took each other in our arms. I was so happy to see him. He was already fourteen and quite strong. His father's traits were now more pronounced, and for a moment I felt Odysseus was back. His hug left me without air. I asked him what was going on there, and he told me that a ship from Pylos had given them the news of my nomination to high priestess. "Think, Mom. People will come to ask your advice. You will need to lead the ceremony to Demetra and Persephone, and you'll be the one to sacrifice all animals. Our island will become famous," he said.

"I am quite well known already," I told him. "And I'm not sure I like to sacrifice anyway." I moved toward the stairs. I was tired, and I only wanted to get a warm bath and sleep on solid ground. After three days on the sea, I simply needed it.

"Maybe you can ask the chthonic gods if Odysseus is already in their realm," I heard the voice of my father-in-law say.

"Laertes," I said, "how nice to see you in good health. I see you did a good job during my absence. Everybody seems well fed and in a good mood."

"I hope you stay more in your place, my daughter, because I'm getting old, and Anticlea is getting weaker every day. The absence of Odysseus and the uncertainty over his well-being is eroding her health."

"I am so sorry to hear that, Father, and though Odysseus is well, he is hiding from the Mycenaean king, who now has seized power and seeks to destroy all those who fought in Troy."

"That is really good news, and I ask you to go to tell her yourself. I'm sure she would love to receive you and learn all about her son and how you obtained the title of high priestess. She is so happy that the title came here to Ithaka."

"I will, Father. This will be my first worry tomorrow morning. I promise."

He retreated, and Polydorus came in to tell me that the boats were in the shipyard and that the palace was quiet. I went to bed, and I was happy to sleep again in my own room after such a long trip. I passed my fingers over the wood of the olive tree so nicely cut and polished by Odysseus. After so many years, it hadn't lost its shine. I felt I was missing my man. A deep feeling overwhelmed me, bringing a sob that I killed in my throat before it reached my eyes.

Cyanea brought me something to eat and helped me get a bath. I noticed she was becoming old. "You should stop going around on the open sea, my lady. These are things for the strong and warlike men. Not for your little body."

"You don't know how much I agree, Cyanea," I said, and I really thought that this was my last adventure on the seas.

"Here there are so many things to do. The palace has so many needs. The young men in the academy have become ever more disobedient. There are so many people who require advice to go on with their lives," she said.

I listened to Cyanea tell me all the news, and it felt good; it felt like home. I was needed, loved, and wanted…and I was missing Odysseus even more. I had no one to share my happiness with, to give my love to and to allot the many responsibilities and tasks of reigning.

I went to bed, and then came the sweet dream. It was magical. It was similar to a divine present. I saw him on that island. Somehow I knew it was an island, but it didn't look like Ithaka. He was walking on the beach, and his feet were submerged in the warm sand at every step. His upper body was free, and I could see the various wounds from the fighting. I searched for the childhood wound on his leg, and I found it, which contented me. His long black hair was waving in the breeze. His beard was well trimmed, and his eyes were eager and inquisitive, as always. Every two or three steps, he turned and looked at the sea. His look was worried and willing, willing to go face the waves, to go back to Ithaka, to his wife and child, to his parents and friends. I wanted to stroke his hair and tell him that we were well and waiting for him.

I felt sad in the dream, fearing that I would not be able to placate his worries, but then I saw a hand touching his hair and heard a female voice telling him exactly the things I wanted to tell him. I woke up scared of my own dream, scared of my own thoughts. What had I just seen? Odysseus was on the island of Calypso, safe and taken care of. Was Calypso sending gleams of Odysseus's life on her island? Were my friends the nymphs helping me again?

Armed with this certainty, I dressed as nicely as I could. Autonoe made my hair, and I put Leda's tiara on and the beautiful golden earrings with the rubies. My hair, black and rich, was put in a beautiful updo and fixed with golden-red ribbons. I was feeling different, and I knew it was Odysseus's love that had shaken me and inspired me.

"You look beautiful, my queen," Autonoe said for the first time, with astonishment in her voice.

A smile of satisfaction filled my face as I looked at her. Then she opened the door of my room, and I went downstairs. In the megaron a few people had gathered for advice and cases of conflict of interest, but I didn't stop there. I had promised my father-in-law to go to talk to Anticlea and give her the news about Odysseus.

I took my horse and left. It was a beautiful morning, albeit a bit cool. It was about a half-hour ride. My guards followed me. I saw the mansion from afar, and I rode faster. Laertes was having breakfast with Eumaeus, Odysseus's swineherd.

"My queen," he said, and he stood up, keeping his head low.

"I'm here as I promised," I said. "I have news from Odysseus to convey to my mother-in-law, if you take me to her."

Laertes nodded with awe. "You are most welcome in my house, with or without news from Odysseus," he cleverly replied, and he showed me the way toward the stairs.

Anticlea was in bed, with her maid helping her to have breakfast. Laertes sat on the bed. "Penelope is here, my dear wife. She has news from our son. She only returned from Sparta yesterday evening, and she rushed to you first thing this morning to give you the news."

She nodded to the maid that she didn't want any more food and wiped her mouth. I hadn't seen her for a while, and for the first time I realized how much older and consumed she was by the absence of her son.

"Come, my daughter. May the gods have sent you with good news, and may they allow me to live long enough to see my beloved son, if he is still alive. If, on the other hand, your news is talk of misfortune and death, then I wish the same for myself, so as to hurry up to see him as soon as possible." She stretched her arm toward me, and I took it.

"No, Mother, the news is good," I said, and I sat on the side of the bed. "He is well. Calypso herself looks after him, and she sends me glimpses of him and his life on her island. I know the only thing he wishes is to come back to us."

Her face lightened up, her eyes sparkled, and those of Laertes did the same. "Oh, it is such a blessing to have you as a daughter, Penelope. For sure the gods love you a great deal if they allow you to watch their makings," she said and embraced me with rigor. "The news you brought me today is the best I have heard in years, since Odysseus had to depart for the great war. You have given our house honor all the years you have reigned on your own. But tell me, how did you obtain the tiara of Nemesis? It is only for the great Achaean priestess to wear, and as far as I know, Clytemnestra should have received it after Leda."

"Oh, Mother, I don't know myself how this could happen. Leda died in bitterness after Clytemnestra and Aegisthus consummated their horrible act. Before she died, she took the tiara to Hera and asked her to give it only to the woman who deserved it. As my father led me in front of the statue, the tiara literally fell into my arms. So Father proclaimed me high priestess of the Achaeans."

"Your father did well to take you there and to proclaim you high priestess. I cannot think of anybody who deserves it as much as you. But be prudent, my daughter, not to provoke the anger of your cousin Clytemnestra. She may take revenge for the goddess's choice."

I understood what she meant, and I nodded. I promised her I would come back with whatever news I had from Odysseus and left the room. Again with Laertes, I transferred to him the greetings of my father, and I handed him the presents, as it was custom.

Back in the palace, I went straight in the megaron. Cyanea, who met me in the yard, tried to persuade me to take lunch. It was already noon. I took some figs on the fly and moved toward the megaron. As I entered, I noticed the people's astonished and inhibited glazes.

I nodded for the first visitor, who described his problem only vaguely, telling me that he didn't want to waste my time with his stupid disagreements with his neighbor. I only advised him to lend an open ear to his neighbor, and everything would be resolved. He bent, kissed my hand, and left. Most of the audiences went like that—quiet, self-conscious, and almost self-resolving. I realized the power of the tiara. People had respect for it. In the presence of the priestess with the tiara, reason and justice were imminent and self-evident. The pronouncements of the priestess were sacred and undisputable. Nobody dared to waste the time of the gods with selfish and egoistic debates, and the risk of failure was just too great, so they preferred to resolve the problems among themselves. I was able to grasp the greatness of Aunt Leda. I was like her—almighty, capable of attracting the attention of gods, able to exist and act in the vague space between the divine and the human.

I worked that day without food and water until late at night and I continued in this way the following days and weeks. I listened to all claims, and I went wherever they asked me to go—their homes, fields, or stables. I visited the sick, the elderly, and women giving birth, as well as those who were inaugurating their businesses. Everybody wanted my blessing, my assistance, or my comfort. And I didn't deny it to anybody, even to those coming from afar. They could sleep in my yard or share the rooms of the servants. I was fully aware of the importance of the power attributed to me.

λ'

The following weeks and months were similar. The tiara had made me a sacred person. It was making me work harder, and it was changing the attitudes of those around me. The effect was most pronounced in the academy. The boys at the beginning of the war were becoming men now. Some had gone back to their families, and others had joined the academy. Laertes had split them into two groups, the young men and the boys—altogether about two hundred by now. Most were staying in the dormitories that had been created for them around the palace at least a few days a week and going back home the other days. The older ones I took with me on some of my trips, and they were fully capable of fighting and defending their country despite their young age. Among them, Antinous and Eurymachus had started developing the capacities of a leader. I was proud of them. I needed good fighters and clever army leaders able to organize a defensive operation. I had to trust that they would defend our trade boats around the Mediterranean and that they would make sure goods, gold, and money would come back to the palace as expected. And they did that.

Often other regions, such as Etolia and Elis and Epirus, asked for our help to fend off invaders from sea. In such cases I dispatched boats with our fighters, and they always came back as victors. Invaders from the sea never dared to attack Ithaka, because they knew that they had no chance against the well-organized army of Ithaka. They were devoted to their queen, and the tiara was giving them the assurance of the victors. I was pleased with this result, because the academy had cost me a great deal of energy and work, but now it was paying off.

Except for Pylos and Mycenae, almost all the Trojan fighters were still dispersed from fear of Aegisthus, so most cities were lacking experienced fighters. That was not the case on Ithaka, due to the existence of the academy, of which my son was also part.

Except for my personal effort, the palace had to feed all the boys and keep the dormitories, classes, and gyms in good shape and clean. The older the boys got, the more difficult it was to keep up with the academy's needs, so I asked the families to contribute with regular shipments of herds of sheep and cattle to feed and dress the soldiers. Each family would take turns to lead the annual shipment of tin. This was important for the preparation of bronze. Tin could only be procured from the markets of the north, and it was a dangerous endeavor.

At the same time, the palace was also full of young girls. My maids and servants had their own children who were also in their teens. Also, other lords in my queendom were sending me their girls to be educated in the sacred rituals. So I had more than hundred girls of various ages living in the palace. They were following the same lessons as the boys except for the training that was done in different gymnasiums. While the boys were trained close to the academy, the girls were closer to the temples at the other side of the palace. Some of them were doing really well in running, riding, and archery, the sports that my mother liked best.

The tiara made a great impression on them, and they often asked me what it meant for me to wear it. "I don't know," I said once. "I just think better when I have it on. Somehow my judgment is more rational and less emotional."

In fact, I had noticed this. The tiara made my blood grow cold. Nothing could excite me. My pulse turned slow and my breath deep. "You are becoming cold blooded like the dead," Melania, daughter of Dolius, told me.

I looked at her with the surprise of someone who just heard his deepest secrets aired in the public. She was right. The tiara was making me cold like the dead. But maybe that had its good side.

I had noticed that the older girls were already flirting with the older boys. That was a blessing, because the islands needed new people. Births had been scarce in recent years. So I talked to the parents, and we arranged for some marriages.

But then a message from my cousin Timandra, queen of Pisa in Elis, arrived with an invitation to me to open that year's Heraean games. She also asked for a delegation of young women from our island to go and compete in running and riding. Both the Olympic and Heraean games had been relaunched after the end of the war. They had been suspended due to the unavailability of men and the workload of the women. Although I had decided not to travel anymore, I was glad for this invitation. It was, after all, a great honor. So I asked to have the boats prepared. I chose twenty girls to participate in the games, and I got the permission of their parents to take them to Pisa. Some parents seemed reluctant, but it wasn't easy to disagree with the priestess of the chthonic gods.

I was glad I could take the girls on a trip. I had often been out with the boys but never with the girls. Of course, some of the boys would have to come with us as rowers and guards, but it was not their call. It was the call of my girls.

It was an easy trip. Pisa was only opposite Zakynthos in Peloponnese. We arrived at Pisa, and Timandra greeted us and showed us our rooms. The stadium was next to her palace. Queen Hippodamia had launched these games when she managed to escape the tyranny of her father, who didn't want her to get married, scared he'd lose his life at the hand of his son-in-law. She had bribed Oenomaus's charioteer to loosen the linchpins of her father's chariot, and he would be allowed to get her for himself. However, Pelops killed the charioteer, and he claimed his reward. Hippodamia was an excellent rider and runner herself, and she invoked Hera's help in freeing herself from her father. She arranged for a group of sixteen women from the surrounding villages to oversee the games and, together with her, to spin the shroud of Hera. As Heracles passed by Elis, he became a witness of the Heraean games, and he established the Olympic games to honor his father, Zeus, and his grandfather Pelops.

In the evening I was sitting in Timandra's megaron with the sixteen women and, to my surprise, my cousin Clytemnestra, Timandra's sister. When I saw her, I understood immediately what was going on. The sisters wanted back what they believed belonged to them—their mother's tiara. But neither of the two was qualified. I was the only Parthenos—that is, a woman with long-term abstinence from the pleasures of love—in there, and people knew it. So, despite their wish, they allowed me to open the games and to carry out the sacrifice as it was planned.

Then Clytemnestra came to me with two guards and asked me to deliver to her the tiara if I wanted to see my child again. Her eyes were dark, her voice deep, her expression tormented. I understood there was no point in discussing it with her. I gave her the tiara without saying anything, and she left my room immediately.

From one point of view, I was happy not to have to kill the animals any longer. On the other hand, I felt pity for her. That same night, an earthquake hit the place. A dormitory collapsed, and many girls who had followed Clytemnestra were buried under the rubble. None of the other girls were injured.

Despite the calamity, Clytemnestra took the rest of the girls, her guards, and the tiara and headed back to Mycenae.

Timandra and I stayed until we had dug up the girls' bodies and given them the funerals they deserved. I knew now that Clytemnestra had entered the path of evil. The peasants interpreted the earthquake as the wrath of gods for stealing the tiara.

Timandra asked me for forgiveness, and together we offered libations to the earth goddesses. After some time, some traders who stopped in Ithaka told me that Clytemnestra didn't dare to put the tiara on her head. She had placed it in a box, which she locked up with a little golden key, which she hung from her neck. No one had seen the tiara ever since.

Some four years after the end of the war, Neoptolemus, son of Achilles and Deidamia and grandson of Peleus, king of Phthia, announced his visit. Neoptolemus had taken the long walk from Troy to Phthia to spare his troops from dangerous sea travel. When they arrived, he was pronounced king of the region of Epirus, since his grandfather was still ruling Phthia. Therefore, he was our neighbor, and we had a common border with this kingdom.

I prepared everything for his visit, as was the custom for the visits of kings. Telemachus could not wait to hear about all the deeds of his father throughout the war. As announced, the vessels of Neoptolemus's fleet blackened the sea of Ithaka's northern coast. Telemachus and I were in the megaron, set up for the king's visit. I wore my deep-blue dress with the golden brooches and the golden belt, present of Odysseus. Polydorus and Laertes were at the port to welcome the king and hero.

I was giving last-minute instructions for the preparation of the sacrifices when Polydorus announced him. He was not tall, but he was well built and robust. His face had mild lines, and his colors were those of Thetis. I realized later also his smile and wit. It was hardly possible to think that this man had proven to be a killing machine, exactly like his father, throughout the war.

He bent his head when he saw me and said, "Queen of Ithaka, wife of valiant Odysseus, priestess of the Achaeans, I came from Epirus to ask for your alliance and friendship, as only with those can we fend off the enemies who seem to want to take hold of our kingdoms. Your husband was a great friend and mentor throughout the last years of the war in Troy, and I know that he is now hiding, as many Achaeans do, hoping that the leadership in Mycenae will soon change again and they will be able to come back."

"It is a great honor and a privilege to host you and offer you my and Ithaka's alliance and friendship. Please have a seat and allow the maids to wash your hands and feet and offer you a glass of our best wine mixed with water to quench your thirst."

When all was done and Neoptolemus and his commanders were sitting comfortably with their mugs of thinned wine in their hands, Telemachus spoke first. "Tell me, great king, what do you remember from my father? I miss him so much, and I have so many questions. I remember only small bits of our time together, and there is nothing that my heart desires more than to see him again."

"I can feel you, boy," he said. "My story was not much different from yours. I also had kept glimpses of my time with my father, but he also had to go to the war, the very same war. I grew up with my mother in Skyros until your father came to collect me two months after we had received the news of my father's death. My heart was burning for revenge, and your father knew how to make this feeling unbearable. My mother tried to keep me away from the war, without success. But I was lucky to come back to the earth that gave birth to my father and to avenge his death. I'm sure your father will come back, and you'll soon have the opportunity to embrace him, something that was never conceded to me," he said.

Telemachus, eager to hear of the heroic deeds of his father, said quickly, "But tell me how he fought in the plains and how many Trojans he killed."

Neoptolemus looked a bit puzzled, but he replied without delay. "Your father was a valiant warrior, my boy, but he will not be remembered for that. More than anything, he was the mastermind of the war. From the moment I met him, he worked untiringly to create the conditions for victory. Fighting only, no matter how rigorous and unconditional, would not have made fall the mighty walls of Troy. He managed to get my father into the war, which led to the killing of Troy's most valiant child, Hector. He brought Philoctetes into the war to kill Paris, the second-most important prince, whose bond with Helen of Sparta made him invincible. Together with Diomedes, he killed the Thracian leaders and stole Athena's wooden statue, which was making the city unconquerable. He kept good relations with most nobles of Troy, persuading them in the end to change sides, but most of all, he conceived the plan of the sacred horse, which confused the bigot Trojans and made them destroy their own walls, opening the gate for the

Achaeans to enter. That was your father—a brilliant mind and at the same time dedicated to our common purpose and scope."

I could see Telemachus and Laertes overwhelmed by pride.

"And why do you, an experienced warrior with your famous myrmidons for guards, think that you need the support of poor Ithaka, deprived of its men and its wealth?" I said, changing the subject.

"I have heard only the best about how you have managed to defend your country and wealth up to now, my queen, and about how you managed to create an army from young kids who are dedicated to you. All Achaeans talk about your generosity and hard work. I came to you also for your blessing, since I'm about to create a new kingdom, and I'd like you to be present at its inaugural ceremony."

"I'll be there, with great pleasure. Now let's go to offer to the almighty gods and the all-caring nymphs what is theirs. And after we have pleased them, let's sit around the table and enjoy our meal."

And so we did. Neoptolemus stayed with us the whole week. He was impressed by the organization of the country and the work at the academy. He wanted to introduce both concepts back in Epirus. He told me that he was not scared of the

Mycenaeans. They would not dare to attack his myrmidons, but he had no intention to enter into a quarrel with Aegisthus. He was simply trying to avoid him as much as possible. I agreed with his positions, and I told him that I'd let him know through my trusted people if I noticed any movements hostile to his kingdom. So our alliance was sealed, and he departed. I reciprocated the visit soon after.

λα'

It was a period of change. In the fifteen years of Odysseus's absence, Telemachus had become a man, and the little boys I had received in the academy had become warriors. Some of them were even quite handsome. Both Eurymachus and Amphimachus had by now twenty-seven years and had taken part in many sea adventures. Others, such as Thoas and Eurydamas, were about that age and were both very strong and robust fighters. Some had taken over the teaching of war to the younger generation, since many of the elders were dead or too old to hold the sword and throw the spear. They had all proven they were valiant fighters and citizens of the kingdom.

I was very proud of them. I felt they were my construct, my creation. I knew I was special to them as they followed my every move and fulfilled my every wish. Whenever they saw me sitting idle in the yard, they gave me the lyre and asked me to sing some of the old stories of Sparta or of the Trojan War.

Their attention became for me more of a problem than a blessing, since I noticed that some were even courting me. This again was making me feel the absence of my husband even stronger. I hadn't touched a man's body for all the period of Odysseus's absence. One day I caught myself watching them with attention as they were training with bare upper bodies in the academy's ring. It was not the watching that troubled me; rather, the desire that was aroused in me. I turned, almost scared, and left for fear that they might read my thoughts. I was the queen and couldn't allow such weakness.

But the next morning, I again caught myself getting dressed with attention, making sure that my beautiful black hair was falling on my shoulders and partly covering my decollete, which I had left intentionally as bare as I could. I had also straightened my belt as much as necessary to accentuate my breasts, and I had made sure one of my legs was coming out of the drape of my dress. My maids, all much younger than I— some of them could have been my daughters—felt challenged. "How beautiful you are, my lady," they kept saying. "Men will become crazy for their queen." I didn't mind their jealousy, not even their talk behind my back. I was feeling more and more a woman wanted and beautiful, and I was missing the male's breath on my neck and the warmth of his body in my bed. As predicted by the goddess, I was ever more beautiful and desirable, and my appeal was difficult to manage.

At least this was what I was thinking, but it wasn't me. The whole palace had been invaded by Aphrodite's fragrance.

There was love everywhere. My boys and girls were flirting with one another. The older ones were even loving each other often in the most appropriate places—in the storage rooms, behind the big trees of the garden, in the dormitories when everybody else was busy with something. Every time I saw them loving each other, it was as if I were relieved from my own desire.

Thekla came to me to complain that these kids didn't bother to keep the palace order anymore.

"What is better than love, Thekla? We need some love in here. It's all too rational, too still," I said.

"At least get them married," she said.

"All right! Whenever you find a couple, bring them to me, and I will arrange for their wedding, even if their parents don't agree."

I didn't uncover any couples. For some reason, I found pleasure in sensing their desire and feeling their love. But Thekla did. Within the next year, we celebrated twenty weddings. Parents usually agreed. When they didn't, I offered a dowry and land for them to build their home and cultivate.

It was during this period that my mind found a weird way to get satisfaction. One night the dream about my husband came back, but it was no longer a reassuring dream for his health and the desire for him to come back to Ithaka, but a dream of crazy passion, primordial instinct, and the quenching of internal fire. He was sitting on the sandy beach again, looking at the far-away land beyond the sea. His only dress was a piece of short chiton around his waist, covering half his thigh. A female hand touched his shoulder. "I miss her, Calypso," he said without turning.

"I know," she said, and he turned, surprised, to see her. But then I realized he was seeing me. I was there with him. "Penelope," he said, and he took me in his arms with a force that left me breathless. We kissed with passion, and we undressed quickly to feel the warmth of each other's bodies. Yes, it was him, my Odysseus, and it felt so good. I was kissing him everywhere, as if I wanted to devour him, to internalize each single part of his body. We loved each other on the beach, and we didn't care about the jealous maids of Calypso who were watching us from afar, or about the indiscrete seagulls that paired with each other all around us, taken up by the clout of our love. And we didn't care about the waves that were now arriving at our feet, threatening to swallow us, as if to seal forever that moment of divine frenzy.

There was so much love and ecstasy in me that I didn't know if I was drowning in it or in the sea that had reached us and was tearing us apart.

I woke up with the need to take breath, fully overwhelmed by the feeling I had experienced in my dream. I looked around, and I realized I was only in my room, on my bed carved by Odysseus on the centenary olive tree trunk. Tears of pleasure and disappointment filled my eyes, and I started laughing, taken by a happiness that I had entirely forgotten in the long years of separation from my husband.

I didn't want to go back to sleep, for fear I would lose the euphory of love. So I went down to the kitchen to prepare my breakfast. Sitting there, I wondered whether it was me or Calypso who had just made love to my husband. I realized I didn't mind. I was not envious of Calypso. I only wished she would share more of these moments with me and eventually send me my man back as she had promised.

The encounter of love made me shine even more and stilled my desire. I regained my power to reign, and I got rid of the weakness accompanied by desire. This was another present I was receiving from my friends, the female goddesses and nymphs. My beauty had multiplied. I had never felt more beautiful before—pretty, maybe, but not beautiful. Some days I thought that even my cousin Helen would faint if put next to me. Then I laughed at my own vanity. It was really an exceptional period for me, and my name as the most beautiful woman in the Achaean land spread quickly. Telemachus was feeling almost embarrassed, and I was happy and laughing with his accusations of forgetting that I was his mum, since there is nothing that can make a woman happier than the rediscovery of her own beauty.

So my young ones were getting married and making their families, and the older generation was diminishing quickly. Anticlea, Odysseus's mother, died one night. Laertes said that her heart was broken for the long-term absence of Odysseus. She was not sick but frail, and she died after a long period of being in bed. We buried her as a queen in the same place where Cephalus and his son Arcesius and his wife, Chalcomedousa, were also buried.

Not much time passed, and then Cyanea died. My faithful nanny and Parthenos guardian. She had been a hard worker with only one mission—to look after me and meet my needs. She fell sick but couldn't stop providing for me. So I ordered her to stay in bed. But then all the love in my dreams and that consumed in my palace by my subjects distracted me. I failed to give her enough attention, and one morning the maids told me she was dead. So a Parthenos had died in a palace taken by the frenzy of love. That made sense. Aphrodite was winning. Would I also have to die? Or maybe I should choose one of the men for my bed. Aphrodite was laughing. She was driving me crazy. She wanted me for herself. I knew. Long enough I had escaped her nets when she had been catching most of the Achaean women. Maybe I should just capitulate. Love was so sweet.

In the seventeenth year of Odysseus's absence, the news that arrived from Mycenae crowned the madness of the times. Clytemnestra was dead from her son Orestes's hand. Horrible news. Blood that brings more blood, I thought. Revenge never finishes; it is justice that calms people down, tames them, and makes them work for the common good.

It was clear to me that I had to stick together with my son. Any decision of mine to marry any of these men would lead to Telemachus's death, or revenge in case he managed to escape.

However, the news wasn't as bad for me. Odysseus could, after all, come back now. So I went to meet the goddesses and nymphs and ask them—Calypso more than the others—to release my man, since the danger from Mycenae had been removed. The graceful Calypso looked me in the eyes in a way that made me become red. "As you wish, my dear, although leaving him on my island might be more beneficial for you."

I knew what she meant, but I said slowly, "For me, maybe, but here there are many who wait for him, among them his son."

Calypso bent her head in a sign of resignation and disappeared. In my dreams some days after, I saw Odysseus leaving her island. She had kept her promise.

λβ'

Although it had been a while since Odysseus had left Calypso's island, he was still not back. I had no news and no dreams, and I was wondering what was happening. Then I started really getting worried.

The frenzy of desire, love, and passion in the palace had even attracted the nobles of Ithaka, who were often coming to the palace to learn news about Odysseus, as they were saying, but in reality they were trying to persuade me to marry one of their sons. They were worried that with all the arranged weddings, they would miss an opportunity. So they were massing around me to promote their sons. I was amused because in most cases, I knew which of my maids their sons were engaged to, and often I was arranging their weddings shortly after the fathers had been there to persuade me to marry their sons. No one ever disputed my reigning over the contrary, but with so many available men around, why should reigning be a woman's job?

I started feeling the pressure when Eurymachus first came to officially ask me to marry him. I gently explained that no news had come so far that Odysseus was dead, so there was no way I would marry anybody. After a while, Antinous came, and then others from the academy.

Suddenly the fear came back into my life. I was faced with a new reality. My possible remarriage. All the glamor that the nymphs had given to my life had led to more men thinking of me as their possible future wife. I suddenly realized what Athena meant by managing my beauty, and I started realizing how difficult the life of my cousin Helen was. Why couldn't I continue to reign as I had been doing for so many years? Ithaka hardly felt the lack of a male ruler. Everything was working to perfection. Everybody was happy with my decisions. People seemed proud of their queen. Why couldn't I continue doing what I was doing so well? I had learned to live without a man. Nobody in the palace was requesting me or instructing me. They were all expecting me to instruct and command, and they were happy with that.

They were feeling part of something bigger. They were not my subordinates or servants. We were all equals, working for our independence and freedom. These were my thoughts one evening sitting next to the fire of the megaron with old Euriclea on one side and Autonoe on the other. They were working the wool to make new clothes for Telemachus and the many babies born around the palace. They were working quietly and harmoniously without making even one little redundant move. Their fingers had captured the wisdom of the centuries, spinning and twisting and combing. I was watching them in the light of the fire, and I got an idea. I would start the funeral shroud of my father-in-law. Nice shrouds took years to make. So, at least for a while, I was able to decline further requests for marriage. I hoped that in the meantime, my friends the nymphs would help me keep my freedom.

The palace and the academy kept filling up with young men coming from all around Greece to ask to marry me. I was the last fortress of female independence. I was the only one of the wives of those who had fought in Troy to not have a new husband. The others had either gotten their husbands back or had gotten new husbands who had chased away the original husbands.

"Polydorus," I asked my good and faithful friend one day, "aren't the people of Ithaka happy with me and the way I reign?"

"Of course they are, my lady," he replied without thinking much. "Wherever I go, they say how just and wise is their queen."

"And why do they all want me to get married again, do you think?" I asked.

Suddenly he looked puzzled. "I…I guess because there is no queen without a king in the other kingdoms, my lady." He looked at me to see if I approved of the answer.

"Is that reason enough?" I asked. "What more will a king bring to Ithaka than what I give it already?"

His face got worried. "I don't know, my lady. Maybe a stronger voice, maybe a warlike face. You are so beautiful and blessed. You can win any war without even fighting it. What is a man worth if he can't fight for what he wants?"

I stayed speechless.

"I don't want you to marry, my lady," he added as he saw my disappointment. "We've had great fun protecting Ithaka all these years. And most of the men who grew up in the academy with you don't want you to marry. But it is the pressure they receive from their families that make them act like that."

I nodded as if to thank him. He left the room. But Autonoe, who had just poured me a hot tea from herbs that she had collected from the surrounding mountains, said, "Stop harrowing everybody. You want your freedom, but every woman needs a man. Particularly a queen as beautiful as you."

"But Autonoe, you are talking about a woman who has been on her own forever," I said. "Only I know how much solitude has cost me. All the nights that I wished to have a man in my bed to warm my feet, all the evenings that I needed someone to counsel me and support me."

"It is exactly that, my lady, with all your travels and responsibilities, all the people who come to find you and talk to you from all around the kingdom. You do so many things, my lady. You have a son to look after and all the palace to run. All of us here recognize your good work and effort to make sure all are happy and satisfied. This is why we want you to remarry and have, for once, someone to support you, to share with you the many responsibilities," she said.

And I realized that some just felt pity for me and saw marriage as a means to improve my life.

The various families of Ithaka, Zacynthus, Sami, and Dulichium kept sending representatives to negotiate a possible marriage between me and a son or grandson, who was usually in the academy, either as a teacher or student. At one stage we counted around 120 marriage proposals. More than once I tried to explain to those people that I had no intention of remarrying because I was entirely convinced that Odysseus was alive and would come back. But this argument was losing its strength with the weeks, months, and years that were passing.

It was then that I started the shroud. My father-in-law was getting old and was so broken waiting for his son. I was telling everybody, "So if the gods didn't allow me to make the shroud for my beloved husband, at least I will make the best I can for my father-in-law." The shroud also gave me a reason to reduce my visibility. It was not as much fun anymore to go around, with all the men watching me as their possible bride. It suddenly looked as if everybody had a right upon me, even those who had already selected their lovers. At the beginning, when I noticed the love plays, I was happy. I thought the young men were, after all, abandoning their hope for me and would make families with the maids. But as time passed and none came to ask me for my blessing for a wedding, I realized that most had relationships with my maids only to know my moves.

Such became their competition and their determination that they didn't leave the palace, not even when there were various jobs to do, such as the harvest or the saw. They were living mainly from the resources of the palace, which was making me even more upset. The palace personnel had to prepare food for all of them daily. Since the academy rooms were full, some were using the palace's auxiliary rooms for sleeping. Sometimes there were quarrels among them that agitated all the palace workers. My boys—those who had grown up with me, with my songs and traditions—were behaving well, but the foreigners were really audacious, creating many problems. I was scared a fight would start within my palace, in front of my eyes.

λγ′

Telemachus was no less worried than I was. He was twenty years old now and keen to mimic the great heroes of Troy. He was passing less of his time in the academy now and most of his time with his grandfather. Whenever a foreigner passed by Ithaka, he would interrogate him about his father—if he had met him, if he knew where he was, if he had heard of his death. But he was receiving no news. No one knew anything about Odysseus, not even my friends the nymphs. His agony was growing day by day, and I couldn't help him anymore. On the contrary, I was becoming more of a risk for him. If I were to remarry, my husband would become the new king, and his children would have the right to claim the kingdom. Although I had no intention of remarrying, he started trusting me less and less, and I knew it. I tried to calm his fears, but then we both realized that neither of us could trust the men of the kingdom. They had entered in a state of ecstasy, thinking of the power and wife that was awaiting them. They seemed able to do everything to push me to marry one of them.

On the other hand, I knew that even if I were to choose one, the others would probably not accept him and would form an army to challenge him. Even leaving the kingdom to my son and going back to Sparta was not an option. It would expose Telemachus. They would unite to get him out of the kingdom in the best case or kill him in the worst. If I could only take them to a battle, if I could have an external enemy to fight against, it would be the best. But since Aegisthus was dead, there was no reason to fight anymore.

Telemachus was trying to put the pieces of his father's life or death together from what he was hearing from the passersby, and he would come to me to ask me if I had heard this or that or if I could confirm this or that. My advice to calm down and find a girl to marry and settle down with was going unnoticed.

My concerns grew even more serious when I realized he was not going to the academy to train anymore. Apparently the others had showed him that he was not welcome there any longer. One day Thekla ran to me to tell me that she had heard of a plot to kill the "young prince," as she called him. This was when I made the decision to send him secretly to find allies among those who had fought with his father in Troy and build with their help an army to suppress the suitors. I told him to start in the kingdom of Pylos. Then to go to Sparta to ensure the support of his uncle Menelaus, then to visit his aunt Iphthimi and ask help from her husband, Eumelus. And, last but not least, to Neoptolemus of Epirus, who was a good friend of both Odysseus and me.

In order to get Telemachus safely out of Ithaka, I told everybody that my father was dying in Sparta and that he had to represent me there. In reality, Father was already dead, but I had kept that for me. Telemachus departed after two days. Now I had only to wait for him to come back with the army. My plan was to intimidate the suitors with the presence of the army that my son would put together and to force them to accept that he was the better solution to reign over the country since he had managed to get so many great heroes on his side. They wouldn't like it, but they would have to accept it. I would leave them with no other choice than going back to their homes and accepting my son as their king.

I wanted to see my friends and ask their opinion about my plan, so I went to find them in the cave. As always, I took milk and honey and fresh bread with me. I called them and offered them the libations. They came, faithful as always. "My dear," Athena said, "it is nice to have you around. Your man is on the island of the Phaeacians—"

"With the beautiful daughter of the king, Nausicaa," Calypso said, interrupting her.

"He will soon be with you, my daughter," my mother added. "You have to be careful now and avoid senseless bloodshed. When men come together, they think only of combat and imposing themselves on each other. They hardly reason and almost never see further than their egoistic drives of the moment."

"Hold firm on your position, and use your intelligence to manage them. Then they will all come at the same time," Thetis said, and they again all disappeared.

So new challenges were coming toward me. I went back to the palace. Approaching it, I noticed men and some of the maids and the personnel of the palace awaiting me at the entrance of the megaron. Eurynomus came to me and said, "Queen of Ithaka. Is it true that every evening you undo all you had woven during the morning?"

I couldn't understand the question, and I looked around. Melantho came forward and said, "I told them, my lady. You are such a pity. You have to choose a husband and get married again. We all think that. We want you to be happy again."

I had no power to complain, to argue, or to discuss. I pushed my way through the people, who moved aside to let me pass.

"You have to choose now, lady. We are here for you. We are all valiant men. Why do you continue to ignore us?" Eurymachus shouted.

"Aren't we good enough for you?" Antinous said.

I stopped. *It is not that, Antinous. It is just that I want to be free*, I thought, but I didn't have the courage to turn and tell him. I continued on my way. Telemachus would come back soon and would bring soldiers. I had to avoid spilling blood for any reason. The oracle had said that men would die for me. I had to develop a strategy to avoid that. These were my boys. I had trained them. I had instilled in them love for the traditions and their country. I had sung to them the deeds of the heroes, and I had taken them on the sea to fight the pirates. I didn't want them to die.

It was a night of turbulence. No one was sleeping. Everybody was discussing the queen's denial. I could see the fires burning until late. But I didn't intervene. I took my lyre, and I started singing one of the old songs from Sparta. The sweet melody went out my door and down the stairs and out my window and spread in the night air. It flew around the yard, and it cracked through the walls into the megaron and the kitchen. The whole palace was now seduced from the beauty of the song. Slowly the fires extinguished, and all of them went to sleep. It had worked. All was quiet, and I was again reassured that I was in control.

During night Telemachus had crept back. He woke me up at dawn. "Mother, they will be soon here."

"Who?" I asked and sat on my bed.

"The army. They all promised to help. Uncle Menelaus gave me his best officer and a small team of warriors. The son of Nestor is with me, and Neoptolemus will come with a part of his army. They will be soon in our port."

"How soon?" I asked.

"In two days. They said they would be here with the new moon. The new moon is in two days."

We went to the kitchen to get some breakfast and discussed what could happen. I told him that we should avoid any fighting. That when he became a king, he should have all these men as his army.

"And what about you, Mother? You will still be the legitimate queen of this place."

"I have to go and meet some people. There are some who still need my help. I will be off on a big journey."

"Your position is here, my queen," we heard a voice next to us say.

We turned and saw him. An old ragged beggar in the corner, almost invisible. He was sitting on the floor with a jug of milk in one hand and a piece of bread in the other. For a moment I wondered, Since when had he been hiding there, and how much of my secret thoughts he had heard already?

"Who are you, foreigner? And how did you arrive here?" I asked.

"Oh, my lady, don't pay attention to him. I felt pity and gave him something to eat. Now he'll go and will not disturb us anymore," Euriclea said and started pushing him out.

He stood up and went out of the kitchen. As he was leaving, he turned and looked at me intently. My heart fluttered, as if the beggar had looked into my soul and had seen my deepest thoughts. Then he looked at Telemachus from top to bottom and disappeared.

We sat, speechless and still, until Thekla put in front of us our jugs of fresh milk and barley bread with nuts and honey. Telemachus told me all his adventures during his absence. I advised him to keep quiet and be as invisible as possible until the army had arrived.

Then I went to get dressed. As I was passing from the veranda of the first floor overlooking the internal yard, I saw him again, sitting on a low stool, with Euriclea washing his feet. More than washing, she looked as if she was examining one of the feet. I thought, "How strange that the old woman takes the effort to wash his feet with such attention." But then I noticed him watching me again with insistent looks, and I turned quickly toward my room.

As I was sitting in front of my mirror with Autonoe making my hair, I imagined the look of the beggar again, but around the eyes, the face of someone else was forming—a younger man, a man I knew. It was Odysseus. My Odysseus. How was it possible? I stood up and ran back to the veranda. There was no one there. I called Euriclea and started to run toward the kitchen, calling her.

"What is it, my lady?" the old woman replied, coming out of the kitchen with her slow moves and all worried.

"Where is the beggar, Euriclea?" I asked.

She looked worried and turned away. "Oh, I don't know, my lady. I did all that was expected of a good host who takes care of his visitors. He moved on toward the academy."

"Oh no," I thought, and I started running in that direction. I saw them from afar. Most of the pupils were there, training with their teachers. I had no lesson at that time; it was training for war time, so it looked strange for me to be there.

Nevertheless, they all stopped to salute me with respect as they saw me. I looked around, searching for the beggar, and Antinous came to me to ask if I'd like to watch the training and if he could get me a chair. Before I could reply, we heard noise from the backyard, and we saw some kids pushing the old beggar around. They had given him a spear, which he held with one hand, and a sword, which he held with the other, and he had a huge shield hanging on his chest, almost bigger than he was. They were asking him to attack, even though the poor man couldn't even manage to keep himself straight from the weight of the weapons. The kids were pushing him and hitting him with the backs of their swords and laughing at him and running around to confuse him.

I felt the need to intervene and said that these were not the manners of noble Ithaka youth and that no one deserved this behavior, in particular not an old beggar who had asked for the protection of the palace.

Antinous immediately took my part and asked them to go and free the beggar from the shield, ordering him to leave and not to come back, since this was not a place for him.

"I came to invite you all to a banquet tonight in the megaron," I said. "Even you, old beggar…are invited."

Antinous asked what the reason was, and I replied, "My beloved son has come back from Sparta, and he has news to share with you. Let's see if he's bringing us any news about our king, Odysseus." I looked at the beggar now intently.

"Ah, when are you going to believe it, my queen?" said Eurymachus. "Odysseus is dead. He will never come back. You have to think of your future and that of all of us."

Eurymachus drew my attention for a moment. "You may be right, but let's see what my cousin-in-law Menelaus advise us," I said, and I looked back to find the beggar. But he had disappeared. Nowhere to be seen.

On my way back to the palace, I once again wondered if that was really Odysseus or if my mind was playing some silly game with me. Surely it would not be easy to reveal himself in this hostile place, in which Odysseus was only a heroic remembrance. With the exception of Telemachus, none of these guys wanted him back, I reckoned. Even I looked at his return only as a way to avoid marrying a young and ambitious man who most probably would restrain my reign in favor of his autocracy. Odysseus was for me more a way to keep my autonomy and freedom than to again have a husband.

But maybe that was a utopia. Also, Odysseus was a man, and he would claim back his authority, requiring his wife to silently support him in all his decisions.

Arriving in my room, I threw my head scarf with anger on the bed. "All these years working so hard to keep them all well fed and educated. Taking out my best self, all my strength, to be a worthy queen and to stand up to expectations. And now that everything is fine and works so smoothly, I have to cede it all to a man, a husband that I don't need," I shouted.

Autonoe, who was cleaning my room, ran scared out of the room. For a moment I thought she would go tell the suitors, similar to what Melantho had done with the shroud. But who cared? I still had to hold on for two days. The army of Neoptolemus would soon be there, and all my problems would be resolved.

λδ′

At the evening banquet, everyone was there. They had mostly come to hear from the mouth of Telemachus that his father was dead. Even the beggar was there when I stood up to welcome everybody and to give the floor to Telemachus. Telemachus told them about how he had first visited Pylos and then Menelaus, who told him how valiantly his father had fought during the war and how he, together with Diomedes, managed to steal the palladium, the little statue of Athena, protector of the city.

Then his aunt Helen and his uncle Menelaus explained what happened to them after they departed from Troy, almost at the same time as Odysseus. But they soon lost him from sight, and since then, no one knew what had happened to him. Telemachus then told the story of Menelaus and Helen in Egypt and described the wealth in the palace of Sparta. And last, he went to meet my sister Iphthimi and her husband, King Eumelus of Pheraes, but he couldn't please him with any news.

"So no one was able to tell where Odysseus is now," Antinous said. "No one can say if he is dead or alive, and no one can explain why, if alive, he is not coming back."

"But also, no one has seen my father dying," said Telemachus.

"Come to your senses, Telemachus. Your father is dead, and the kingdom needs a strong hand to govern it now that all kings are back and have resumed their duties. It is Penelope's duty, as queen and legitimate lady of Ithaka, to choose the next king. What are we waiting for?" said Eurymachus, who was red from excitement.

All exalted him. And for a moment, even I thought they were right. They could see my decision was imminent, and they started banging their wine jugs on the table, as if to push me say a name. Eurynomus felt my hesitance and said, "My queen, whomever you choose, your decision is sacred for us. All of us will stay your faithful servants as we have always done, and we shall swear allegiance to the new king."

His words sounded fake to me, and I said, "Are you sure, Eurynomus, that you are talking on behalf of everyone?"

My words raised a murmur. I stood up. I had to gain time. "I'll announce my decision tomorrow by midday," I said, and I left the room. I noticed none of my maids followed me. This was a clear signal of what was happening in my own palace.

I went to the kitchen and asked Thekla to monitor the situation in the megaron and come report to me.

She did as I asked. After she came back, she told me, "Do you really want to know what's happening in there? They're behaving as if they will be kings tomorrow. They are drunk, and they're disturbing the poor beggar. Some of them are playing dice, as if the one who wins in that will also marry you. And the maids, already coupled, each with one of them, can't wait to see their own lover winning and having his favor or becoming his official concubine. This is where your indecision has led the palace. You should have decided much earlier and had your maids get married quickly. Then you wouldn't have these problems," she said.

I couldn't listen to her accusations any longer, so I told her to go to bed.

Then Telemachus came to me. "Mother, why haven't you told me? Why say a name when in two days our friends will be here?"

"Shh." I put my fingers on his mouth. "Close the door and make sure no one is hiding anywhere close."

He did as I asked.

"I'll organize a contest with the bow. The bow is of Apollo himself. Iole gave it to me many years ago, and only those whom I want can bend it. The bow will bend only for you, Telemachus," I said, and I took out the bow that I had gone to collect from the armor storage room the other day. "I'll show you how to bend it. If one tries the normal way, this bow cannot be bent. So you'll be the only one to bend it and will win the contest. At the same time, Neoptolemus will arrive and will demand they honor the agreement. So everything should go smoothly."

He looked puzzled. He then realized that I was holding to him and I would never let him down. He took me in his arms. "What would I do without you?" he murmured.

"You will be the king," I said.

He left, and I hid the bow again. Melantho came to my room to prepare me for bed. "My lady, what a wonderful day. Everybody is so happy since you decided to announce the name of your future husband," she said.

"Yes, I can imagine, my dear. I hope the young men still know how to behave in a palace despite their happiness."

"Well, they are so agitated. They may have gone a bit over the top, but I assure you, it is only for today. Then this beggar seems quite cheeky. He doesn't seem to know where his place is."

I looked at her and tried to understand what made this girl so profoundly dedicated to me to not see the obvious. I took a deep breath and turned to the mirror. I watched her happiness. She was obviously expecting her own marriage once mine had been settled. Who could blame her for that?

The next morning after breakfast, I asked to see the beggar. He came limping to me. I watched him from afar. Now it was me watching him, because I knew he was hiding Odysseus behind his appearance. Why wasn't he revealing himself to me? Obviously, he didn't trust me. He was there to study me and the others. He was scared for his life if he were to reveal himself. Everybody was faithful to me and no one to him. They didn't know him, and he didn't know them. Some had even been born after he had left.

"You asked for me, my queen," he said.

"Yes. Please sit down and share with me this wine mixed with water. I hope people are treating you well here in the palace and you're receiving everything you need. I gave orders to everybody to look after you; Zeus should find no fault in how the Ithakan people have hosted you. But tell me more about you—your name, where you've come from, and where you are heading."

"My lady, your hospitality and care for those in need is legendary in all the Achaean land. You are our high priestess, and Zeus will ask first your opinion about a poor man like me and then my opinion about your hospitality. I'm from Crete. Aithon is my name, and I came to you to be blessed. You see, I was away from my home for many years, following the army of King Idomeneus to Troy. When we came back, the king found out that his wife had been forced to marry his nephew. The new king and queen didn't allow him to disembark, so we all sailed to Italia.

"After a month of traveling, we arrived at a beautiful beach and went on land. The king asked the local lord to give him shelter, and he would teach him all the secrets of war. The lord accepted us and gave us all we needed to live. Some even got married and started new families. The lord gave us some land to live on and cultivate, and we named it Neapolis.

"But my heart was burning from desire to see my wife and child back in Crete and was weeping every evening in their remembrance, so when I got the opportunity, I asked Idomeneus for permission to go back. I went on the first merchant ship I found, and after many adventures, I managed to reach again my village. None could recognize me any longer. When I arrived in my house, it was changed, and I noticed that she had had another man in the house. I wanted to shout, 'Eh, look at me! I did everything I could to come to you earlier,' but I couldn't.

"I went to the kitchen to meet her. I told her who I was, but she escaped to the bedroom. I followed her, reminding her of the nights we had spent together in that bedroom. She was crying and screaming, and her man arrived and pushed me down the stairs. I broke my leg and have had a limp since then. The leg gives me a lot of pain, my lady, but most of all, I can't manage to get along with the pain of her betrayal.

"I left Crete and went around ragged and poor, and kids laughed at me and passersby pitied me," he said with his head low and without looking at me.

"I understand your pain, Aithon, but I also understand your wife's decision to get married again. Believe me, it was not easy during the war. Men were absent, and women had to do everything themselves, along with protecting themselves from the pirates who were kidnapping them and selling them as slaves. Here in Ithaka, I lost a full village of women and kids to the pirates during the first year. But then I learned how to protect them."

I wanted to continue, but he interrupted me. "You seem more in need of protection now, my queen, from all these suitors around you."

"Oh no, you misunderstood," I said. "These men were all trained in poetry and singing by me. I gave great importance to their education as soldiers because since a young age, they followed me on most of my trips to fight off pirates and protect the land and Odysseus's gold shipments. Believe me, I have nothing to be scared of from these men. They will obey me to their death. Nevertheless, they want me to marry one of them in order to have a king and be on equal terms with the other Achaean kingdoms. These are also the views of the elders of Ithaka, who also push me to get married," I said.

"You know what I should have done, my queen?" said the beggar as if illuminated. "I should have killed him. The husband, I mean. Now she would be mine, and I would live again in my house instead of going around asking for alms."

I shuddered because I knew he meant it. "No," I said. "We don't want any more killings. Go to the temple and stay there and fast for three days. If you find a way to forgive, then I'll bless you, and you can go to live your life from the beginning. If not, dammed you'll be."

He looked at me intently and left limping, as he had come. Was he Odysseus after all?

I called the people to announce my decision on whom to marry. I was carrying Apollo's bow with me.

"As promised, the queen will announce her decision." Telemachus said. "I say that this man will be the king of Ithaka and only this: who will manage to pull the string over this bow and shoot an arrow through twelve consecutive ax heads. The contest will take place tomorrow morning with the first sunlight, in the military academy yard."

I heard them all talking agitated to one another as I turned to go back into my room. I had no intention of either going out until next morning or of having any of my maids in my room. The only person who was allowed to enter my room was Thekla. I trusted only her after Cyanea's death.

"What are you going to do if the only one to win the contest is that ugly beggar? Why couldn't you choose your husband as every woman would?" she asked me when she came in.

"Don't worry, my dear. I take only calculated risks."

"And if more than one manages to do it?"

"Then I'll give them another contest."

"So this is your new trick to keep them busy for another while, with the hope that they will marry and leave you alone. Forget it; it won't work," she said.

"Maybe you are right," I said with a frown. "It didn't work with my father's contest, but the adversary was Odysseus. We shall see."

The next morning, I asked them all to form a line, and I passed in front of each man. "I expect fairness," I said and declared the contest open. "The contest will last until midday."

With pleasure I saw them all failing. They tried again and again but could not manage to even pull the string of the bow. "So, the spell still works," I thought. I saw them using all their power and sweating and failing again and again. It was getting to be midday, and I was looking around for Neoptolemus. He should be arriving by then. Where was he?

I stood up. "Let's see if Telemachus can do it," I said.

Everybody laughed. Others who were much stronger and more muscular than Telemachus had tried and hadn't made it. From the end of the yard, though, I heard the voice of the beggar. "Let me try before your son, lady. I am by far not as young and strong as your son, so I will fail, but a curiosity has taken me by surprise. I hope you don't mind, my queen," he said limping in front of me and taking the bow from the hands of Telemachus.

His hands, which previously had been trembling, moved decisively. His body took a position that I knew and had seen before. His fingers pulled the string over the bow and with ability fixed it in the opening. I heard an "Oh" from the others, who certainly had not expected this. He then straightened his body, which suddenly appeared strong and well trained, and he shot the arrow, which passed through the twelve ax heads.

Telemachus took me and led me to the exit of the yard. I was looking back as he was pulling me. The man, the beggar, was nowhere to be seen anymore. Instead, Odysseus was standing there shooting one arrow after the other, and my suitors, my soldiers, my boys, were falling dead, one after the other. Some tried to grab him, but I couldn't see any more because I was already out of the gate.

All gates locked immediately as I exited. I could hear thuds and shrieks from inside, but Polydorus, together with Thekla and Autonoe, took me back to my room. "Come, my lady. These are not things for your eyes. It looks like others are taking command now, and you have to go their way," Thekla said, but then she soothed me. "Don't worry, my lady. Everything will be good again."

I was worried and then angry. How could he dare? Making a bloodbath in my palace. All for what I had worked for over the years. Ithaka's young men were massacred. The feelings of anger and my inability to help made my blood boil, and my eyes filled with tears. Where was Neoptolemus? I looked toward the sea, but it was desperately blue. Why did he need so long? In my room, I heard lightning strike. I sat on my bed. Outside, the rain started. The sky was as dark as my head, and the raindrops were as heavy as my tears.

I tried to look toward the sea with the hope that I would see the fleet arriving. In vain. The sea was even blacker than the sky, and the waves were getting bigger and bigger. Thekla brought me tea, which made me sleepy. I fell asleep quickly.

I woke up early the next morning, and everything was quiet. Suspiciously quiet. I put on my robe and opened the door of my room as quietly as I could, for fear I would wake the dead. I looked down from the veranda. Fires were burning, and some of the servants were busy cleaning. There was a smell of death, blood, and burning flesh. I went down the stairs, and I heard voices from the megaron. I went toward the entrance, and I heard some of the discussion. "It was not a clever idea of you to kill them all, Odysseus. What are you going to do with their parents now? Kill them as well? And even the maids. What for?" said a voice that I recognized as that of Neoptolemus. So he had arrived during my deep sleep.

"They would have never accepted me back. You know that. I had to clear the place. They would have always been a source of trouble."

I went in, and they stopped. Neoptolemus smiled and tried to greet me, but I ignored him. I went to Odysseus and said, "Damned are those who cannot forgive," reminding him of our previous discussion.

"Woman, be happy that we cleaned the palace of these individuals. They were overblown, useless sacks. No one will miss them, really."

My anger made my throat swell, and it was preventing any word that was formed in my mind from coming out. I left the room and went to see the bodies. Tears formed in my eyes, and the sobs in my breast multiplied with every body I'd see. The academy was full of them. In my palace, ten of my younger maidens were slaughtered like sheep.

I went back to the palace, feeling my way along the walls because I couldn't see anything from the tears. Odysseus came toward me. "Penelope…we are now free to reign as we wish…as you wish."

But I didn't want to hear that. I called Thekla and told her to start the preparations for the funerals. I felt that I was the only one who could give these people a proper funeral and honors for the dead. I started the preparations for the libations, the burial places, and the remembrance feast afterward. I gave the orders to start cleaning the bodies of the dead and preparing them for the funeral. Then I went to the temple of Zeus to pray.

λε′

He was there as I walked out of the temple. He had nothing in common with the man who had saved my life many years ago. It almost felt as if he was not the same person.

He cried my name. "Penelope."

My eyes filled with tears again. I didn't want to talk to him.

"Penelope, I need to talk to you."

"I have nothing to say," I said.

"You are my wife. I know you have been faithful to me. I know you have worked hard to keep the kingdom. I do acknowledge your dedication to me and Telemachus. Now I'm back, Penelope. We belong together. You have to officially announce the return of the king and your subjection to him."

I turned and looked at him. His image hurt me so much. "The king of whom? You killed all those you could subject. I'm only the will of the goddess, which cannot be subject to any mortal."

"But Penelope, they would never subject to me. They would see only you."

"So you killed them to revoke power from me and not to protect yourself, as you claim. You were not sure about me, about my preparedness to receive you back…"

"But look what happened to most of us. It was the wives who rejected them, who sent them to exile or even killed them. How could I be sure?"

"Yes, it is your lack of trust and faith that haunts you, Odysseus. That didn't let you find your way back to me. While your overblown ego is telling you that I esteem power as much as you do." I turned to him again. His eyes seemed filled with shame. "Well, learn now that it was a deep sense of duty that gave me the power and the humility of service that attached respect to it. Yes, you won the war, but not the people."

I left him standing there, as if struck by thunder, and I ran back to the palace.

In the evening he tried again to approach me. He seemed to change his tactic. He opened the door of my room and came in quickly to avoid being seen. He closed the door but stayed there, not daring to come closer. "Penelope, I didn't think these people meant so much to you. I am sorry. I'll do what you want me to in order to purify myself and be worthy of your love. Please have me back in our room and in our bed. The bed that I, with my own hands, smoothed from the trunk of the olive tree."

The face seemed to have lost its arrogance. It almost looked familiar now. Was it real, or was he just changing tactics? He noticed my hesitance, so he came closer. "Oh, Penelope, in the name of our love at the time of Calypso," he said, and my whole body lit on fire.

He knew about it. He enjoyed it as much as I did. He knew what I was thinking, and he took me by the waist. "Be again my wife, Penelope." He lowered his face to mine. I just wanted to give in, to feel his strong body pressing on mine. I wanted him to make love to me. "On this bed that hosted the love of our youth."

I closed my eyes to fully taste the kiss he was giving me on my lips, and for a moment I thought this was the best thing that had happened to me in the last twenty years. But then I heard a voice inside me. "Old good Odysseus—you can't be so stupid as to believe him."

I opened my eyes, and I saw it. The statue of Athena in front of me. It looked as if it had been set on fire. The face of the goddess was severe. I heard her voice in me. "None of this is genuine."

I pushed him away. His face was full of surprise. I stepped back. My answer came back as hard as the ax I had used to sacrifice the bulls during my time as a holy priestess of the dark gods, when I knew the blood would splash on my face. "This time the bed will host you and the shadows of the dead that you, with your own hands, so ruthlessly have murdered," I said with all my power.

We looked at each other for a while. I was ready to go out, and I had already decided to change rooms when he stopped me, saying, "You stay. I'll not disturb you anymore."

As he was going out, he turned and looked at me, surprised again. "No wonder they cherished you…" he murmured as he closed the door.

I stayed on my own. All my rage became sadness, and then I realized that I had just sent away the only person I had longed so much to have next to me all these years. My eyes filled with tears, and my mind played me all scenes of love that I had lived with him and I had dreamed of over the years of his absence. "Where is the man you promised me?" I asked the statue of Athena. I fell on my knees in front of it, and then, leaning against it, I cried until sweet sleep covered my face and forced my mind to calm down.

The news spread, and the relatives of the dead started arriving. They declined to give honors to Odysseus. Fathers, grandfathers, and other male relatives went to Neoptolemus to complain about the deaths of their young people. Neoptolemus camped with his troops just outside the palace perimeter. There was also a small troop from Sparta and a smaller one from Pylos. They could not depart as long as there were funeral ceremonies. Since they were there, they had to stay.

Neoptolemus was profiling himself as the new leader of the Achaeans now that Mycenae was practically ungoverned. Yes, Menelaus had taken over, but Orestes was still in a state of craziness, going around the country asking forgiveness for the murder of his mother. Neoptolemus had taken Hermione, daughter of Helen of Sparta, as his wife, and that legitimized him even more. In fact, Hermione was to become the new high priestess. But none knew what Clytemnestra had done with the tiara, and there had been no official ceremony to hand over the power yet. Things were difficult for the Achaeans. They needed religious and political leaders soon, and Neoptolemus was up to that role.

Mothers, grandmothers, and female relatives of the dead were coming to me. I was dressed for mourning and not for celebration, as Odysseus was expecting. I left my hair uncombed, and I led the lament.

It took a full week to carry out the funerals and the related celebrations. Odysseus appeared on the first day. He could not enter the temple because he was impure. He was there when the fires started. All looked at him with disdain, and I had to stop the ceremony. He had by now realized that he would never be the king of these people.

"What did you want me to do?" he shouted. "They were reducing my birthright to nothing. Showing no respect, preferring me to be dead. I had gone through so many difficulties, and my only dream was to come back to my island, to my family, to my people. I went through the Tartarus to be able to come back. And as I arrived, I realized that everybody wished me to be dead. What did you want me to do?"

Aigyptius, very old now, said, "These men you killed without mercy helped retain your kingdom for almost twenty years. They lost their fathers in the war and during your wanderings, from which you, as the only one, came back. What did you want them to do? Rightly they expected to become kings and reign over the country that they loved. You should have consulted us, the queen and the great king, before acting. Instead, you killed the youth of Ithaka exactly as your stupid arrogance killed the previous generation by taking them to a futile war. None of us wishes to see you here any longer."

Odysseus fell sick the same evening. Euriclea died two days after that, and my father-in-law another two days after. Only Thekla took mercy on Odysseus. She tried to feed him and keep him alive, and she was hoping that I would save him and accept him again as my husband. Telemachus, seeing his father sick, got scared and came to me to cleanse him.

"Did you kill?" I asked.

"No, but I helped," he said. "I locked the gates and gave him the spears," he admitted with horror, understanding then the weight of his deeds.

I took him to the temple of Athena, and I told him to stay there for three days without food or water. If he came out sick, he was guilty. If he came out well, he was forgiven.

After the funerals, Neoptolemus called me to his tent. "I was asked by the people to be the judge in the name of the dead. Tomorrow I will give my sentence, but before that, I'd like to hear your view," he said, and I knew he meant it.

"I am glad that you are here, and you will define our future, since I know that life has taught you great wisdom," I replied.

"Thetis, your grandmother, follows each step you take, advises you, and protects you, similar to how she does with me. I will follow your advice and obey whatever your decision will be, because I know it will be the best for all. I have nothing else to say," I said.

He looked at me as if he at that specific moment knew all about my secret encounters with the nymphs. Probably he had had some himself.

The next day, he announced his sentence. Odysseus had to leave the country, go to cleanse himself for the killings, and come back only then. He entrusted the country back to me, as the legitimate ruler since the time of King Perseus, with the requirement to appoint the new king sooner rather than later. He asked all Ithakan people to follow this decision since it was the will of the gods, communicated to him directly by his grandmother Thetis. "The people would have to accept and honor whatever decision I made about the future king, since that would be a king, blessed by all gods," he said.

Neoptolemus left after three days, and so did the troops from Sparta and Pylos. I knew these were Ithaka's long-term friends and supporters.

I was happy with this decision, and I could now without hesitation move on with my plans. Odysseus was sick, but I knew this was a sickness of soul more than a real physical one. I had to find a way to cleanse him and make him get rid of his arrogance. This arrogance had fascinated me at first and later disturbed me, and now I loathed it. It was my duty now to take back the treasures he had stolen from the others. This was my accord with the goddesses. They would help me if there was no harm to other people. Now was the time to make well what he had done wrong during the twenty years of his absence.

I gathered the people and communicated to everybody my will. The future ruler was my son, Telemachus, who hadn't killed any of the men and had survived the three days in Athena's temple. He would rule according to my will.

Odysseus and I had to leave. A part of Ithaka's treasures would have to be given back to their legitimate owners. This would purify the whole island from the curse of the war. The elders agreed with all and spoke positively about this to the people. All wished me good luck. I prepared two ships. I put on all the gold that I had received from Odysseus's looting and from Odysseus himself, who couldn't walk on his own anymore. One nice spring morning, I departed with a few soldiers and a sick and broken man. I was ready for that. I had been waiting for that for my whole life. I was holding his head on my lap and was stroking his hair as Ithaka slowly disappeared. Nostalgia overwhelmed me. Would I ever see my home again?

λς'

We headed toward Epirus to Ephyra. There was the nekromanteion—the oracle of the dead—of Hades and Persephone. My aim was to make Odysseus regret his arrogance and his aggression and ask all those he killed for forgiveness. I considered this the only way to save him from the guilt and to save Telemachus from future acts of revenge from the families of the dead. The nekromanteion was next to the Acheron River, the river that transported the dead souls to Hades; it was beautifully situated close to the river's springs. It was also adjusted to the swamps. Farther downriver, another river, Kokytos, joined the River Acheron, creating an extended region of swamps from which the fumes of rotten material were rising. It took us two days to arrive, one traveling by boat and one on foot. Acheron, after entering the underworld, flowed into the mighty River Styx, which circumvented Hades.

Odysseus was almost unconscious from fever. The guards were carrying him on a stretcher. Polydorus, my good friend and consul, was with me, along with five guards. Another fifteen rowers were left to look after the boat. I had taken with me only the absolute necessities, since the boat was full of the gold that Odysseus had sent to Ithaka from the sacking of

Thrace and the other cities he and the Achaean armies had destroyed. We never received any gold from Troy, since that disappeared with Odysseus's boats during his trip back. I had promised the nymphs and Athena to bring the gold back to those from whom it had been stolen. And now was the time to execute this promise. I was determined to do this with or without Odysseus. I was expecting that if the goddess were to let him live, she would give him enough wisdom to carry out this labor with me. At times I was scared he would die before reaching the nekromanteion, but in the end, we made it. Since he was not capable of walking, I had to enter with him. But that was all right. I was not scared of the dead and their shadows. I had learned that from carrying the tiara, even for a short time. And I knew I couldn't die before I had executed my mission.

The necromanteion priests purified us, and we entered the first chamber. We ate barley bread, dried pork, and beans, the only food allowed in the caves, and we slept. We knew Polydorus would carry out the sacrifice on the top—every day another sheep. Every time a sheep was sacrificed, a gate would open to go to the next chamber. Every chamber was different, since it represented another stage of the way toward the reign of Hades. The deeper we went, the darker it became. The frescos on the walls were becoming darker, showing the various stages of the souls in the underworld.

In each chamber, the priests had left water and a beverage made of boiled barley with herbs and honey. The food was becoming ever simpler and less. I was almost carrying Odysseus by the time we entered the final gate. We sat on the wet earth, and then he started seeing the dead men of Ithaka passing in front of him and asking him why he had killed them and if he couldn't have spared their lives and talked to them. Odysseus's eyes were swollen and seemed as if they would pop out his face. Sweat was dripping almost like water from all his body.

I was sitting next to him, imaging him upright and strong again. I knew he could see things I couldn't see, and I knew he had to ask for forgiveness if he wanted to get out of there alive. I gave him water, which I was collecting from the walls of the cave. I couldn't sleep, and I couldn't stay awake. The air was heavy, and at times I thought I was dead myself. I couldn't tell whether it was day or night outside, and it was impossible to say how long were we in there. Was it only some hours, or days or months?

Then he started recovering, his dreams ceased to torment him, and he stopped shivering. Suddenly a piece of the wall opened, a door that we had never noticed. I managed to get him up, telling him that it was time to go back. We dragged ourselves to the opening. The cave, full of shadows before, seemed a quiet little room. As the door closed, we noticed daylight at the other end and moved toward it.

Odysseus was free of fever but very weak. The light was becoming stronger, and upon reaching it, we realized we were out of the caves. I was supporting him as the sun's rays fell on our skin, making us feel alive again. But our eyes couldn't bear the light, and the priests gave us head covers with low brims to protect them. They told us to go and wash ourselves in the purifying waters of Acheron. Failing to do so would mean no contact with other humans.

Polydorus was watching us, but he didn't come close to help me. So I turned toward the river despite the weakness I was feeling and the weight of Odysseus on my shoulders. Before we entered, we were asked to undress and burn our clothes, so I helped Odysseus take off his clothes, and I took off my robes. Polydorus made a fire, and Odysseus and I walked with fragile steps into the river. It was cold, but a feeling of lightness took us by surprise and gave us strength to submerge ourselves completely. We felt the spirits of the dead leaving our weakened bodies and giving them new strength. We looked each other in the eyes, and we saw our souls clean and keen for a new life.

On our way out, Polydorus passed us new clothes. We moved toward the camp of our soldiers, who welcomed us and gave us milk with honey to drink. Although they were curious about what had happened in the caves, they didn't ask, and we couldn't say anything.

During the evening, around the fire, I took the lyre and started singing my story as queen of Ithaka. Odysseus sang his adventures of coming back to his island. It was the moment of truth. We sang our lives to each other, and it was the first time that we felt we were reunited.

By the next day, Odysseus had recovered, and I knew his life was spared. I told him that we had to go to Thrace to give back the gold he had stolen, and he agreed. However, he said that Persephone herself had given him two jobs. First, to find Queen Callidice and enter into her service to fend off her enemies, and second, to find his old friend Diomedes and collect the palladium, the wooden statue of goddess Athena, and deliver it to Aeneas for his new city.

λζ′

So we went to the city of Ephyra, the main city of the Thesprotians, very close to the nekromanteion but in a location where the citizens were safe from the swamp's deadly fumes. The city was in turmoil. The old king had died, and the Brygians had camped outside the city walls and were asking the city to surrender.

We approached the city from the swamps, since the Brygians were scared of them. We were allowed to enter and find refuge within the walls of the city. We noticed the army was in disarray, and it seemed that the palace had been abandoned. We asked one of the guards where the king was, and we were told that he was dead and that his daughter, Callidice, had asked King Neoptolemus for protection. However, he had since been murdered in Delphi by Orestes, the crazy son of Agamemnon and Clytemnestra. Odysseus and I looked at each other as if the ghosts of the Achaeans had come back to haunt us after all the effort we had put in to get rid of them.

"And where is the princess now?" asked Odysseus.

"In the temple of Dione. She went there to ask for protection. She is pregnant, you see, but no one knows who the lucky father is." And he stopped with a grin. "I have to go now. The Brygians are not known to spare the lives of Thesprotian men." He tried to go, but Odysseus grabbed him by his sword belt. "You are not going anywhere farther than the army camp. I need to find the one in charge of the army."

"But I told you, the king is dead. There is no army. Everybody is abandoning the city, even the princess herself," said the man, almost crying from fear now.

"I'll go to find her. You take care of the Brygians," I told him.

The man was not happy, but he realized he could not escape. He took Odysseus to the camp. Once they arrived, Odysseus spoke to the men. "I am Odysseus of Ithaka, the destroyer of Troy. I am here to lead the war against the Brygians. Behave like an army, and get ready for war. We shall face them the day after tomorrow at dawn."

The message went around the city that King Odysseus would lead them to war, and everybody start gaining confidence and coming back. I left the city with a small troop of guards. We went to Dodoni, a two-day trip from Ephyra. My job was to get Callidice back to her city and ensure her reign.

When we arrived at the holy oracle of Dione and Zeus, we asked for Callidice, and we were taken straight to the temple of the goddess. Callidice was in labor, which seemed to be a tough one. The labor had started two days before, but the baby was not coming. Poor thing—she was so young and scared; her father was dead, and no husband in sight. I went close and presented myself. She took my hand as if she was asking for help. I put my hands on her belly and asked the goddess to guide me. The priests of the temple left the room except for one, old and half-blind. "The baby is alive," he said. "I have given her the tea of birth, but she suffers more than she deserves."

I asked the servants of the temple to make a relaxing tea and the midwife to apply leaves of Artemisia to the vulva to relax the muscles. I realized it was her fear that was not letting her give birth. The fear was restricting her whole body, and it was threatening to kill the baby. As she started relaxing, the labor pains started coming more often, and the baby was born the same night—a fatty baby boy who was bluish from staying too long in the channel. The old priest put the baby at her breast, and they both fell asleep, exhausted.

It took her two days to recover from the difficult birth, but she was breastfeeding fine and was able to stand up and walk on the third day. I told her that Odysseus was fighting the Brygians back in Ephyra and that she would soon have to go to encourage her people.

She looked at me, confused. "How can I go back there? Neoptolemus, the father of the baby, is dead. I cannot reign on my own," she said, unsure.

"Of course you can," I told her. "It is essential that you do. You are blessed to have a son. You have to take up the kingdom until your son is old enough to get married and take over from you. You can make it. The gods told us you can."

She looked confused.

"We shall go back as soon as you can undertake the journey," I told her.

In Dodoni, priests had a lot of information about what was happening in the various Achaean kingdoms. It was a crazy period. Neoptolemus was dead, and Orestes was still haunted by the furies. Menelaus was in Mycenae, and Helen was in Sparta. There was no sign of a leader after the death of Neoptolemus. Yet the Achaeans had no enemy; nobody wanted to challenge them. The fame of the great warriors of Troy was still alive, and all knew now that these people could unite and face all possible enemies. The priests were talking about the new era. The new time of greatness of the Greeks. They would become a whole new kingdom, if only they had a king and a sacred priestess in Mycenae.

Another three days, and Callidice could take the trip back. When we arrived, Odysseus was fighting the final battle. He had managed to fend off the Brygians, who were now heading back to their villages in the north having lost any faith that they could defeat the army led by Odysseus. When the army came back almost a week after we had arrived at the palace, all were cheering and rejoicing. Odysseus had saved their city.

I was afraid of his reaction. Would he fall back into arrogance? Would he want to stay and forget his responsibilities toward the gods and me? I was prepared to leave him and continue the trip on my own. Callidice had felt the cold of our relationship. And she was hoping to keep him there as protector and king. I was standing quiet, expecting the worst. It was not up to me to intervene, to talk to, or to persuade him. His life had been spared only to fulfill a mission, and he knew that.

He gave his speech to all Thesprotians outside the walls of the city. Callidice was there holding her baby. I was preparing the boats for departure. We had to go and find Diomedes, who had established himself in Italy. I didn't know where to go or how to find him, but I was sure the way would be clear once I had started the journey.

Then I heard a voice behind me. "How blessed are the heroes of Troy. Odysseus here a king, and in Ithaka his son, Diomedes a king of Daunians."

"Do you mean Diomedes of Argos?" I asked.

"Yes, my lady. A clever man. By far the most intelligent, after your husband. It was here that he came and asked the help of our king Thoas, father of Callidice. He gave him boats and food and me as a guide to take him over to the kingdom of the Daunians. Their king, Daunus, was good friend of Thoas, and they had engaged in trade. When Daunus died, Diomedes took over. A very clever man indeed, this Diomedes," he said.

"Can you take me to him?" I asked with hope.

"Of course, my lady. When should we depart?"

"Now," I said. "Let me check the boats. They must be ready by now. We depart as soon as possible." I went off to check how the preparations were going. I wanted to depart sooner rather than later.

Then I went to find the old man. "We are ready," I told him. "We can depart with the first light tomorrow."

The next day, he was there. He jumped in the boat with ease despite his old age. "We shall depart as soon as the king is here," he said.

"No, the king will not come," I said, sure that Odysseus had fallen victim to his big ego again.

"And whose hooves are those that make so much dust?" He gestured inland. "I think only a king's hooves make so much dust, lady," he said with a grin.

I looked that direction with hope. Indeed, Odysseus was arriving, and the old man, whose name I hadn't asked yet, asked the crew to release the ropes and put the sail on. Everybody was following his requests without discussion. I was suddenly very happy to have Odysseus back. My heart warmed up a bit. He had passed the first challenge.

λη′

It took us five days and nights to arrive at the coast of Apulia. Throughout the trip, Odysseus was telling me stories of his wanderings. He used every opportunity possible to confirm how important Ithaka and I were to him. As we reached the shore, he felt unsure, and at the beginning, he didn't want to disembark. He insisted that this shore was very similar to the one on the island of Helios where he had lost many of his men.

The old man went off to buy horses, and he came back with two soldiers who spoke Greek and claimed to be Diomedes's guards. Only then would Odysseus wander inland. It took us another two days to reach Argos, the city Diomedes had founded in Apulia and named according to his home city back in Greece. The landscape was so different from that back home. There were plains and only a few hills and fields cultivated with wheat and barley among the woods of poplars and willows. The land close to sea was sparsely populated, but farther inland we saw villages without protective walls.

We soon arrived at Argos—Hippium, as it was called. The old man explained that Diomedes was breeding horses that originated from the horses he had stolen from the Thracians back in Troy. The city looked like a Greek city, with walls and a citadel for the temples.

We moved toward the palace, and as we tried to enter, an old man came toward us, almost running, and fell into the arms of Odysseus. "Odysseus," he cried. "What brings you here? Have the Achaeans thrown you out of your city, similar to what they did with our master Diomedes?" He then relaxed his embrace and looked at him.

"Sthenelus, my friend," said Odysseus, surprised, almost without breath.

But Sthenelus just continued his monologue. "It is so nice to see you again. I never hoped for so much luck. Seeing you is like going back to the years of Troy and our common adventures. Diomedes will be delighted. Poor him—he had to suffer so much after his return to Argos. First, they didn't let us in the city. Then they threatened to kill us all. We lived like wild animals in the woods or fighting as mercenaries for other kings. Then we arrived here. We found a new home and settled down. Now he is the lord of all the area, with more than ten fortified cities. And he has enormous wealth, but what a struggle it has been. Come; I'll take you to him."

And he showed us the way, which took us behind the palace to the stables, where we got new horses. And we rode to the fields outside the city. There were people training for an open-field battle. There were riders and hoplites. Diomedes had divided his soldiers into two groups, and he was training them in battle, both with horses and without.

We were told to wait until Sthenelus went toward the scrum. We heard a voice halting the fight, and then we saw him. He rode toward us, and as he arrived, he stopped to look at Odysseus. Then they both got off their horses, and they embraced like two brothers who hadn't seen each other for long time.

I stayed on my horse. They were two heroes of Troy, and I didn't want to take part in their arrogant alliance. But as they were embracing, I realized that the bonds between these men were deep and strong and that there was a lot of pain in their hearts that needed still to be shared. Polydorus led his horse next to mine, and we both watched them.

"Are you alive, my brother?" Diomedes asked. "I had so often heard that you had perished, that Poseidon had claimed your life. It is so good to see you. What brings you here? Have you come intentionally, or has some god thrown you to our coasts as punishment?"

"Diomedes, my friend, all the years that have passed since the end of the war seem not to have touched you at all. Except for some more gray hair, you are as vital and strong as always. Sthenelus told us that you had to endure great hardship, but now I see you well and happy, and this gives me great satisfaction. I don't wish anybody the sufferings and grief that I had to go through these years."

"Come, my friend," said Diomedes. "Let's go to the palace and talk about everything. Sit with the company of good wine and gentle lyre. But tell me, who is the beautiful lady who accompanies you?"

"That's my wife, Penelope, with whom I reunited only recently. She has joined me in this trip to you."

Diomedes bent as he greeted me. "You are most welcome, my lady. I'm sure my wife will be delighted to meet you and show you our customs."

We rode back to the palace, and after the servants washed our feet and hands, we were given a rich lunch of grilled game and vegetables. He asked his musician to play the lyre softly, and he filled our goblets with wine thinned with water.

"As I arrived at Argos," Diomedes said, "I was refused entrance to the city. The gates remained closed, and my messengers were sent back with threats that if I dared to attack the city, there would be war. Then Egialea sent me her messenger to let me know that my army and I were not welcome in the city and that soldiers could join their families only if they would renounce me and give honors to the new king, Cometes. My soldiers were confused, but they stayed faithful, and we continued camping outside the wall with the hope that all this would change once Agamemnon came back.

"It took another month for Agamemnon to arrive, and we were sure the big king would resolve the problem. But that same night, he was dead. Soldiers went all around Argos, Tiryns, up to Corinth, and as far down as Sparta to announce that the great king was dead and we were subjects of Aegisthus and Clytemnestra.

"I understood that things had changed a lot since our departure to Troy and that there was no place for people like us. I asked those of my troops who had families who were expecting them to go back and do as they were requested and live in peace with their families.

"I took those who wanted to stay with me and went to Aetolia, to my grandfather. There we stayed and helped my cousin Andraemon win some battles, and he allowed us to stay and make a living. But soon it was clear that he didn't want us there. Everybody was scared of a well-trained army with war experience. We were a threat to all kingdoms and, most of all, a threat to Mycenae's new rulers.

"During those days, representatives from King Daunus from Apulia visited Aetolia to buy wine and ask for help to suppress their enemies. I decided to go with them, so I took my soldiers, or whatever remained of them, to Apulia to fight as mercenaries against the Messapians. It was the perfect opportunity for me and what remained of my army to find a new home, so we agreed to go.

"However, I didn't want to be driven out, as it had already happened so often, so I asked the oracle. The oracle warned me that Aphrodite wouldn't let me settle unless I bestowed her honors, so I stopped in the islands just off the coast of Italia and sacrificed to goddess Aphrodite for protection. For the first time it was not Athena the goddess I asked for protection but the one I always despised, the one I had wounded in Troy in my arrogance and pride—Aphrodite.

"I then disembarked on the new land, and I put myself in the service of the king. I helped him receive great honors from his enemies and make peace with his neighbors. And he rewarded me by giving me lands and allowing me to build my own cities. I founded Argos and Aphrodisia and Brendesium and Canysion, and before anything I did, I offered to the goddess rich sacrifices, to receive her approval and to tame her temper, worked.

"Daunus gave me his daughter Euippe for my wife. Her eyes are full of love for me, and since then I've been living here, and I have never again engaged in wars. I am only honoring life and love."

He drank, and we did the same. His words made sense to me, and then I knew that none of the gods liked to be laughed at by mortals, and Aphrodite even less, and it was she who governed the most primordial needs of human race. Diomedes had gotten his life lesson, but I was not sure if Odysseus had gotten his.

But now he took the floor. "Diomedes—you, my friend— you suffered similar to me. Here is my story; judge for yourself. Terrible storms battered my boat from the moment I left Troy and threw me from one hostile place to the next. I met all monsters that you can imagine, and I only managed to escape due to her help—Athena, the goddess who has always helped us. She always showed me the way to get out of danger and survive, but my men were always getting fewer.

"My woes didn't seem to have an end. It seemed they would go forever. I didn't know anymore how much time had passed or whether it was summer or winter. And every time I was out on the seas and my heart was yearning to reach Ithaka's green shores, a new storm would come with winds and rains and hail, every time worse than the time before. The storm would throw us onto a different beach every time, and then the storm would abate and the sun would come out. And it seemed spring, but then the monsters would come to test us again and again. This was going on without end, and monsters would appear sometimes in the seas, as if the gods were laughing at us and at our confidence in using our minds to get out of it. I thought that was my punishment for being too clever, for relying too much on my own mind and the help of Athena.

"And when I was ready to die, Leukothea found me and took me to the island of Calypso. I was the only one left, and she took care of me and managed to get me back in shape. I asked her why she was doing that. Why couldn't I die, similar to all my friends? She said that she was doing it because my wife, Penelope, had asked her to.

"For the first time in my life, I was surviving not because of my own wits but because of love, someone else's love. I asked why I wasn't allowed to go back to my wife then, and she said that she had to keep me there until Penelope told her it was safe to go back. When I had fully recovered and started going around the island, my wish to leave was becoming stronger, and I was trying to build my own boat to depart as soon as possible. I was again using my mind to escape from love.

"But every time I had a raft ready, she destroyed it with one little move of her finger, and then she was using visions of Penelope to make love to me. That was so relaxing and beautiful that it was making my wish to go back to Penelope ever stronger.

"I don't know how long I stayed with her, and for some time I thought that I was condemned to stay there forever and never see my home and beloved wife again.

"One day she told me that now was the time for me to go. She gave me a boat and provisions and made sure the wind was in my favor. She told me that the wind would take me straight to Ithaka if I wouldn't interfere with it. She didn't come to say goodbye. So I left.

"But there was again my mind. Fear came all over me. Every little change of the wind, every slightly higher wave was making me think of storms and monsters, and I started changing the route until the storm arrived and again threw me on an island.

"But again it was love that saved me. The princess of the island was also a nymph, and she knew about Penelope waiting for me. And she again helped me recover and regain my forces, and she sent me straight to Ithaka, which I found now without big problems.

"But what a terrible fate was awaiting me again there. My house was full of suitors and other men who were courting my wife, the woman who had saved me. I again put my master mind to work. I knew how to do that. I was a war hero. I conceived a plan, and I carried it out. I asked the help of Athena, who made me look like a miserable beggar. But I couldn't hide myself from Penelope, who warned me that these men were her guards whom she had trained and prepared for war. But my egoism prevailed, and when I got the opportunity,

I killed them all. All hundred and thirty. A full army of men I could have used to protect Ithaka.

"Holy disease overwhelmed me, and all the families of the men I killed came against me, and the only way to be saved was to leave Ithaka again.

"My dear wife took me to the nekromanteion of Ephyra to find the souls of the dead and ask them for forgiveness. They told me that I would be cleansed of the crimes if I would come to get the palladium from you and take it to Aeneas to build his new city and if I would give back all gold that I had stolen in the raids in Thrace.

"So here I am. I came to find you and ask you to give me the palladium to take it where it has to go."

Odysseus stopped and took a sip from his cup without looking at Diomedes. There were a couple of minutes with only the sound of the lyre. The fire was crackling the wood. The heads of the deer on the walls were watching us with fervent eyes. The shadows on the floor became longer and were also awaiting the answer of Diomedes. Would he agree, or would it be war? The servant again filled the cups.

"The palladium is on the island. I didn't dare bring it here, for fear it would create hatred among my cities. You see, here I am lord of the whole region, not only one city." He stopped thoughtfully, and then he added, "I don't think anybody will miss it here. You can have it to take it where it's supposed to be."

The shadows on the floors faded, and the deer heads looked again, uninterested in the empty space. I felt relieved.

Then he added unexpectedly, "Aeneas is here. He arrived here with the Trojans, who have deserted the destroyed city, looking for a better future. Aeneas has become the lord of Sicily, an island at the very south of the peninsula. You'll have to take it to him."

This was a surprising turn, and Odysseus and I looked at each other as if to get each other's agreement. Odysseus nodded.

"You will collect the palladium from the island where I left all the things I brought from Troy. I even buried the horses there."

Odysseus nodded a second time.

We stayed almost a month with Diomedes. He took us around to show us his kingdom. He had founded several cities, and he was governing with justice and respect to the gods. People were prospering in this fertile land, and trade was rich and profitable. He took us as far south as Bredisium, and then he showed us the land governed by Idomeneus, former king of Crete and another hero of Troy, who was not allowed to return to his city. To the west he showed us the land of Philoctetes, the king of Meliboea in Thessaly, the bearer of Hercules's bow, and the killer of Paris.

I was stunned by how many of the Achaean heroes had ended up exiled in Italia. "How strange," I said. "Trojans who came along with Neoptolemus have established themselves and prosper in Epirus, and those whom Agamemnon brought along founded Tenea, but Greek kings had to leave their homes behind and find new lands to settle."

"Yes, my lady," he said. "Once you leave for war, you never know where you'll end up."

Odysseus, Diomedes, and Sthenelus were spending many hours per day together, talking about the times of Troy. I noticed that it was neither happy talk nor proud. It was as if they were now trying to elaborate and understand the deeper meanings of the events of those times. They were saying that the stealing of the palladium deprived Troy of its common sense. It was easy to fall into the trap of the horse after it.

"No," said Odysseus. "It was Priam who became an old fool. That's why most of the good Trojan families turned against him in the end."

"Yes, and we exploited that to the maximum, didn't we?"

The more they talked, the clearer the events that had led to the fall of Troy became. It wasn't the fighting techniques of Achilles or the strategic leadership of Agamemnon, but the shrewdness of Odysseus and the combined intelligence of these two men, Odysseus and Diomedes, that had forced the Trojans to their knees. They managed to break through the Trojan alliances by killing the Thracian leaders, stripping all Trojan symbols of their meaning with the theft of the palladium; dismantling all their legacies by moving Pelops's collarbone; invoking in the war Neoptolemus and Philoctetes; and, last but not least, building the horse itself, the gift to Athena—Athena, who had helped them along the way. It wasn't that Odysseus was more devoted to her than to any other god. He used his mind, and he refrained from faith. Faith was for him an excuse not to use one's mind. It was a sweet poison that led to inaction and eventually to one's annihilation, slowly but surely, as it had done with the Trojans, who destroyed their wall to get the horse into the city. All his traveling and all his adventures were his paean to the greatness of mind. He was using it, and he was winning.

I looked at him, and I realized suddenly who he was. Yes, suddenly I knew him inside out.

He returned my look as if he understood and said, "But what price we paid, wandering in foreign lands, all alone and empty. Only able to wait for the next challenge to receive the happiness of resolving it, to feel the greatness of our mind. And sometimes the solution was driven only by egoism, by avidity, by vengeance—all feelings that bring a man to his damnation even if he wins the battles. Using one's mind is important, but only if the underlying reasons are noble and virtuous.

"I failed when I killed Penelope's suitors. I had no right over their lives. But I was blinded by rage and hatred. I wanted back what I considered mine—my kingdom, my palace, my wife—without considering that all these people had also a stake to the same things, since they had lived there so many years without me. I should have shared and I should have acknowledged, but I failed to do it. Now I have to pay my debts and make sure the dead can rest in peace."

I took his hand in my hand. "I'm here to help you," I thought, but I didn't say it.

λθ′

One day a messenger arrived. He had been sent by King Turnus, the king of the Rutuli, from the other side of the peninsula. He was a son of Daunus and brother of Diomedes's wife. He described how a new tribe had arrived and settled down in Sicily. These people, however, did not want to recognize the great king Turnus as their lord and master and swore faith only to their lord Aeneas, who had led them there after their city, Troy, was destroyed and abandoned by the gods. So the great king, Turnus, was soliciting the help of Diomedes as lord of what before had been the land of Daunus, his father. The messenger said, "King Turnus agrees to leave you as the lord of what was legitimately his, because of your braveness, valor, and honesty; and through your marriage with his sister, he knows he has a worthwhile ally for life. Now it is the time to honor the alliance and go with him to Sicily to demand that Aeneas and his people submit to him and to even enforce that if it is necessary. Then there can be no new people who don't obey the old rules and lords of the land unless they conquer them. But for that they would have to fight bitterly and see their already decimated population decrease even further."

Diomedes asked the messenger to stay for dinner, wash, and sleep, and in the morning, after he had new clothes, horses, and breakfast, he could take his answer back to Turnus.

During dinner Diomedes said, "I was full of hate in my previous life—first hate for those who had killed my father in Thebes, then hate for the Trojans, and last, hate for the Argives and Egialea, who locked me out of my kingdom. I destroyed the first two cities, Thebes and Troy, and as I arrived here, I had only one wish: to destroy Argos."

I noticed the hand of Euippe taking his hand and him responding positively to this move.

"But here I found everything I needed," he said, kissing Euippe's hand now. "The most wonderful wife; I am lord of an area larger than Peloponnese itself; people love me and honor me. And hate has disappeared from my soul, and I only wish such a life for every man and every warrior who is tired of the battlefield." He looked around and saw approval in the eyes of the others, and, more than all the others, Odysseus himself.

He continued. "Even for Aeneas and the Trojans I wish this fate, and by no means do I want to go back to fighting against them. After all, I have made peace with Aphrodite, and fighting once more against her son would mean my bitter end, no matter how much Athena supports me."

Odysseus took the floor. "You're right to wish for the Trojans a better life, Diomedes. I wish that myself. Nightmares often haunt me of the destroyed city and the people left there in abasement and contempt. Men killed, women raped, kids orphaned. Burned land, looted temples, destroyed houses. This was what we left behind. How can one recover from this? How to build a new life out of blood and tears? I can understand why Aeneas took them away. He wanted to give them the possibility of a new life, and here they can have it. Here land is available and fertile. There is an abundance of food. People are simple and not as warlike as back in Greece. There is enough for everybody. Don't give in to Turnus's request. On the contrary, help him to understand the Trojans, and ask him to give them autonomy, so as to rebuild their lives. This will make them his friends eternally."

"I'm afraid my brother-in-law is too hotheaded to take any of this advice, but I'll try," said Diomedes.

Once again, the words of Odysseus made me proud. Now I was sure about his true feelings, and I knew he was the man I wanted—free of arrogance and pride and full of compassion.

He was becoming the man I wanted to have on my side, my Odysseus. And with these thoughts, we all went to bed.

"I hope Aeneas will be spared the fight with Turnus," I said.

He stroked my hair. "This is not our story anymore, Penelope," he whispered. "I only wish to be close to you and to continue this great voyage with you."

We made love. Tender and affectionate love, as if we had just met and all the years of suffering hadn't been and we were still young and full of dreams of an elusive life.

The next day, Diomedes replied to Turnus, saying that he had fought the Trojans enough, and he didn't wish to start again. He also advised Turnus to give Aeneas a chance before he acted against him.

In the meantime, we were preparing for our trip to Sicily. The day before our departure, we heard that Turnus had started his campaign against the Trojans. He was also sailing to Sicily, but from the western side of the peninsula.

We had to depart; otherwise, we risked ending up in a new war—the one between Turnus and Aeneas. We had our two boats, and Diomedes gave us another two full of provisions and presents. We greeted Diomedes and Euippe and wished them an eternal life of happiness.

We sailed to Diomedes's island first and collected the palladium. We placed it in our vessel, since it was not big and we wanted to keep an eye on it. We then sailed south with the hope of arriving in Sicily before the troops of Taunus.

The old man who had been with us since our departure from Ephyra told us that he knew where we would probably find Aeneas. We headed south along the coast until we found a large gulf, which we crossed. We continued south and crossed the Straight of Sicily, but we didn't enter it, since Odysseus became extremely worried, and he didn't want us to cross it. So we continued all the way around the island until the old man told us that this was the place.

We hid the vessels and disembarked. We decided to move carefully, since we suspected that Taunus would be already there. Indeed, after some walking, we saw his troops moving up and down the mountain that went sharply up from the coast.

"Up there he is," said the old man.

We needed to be careful to avoid Taunus's guards on the one hand, but we hoped to find the guards of Aeneas on the other. Odysseus surprised me again. He said that Aeneas for sure must have established a shrine to his mother, Aphrodite, and it should be close to the shore. We searched for it, and indeed, we found it. We only had to wait for someone to come with libations and then ask that person to communicate to Aeneas that we were there to hand him back the palladium.

After two days, an old man with two boys appeared from the woods. We were hiding, and we overwhelmed them immediately, since there was no other way to get their attention without alarming any army. We explained to them what we were there for, but the old man recognized Odysseus and didn't want to believe anything we said. The recognition was a good sign. It meant that we were at the right place. Now we had to persuade the old man to deliver the message. "Tell Aeneas that Odysseus is executing the request from his old father, Anchises, to bring the palladium to him. Will you tell him that?"

"You stole the palladium in the first place," he said and then added, "There is none more canny than Odysseus. Who tells me that you are not helping Taunus now? You are here to kill us all, those who survived your avidity back in Troy. We have no gold to give you and no land of our own. Go and leave us alone."

Odysseus didn't despair. "I saw his father in the underworld. I know he died from old age here in this place. I saw his wife, Creusa, who was killed in Troy by his compatriots on accusations of treason, and I saw his trumpeter, Misenus, who was drowned by Triton. Tell him all this, and I'm sure he will want to see me."

We let them go and waited. Two days later, Aeneas appeared. He was suddenly standing in front of us with two of his soldiers.

Odysseus was stunned. "You've changed," he shouted. "In Troy you seemed more like a spoiled child. Here you seem a great warrior. A lot must have happened that contributed to such a transformation."

Aeneas said, "You seem the same, Odysseus. Just older and consumed. Was your regret so great that you now want to help me?" he asked.

"I don't care about helping you, Aeneas. You have your own destiny to fulfill, and it is not easier than mine. I just execute the will of the gods before I die. Their will is for you to have back the palladium and build the city and the home that the Achaeans deprived you of. So here it is. I leave it here for you, and I hope it will help you. I only ask you to sacrifice for me and Diomedes a bull to your mother, who governs all love. We both got a great life lesson from her."

Aeneas didn't say anything more. We left the palladium and retreated. We went back to the boats and left as quietly and as fast as possible.

μ′

We started the long journey to Thrace to fulfill our last objective: paying back our debts. We went southeast and passed by Ithaka, Zakynthos, and Pylos, where we stopped to get provisions. We stayed only for a week, guests of Pisistratus, son of Nestor. We took the opportunity to offer libations to Nestor's tomb.

We asked Pisistratus if he had any news from Telemachus, and he said that he was doing fine and that he would marry soon. He said that he was selling a great deal of timber and wooden equipment made from the precious wood of cypress. We were relieved to hear that he was doing well and prospering, although the idea of not being in his wedding made us grumpy. We realized that we had been away from Ithaka almost a year, and we weren't sure when we'd be back again.

However, we had to move on and complete our mission. So we passed the Messenian Bay and then that of Lacedaemon, where my heart fluttered, thinking of Sparta and Amycles and my cousin Helen, the only daughter of Tyndareus still alive. We sailed around Maleas, the terrible cape, and sailed north toward Athens, where we stopped again for water and food. The king in those days was the young Oxyntes, grandson of

Theseus, who hadn't fought in the war and was very happy to host us for five nights, the time it would take to load the vessels with new provisions.

We offered libations to Athena. In the temple, another palladium, the Athenian palladium, was exposed. This was different from the Trojan one. It was taller, and Athena was wearing a helmet and armor on her upper breast. While the Trojan one depicted a beautiful woman, this one depicted a female warrior with gray eyes and a severe expression.

We left Athens and headed toward Tenedos. Odysseus knew he was coming ever closer to Troy, and he started having nightmares and visions of death. The trip was tranquil, and the wind was favorable. No sign of Poseidon's rage. All forces had agreed to allow him to fulfill his mission and pay back his debts to the destroyed villages. On Tenedos, we anchored at the little port and headed toward the small community living on the hills. The countryside was arid and stony, and there was no sign of cultivated land.

As we arrived at the small community, Odysseus was struck to see that it had declined despite the almost eleven years since the war. We went to a city that displayed something that once must have been a citadel. There were some signs of a burnt palace and some temples abandoned to nature's will for destruction. At the palace gate, there was one guard, who started running when he saw us. We didn't hold weapons, only the jar half-filled with gold. This was Odysseus's part for raiding Tenedos.

Since the palace was empty, we moved toward the temple, and then we saw the guard with another man arriving. Other people were following them. It was obvious they were working in the fields, as they were covered with dirt.

"Welcome to our island," the man said. "I'm Corianus, the last of Cycnus's sons and the only one still alive. Are you here in peace, or did you come to steal? Since the great war, there is nothing here. Not even enough food to fill our bellies. The Greeks have killed our men and taken away our women. We survive at the pity of Apollo the plague bearer, and people come to offer to him to save themselves from the bad disease." He showed the way toward the entrance of the temple.

Odysseus said, "Honored king and son of Cycnus, who was impossible to spear, we didn't come to steal but to give and donate. I'm Odysseus, and this is my wife, Penelope."

Hearing his name, most of the people stepped back in horror.

"Yes, I'm the same Odysseus who, together with Achilles, killed Tenes, raided your city—this same city—and burned the palace. The gods cursed me for all my deeds, and many harms thrashed me. Then, one day, the gods asked me to give all my plunder back to those from whom I had taken it. So here I am to return the gold I took from your palace and which was my part of the claim. I ask you to accept it, since this will help your people survive in the next years, by buying all you need to feed them and dress them in warm clothes."

"How hated is your name, Odysseus, around here. You certainly don't have any friends. We only want you away from this place as soon as possible. And take the gold with you. We shall not accept anything that will make you feel better for destroying our cities and killing our children."

"If you will not take it from him, then take it from me. When I received this treasure back in Ithaka, my people were also starving and freezing. It was a present from heaven, but as I raised my eyes to thank heaven, our lady Athena came to me and made me swear that once all had finished, I'd take it back to the people from whom it had been stolen. And this is why we are here. You cannot deny obedience to the goddess, since all gods will turn against you." I noticed his worry, and I pushed more. "Let's offer it to him, then, along with libations, our god Apollo. If it is welcome, nothing will happen. If not, within three days I'll be cursed and die from the plague."

So I said, and Corianus didn't know how to oppose this offer, so he made way for us in the temple. We washed our hands and offered libations and gold to the god and waited three days. During these days we stayed in the palace in a half-burned room that Odysseus tried to fix as well as he could. The food was poor, and there was hardly milk and honey. Even wine was distributed in rations. People were in the fields the whole day, and only the kids were available to talk to. So I tried to have them around us as much as possible. They appreciated my songs and paeans, but when the parents were back, they were calling them away from us.

When the three days were over, the king examined me carefully to see if I had any signs of the disease. I was free of any symptoms, so we departed. On the way back to the port, Odysseus showed me the cave in which they had abandoned Philoctetes, in all his pain from the snake bite. "We thought he'd die," he said. "But not only did he survive, he also helped us to win the war."

None of islanders waved goodbye; none gave us presents. They were relieved to see us going, and we were also so. The next place to visit was Thrace.

We at last reached Thrace. We took our load, and we claimed we were under the protection of Hermes and the dead. So no one came close to us. We moved inside the land, and one night we were assaulted by thieves who sensed the value of our load.

But Odysseus's clever moves saved us. He had placed the guards wisely, and once the thieves came closer, they were trapped. He disarmed them quickly and took their horses. He told them that they had the choice to be tied down and left there to be eaten by the bears, or to run as fast as they could to announce the return of Odysseus to Ismarus. As planned, they left running. I didn't understand why Odysseus had announced his return in this way, but I asked no questions.

The next morning, as we continued our trip, he explained. "The place is full of thieves. But around here, everybody is scared of me. They will go to hide in the city, but I know how to make them open their gates."

We continued our trip without meeting anybody until we reached the city of Ismarus. The city gates were closed, and we could see the archers on the crenellations, ready to shoot. But Odysseus led the convoy west, bypassing the city. Soon I understood why. He headed toward the temple of Apollo. It was quite an isolated location behind a hill, in a grove of oak trees, difficult to find if one didn't know the way. We stopped at the entrance and looked around. There was no priest around.

We went in and noticed that the sacred fire was burning. Somewhere in the back, we saw a little shadow moving.

"Agathon?" cried Odysseus. "It's me—Odysseus."

"Agathon is dead," cried the shadow. "Why are you back, Greek? Haven't you killed enough? Are you still bloodthirsty? There are no men left here, and those left are only shadows of men," said the man, and he came forward. He was so thin that he could hardly walk. I felt sorry for him. "You left behind burnt land and sorrow. What can you still claim?"

"You are Phives, aren't you? The little boy who was helping Agathon," said Odysseus. "I didn't come to claim. I am here to help. Penelope, my wife"—he raised his hand toward me—"and I are here to give you your gold back. All the gold that was taken from this temple and from the palace. It is outside in the wagon. We traveled many months to bring it here, and now we ask you to accept it back."

The man's face changed expression. "All the gold of Ismarus you brought back?" he asked, trembling.

"Yes. In the name of the gods that govern us, in the name of almighty Zeus, Hermes the walker of the dead, Apollo and his sister Artemis, gray-eyed Athena, and the nymphs that helped me, this gold has to go back to Ismarus, and it is your job to do it."

Phives advanced, or rather drifted, toward the exit. He opened the cover of the cart and opened the jars. He reached into a jar to check the contents, and he realized what Odysseus had said was true. He turned back and looked at me and Odysseus, standing straight behind him. "Indeed, the gods have sent you to save us, Achaean. Yes, I'll take this gold to Ismarus, and I'll ask the king to purify you from your deeds and to sacrifice many bulls in the name of Zeus, Apollo, and Artemis, and to the gray-eyed Athena and all the nymphs who saved your life and made it possible to accomplish this task. Wait here until the king sends his guard to get you," he said, and he jumped onto the cart, as if the spirit had suddenly received bones and muscles and resumed its human nature. He disappeared behind the hill, and we knew he'd do what he had promised.

From behind the trees, our people came forward with the horses. We left. We had no need to hear their gratitude, and we had no need to be purified. We had been purified already by the dead. So we disappeared silently, headed to the boats, and departed quickly. Besides, Odysseus was scared that not all were happy to receive us there, despite our bringing presents, and we sooner or later would have to fight for our lives. With great relief, we started the trip back to Ithaka. We had both survived long enough to accomplish what the gods had asked us to do. We were happy and unfettered. We didn't care anymore what would happen to us. We had left our destinies in the hands of the Gods, already freed from our human natures, already ascended to Olympus.

μα′

We headed south and stopped only for food and water on the island of Skiathos. We then managed to arrive at Lacedaemon, and I asked Odysseus to let me out in Gythion.

"You ask me to give up on you? We are not young anymore. Leaving you now means risking never seeing you again," he said.

"I have to go back. You have everything you need now. You are purified, and our son is a king. Your name will be remembered forever. But Sparta is calling me. Greece needs me. If I have to die here, I am a child of Sparta—"

He put his finger on my mouth and looked deep into my eyes, but he didn't say anything. Then he made a sign to the rowers in the direction of Gythion. When we arrived, he prepared two horses. "I'll stay with you as long as needed, and then we go back together. I'm not leaving you. There is no life for me without you, either here or in Ithaka."

I forced myself to smile. Odysseus gave instructions to the stewards, and we proceeded inland, followed by six guards. We moved without talking until we reached Amycles. In the palace, my home in young age, we found only the guard with his family. Everything was clean and ordered. The guard was taking good care of it.

"Does anybody live here?" I asked him.

"No, my lady, but our queen Helen wants it clean and ordered because she says that her cousin, Lady Penelope, may come anytime, and she will need it."

I smiled. I knew Helen was awaiting me. We turned the horses toward Sparta and continued riding. The peasants along the river were working in the fields. On a plain farther uphill, we saw young men training for battle. Toward the temple of Yakinthus, some girls were exercising, dancing at the riverbank, and some others were decorating the temple of Yakinthus. I remembered that the fest to his remembrance was close.

Everything seemed quiet, so we continued our relaxed ride. The city was busy, but people did stop to look at us.

We arrived at the palace gate. Odysseus announced us, and we were shown the way to the megaron. A man welcomed us. He was Menelaus's son, Nicostratus, and he led us into the megaron. I saw again the huge walls with the beautiful paintings that so much had marked my life. The room was beautifully decorated, and there was an abundance of gold. He said he would send immediately to inform the queen, but I grabbed his arm. "I'll go myself. I know this place very well." I couldn't wait to see Helen, and I couldn't stand to be announced in the place I had grown up in.

I ran up the stairs and down the corridor until I reached the door of Helen's room. I opened it without knocking. She was there in front of her bronze mirror. Tall and slim with her golden hair, as if all the years had never passed, as if the war had never happened, as if she would live forever. I went closer slowly, as if not to scare her, but then she turned. "Penelope," she whispered. Her face was as beautiful as ever. Time, though, had left its mark. It was as if it told all her story, all her worries and dreams.

We fell into each other's arms, with eyes full of tears. "Thanks for coming," she said as she was still holding me. "I missed you so much, cousin."

"And I the same," I muttered.

We sat next to the fire. "You still look great," I said.

"It is only the will of the gods. I have no merit. I did all I could to anger them, but all my mistakes seem to be excused," she said.

"You make no mistakes, Helen. All you do is execute the will of the gods," I said, watching the fire.

"You and I know it. But men will talk about Helen the adulteress, not Helen the powerful, and women will get behind them to save their lives," she said. "No one will talk about Helen the mover of men. Helen, Zeus's last child, the desire breaker, the healer, the servant of the poor."

"And I guess no man will talk about me and how I reigned over the terrible years of the war Ithaka. How I filled the bellies of my subjects when there were not enough hands to cultivate the earth and how I protected them from all enemies. I saved Odysseus's soul from Tartarus after he killed all the young men of Ithaka, and I went back to Thrace to pay his debts. And I didn't do all that because I wanted to be the leader or the most powerful. I did it from a feeling of humility and responsibility. Men will only talk about Penelope the faithful, not Penelope the free spirited. And probably women will get behind them to have their favor," I said.

She stopped and took my hands. "Oh, Penelope, I've wished I were dead so often. And now, having you here next to me, it is as if I am being rewarded for all my suffering. What will happen with our people, Penelope? I'm so worried. The time of the heroes seems to be over forever. And we women seem to have lost our power. No other woman will ever claim again to have conceived by the gods. We are the last generation of gods' children," she said, worried.

"My life has showed me that we are all children of the gods. We can all talk to them, and they look after every single one of us. Look at Odysseus—not from god born. He has always invoked Athena, and she has always helped him—until that same help became his downfall, since he became too proud and intolerant, too disdainful of other peoples' lives. Both he and his son would have been wiped out if I had not gone through Hades with him to save him. And similar was the fate of Orestes. He revenged his father, because in his eyes, he was a hero. Only Clytemnestra knew his true nature—a killer without mercy and, more than anything, one who would never be punished," I said.

"Poor sister," muttered Helen. "You know Orestes came back to his senses. He is a good and fair king, and everybody seems to respect him, though people are tired and don't want to oppose him and women are shadowed by his will. It used to be different in our time. Reigning was a job carried out by consensus—consensus among the lords and consensus among male and female values. They wanted war, but we pledged to honor the gods so they would stop war to satisfy our will. They wanted revenge, but we advocated for justice in the name of the gods. They thought that they could eliminate disease by killing the sick, but we showed them that healing is the way.

"We keep the traditions and our history in our songs, our tapestries, and the good-night stories we tell our kids. We are the souls of their existence. And when our thoughts are bad, we drive them to their disaster. When they are absent, they seem like ships without captains, and they'll crash on the waves no matter how large and proud. But when our thoughts are noble, they know what to fight for. They have a reason for existence and can exert value. The war made them think that valor is demonstrated on the battlefield, but valor is demonstrated only in the genuineness of the purpose," she said.

I took the floor. "Bringing you back was a genuine objective, but it never justified the atrocities of Troy. All Achaeans suffered because of that. Now our aim is to remove the guilt from their minds and to make them again proud of themselves. They have to learn again to follow the path of the gods and to regain their happiness in pursuing the simple joys of life, such as a good harvest, the birth of a child, the wedding of a fair daughter, the successful defense of their land."

We looked at each other, surprised by how similar were the lessons that life had taught us both.

"How are Hermione and Electra?" I asked.

"Hermione reasonably well. She has a little son, and she is busy with him. She is learning from me healing and reigning. But she has to still learn to give herself up to entrust herself to the will of the gods." She stopped and looked at me, and I nodded to show her I understood what she meant. Then she continued. "Electra cannot forgive herself for the death of her parents. She thinks of herself as cursed, and she refuses to have children, to avoid the curse being transferred to them. Pylades is always around. He wants her and reads her every wish from her eyes, but she discourages him, always telling him that she won't spread her curse also to his children. She has never come to me for advice, at the beginning because she considered me an adulteress and later because of guilt for the murder of my sister. I'm so glad you are here. I truly believe you are the only one who can help her."

"I will," I said.

A servant knocked the door and told us that supper was served. We went downstairs and met Odysseus and Nicostratus. Odysseus hadn't seen Helen since the ruin of Troy. He watched her approach him with interest. Helen was not the glitzy queen of her youth but was still of immense beauty. Her beauty reflected respect rather than the passion it once had. She stood in front of him, with me next to her but a bit behind her.

"Welcome to my palace, Odysseus. Thank you for accompanying my cousin here. Her arrival gives me great joy," she said with confidence.

"It is a pleasure to see you back where you belong, my lady," he replied, as if to try her.

"Ah, don't be silly, Odysseus. We don't belong to this world anymore, and you know it. Our bodies are buying time until we finish our long-standing commitments. But sooner or later, they will follow our already gone spirits."

I smiled, and she showed the way to the table. Odysseus lowered his head and moved along.

"I hate it when she talks like that," said Nicostratus. "I never understand what she means, and I'm worried I'll do the wrong thing."

Helen smiled. "You always do the right thing, my dear. Stop worrying."

We sat, and the servants brought lamb-head soup, toasted bread and honey, walnuts, and apples. They filled our goblets with red wine thinned with water.

Helen was hardly eating. "I'm worried, my dear, for the future of our kind. I've traveled a lot and seen many people. The Egyptians and the Libyans, the Ethiopians and the Assyrians, the Phoenicians and the Phrygians. Their kings are mighty and rich. Much richer than we have ever been. Their kingdoms are huge, and they dispose of the lives of their subjects as they wish. Their gods are cruel, and they renounce logic. We are different. More independent and free. You, Odysseus, didn't want to go to war and tried anything to disobey Agamemnon. Achilles was the lord of himself, and he never gave in to the demands of the chief. Nestor, and also you, had to tap into the logic of Athena to persuade the others how to behave and what to do. Agamemnon failed as king because he led the Greeks to an unjust war by using indecent means and living in an improper manner.

"This has now changed. Orestes has been reborn and has renounced his father, despite having killed for him in the first place. He has been brought onto the right path for reigning over all Greeks, and I give him the force and reason to succeed. But my days in this world are coming to an end. And someone else needs to do it." She turned to me and took my hand. "It has to be a female who has realized her powers and has no fear to teach other women. You, my cousin—you know how."

Odysseus took the floor. "Helen, your actions and adventures seem to have brought you wisdom. What you propose makes sense to me. As you know, I had many adventures, and I risked losing my life many times. I lost all my friends who followed me in Troy, because I thought I was invincible and that my intelligence would rescue me from all. Indeed, it rescued me, but not my friends. When I went back home, I killed all those who were dreaming of taking my place as king and husband of Penelope because I thought they were my personal enemies. I didn't realize that Penelope was preparing them to take over the kingdom, to protect and defend their land, and to be faithful to their queen or king. I realized all this when I spoke to the dead, and I turned all my life upside down.

"It looks as if you women can see farther than men, and you are able to consider more information in your decisions.

To us men, your talk seems weak and watchful, and it does not combine with braveness and valor. What you say, to our ears, resonates with fear and irresolution, while you talk about inclusiveness and the courage to face the day after the battle more than the battle itself. I don't know how to combine these things in order to lead a fulfilled life, but you, Helen, in the wisdom you share with your father, Zeus, seem to have found the answer. I am pleased to do what you ask and to help you reconcile the genders and their capabilities."

We all took one another's hands, and I sang the hymn to Apollo and Artemis.

The next day, I found Helen sitting next to Eurotas in the place where we had always gathered when we were young. She was sitting there, immobile, with her eyes closed. I didn't want to disturb her, so I sat a short distance behind. The river was unusually quiet. The water was simmering gold from the sun's rays. The air was still with a wonderful scent of roses. There were no roses around, so I reckoned the scent was coming from Helen's hair. She liked it on her hair. Everything around us started becoming ever glossier—the trees, the grass—and I noticed a smile on Helen's lips.

I noticed a silver light coming downstream, and slowly I recognized the bodies of flying swans. Their necks seemed so strong and white. They started circling over Helen until her body started moving upward. Her body was moving inside a column of gleaming, dazzling light. She opened her eyes only to see them, and she moved her arms to touch them. I wanted to call out to her not to touch the swans, because they were there to take her away. But she was so willing. She put her arm around the neck of one swan, who with a move put her on his back and then flew north. The others followed. I watched them as they were disappearing on the horizon. It was a beautiful sight. The farther they flew, the darker it became, until I couldn't see them anymore. Earth became normal again. Colors turned as we know them, the river continued its flow, and a light breeze hit me in the face, as if to bring me back to life.

I went back and announced to the palace the ascension of Helen. Nicostratus asked if he should prepare everything for the funeral. "What funeral would it be, without a body?" I said. "Prepare everything for a thanksgiving. Our thanksgiving to Helen, our goddess of consolation."

We held a five-day fest for the ascension of Helen. We sacrificed fifty bulls, and all Lacedaemon was invited to eat and pray for her soul, safe now in Elysium. Hermione with her husband and little son came from Mycenae, along with Electra and Pylades. It was a beautiful fest without exaggerations, without tears—a spiritual journey through Helen's life and her achievement to unify the Greeks for the first time under first Agamemnon's sword and then Orestes's justice.

μβ′

I knew my time was also expiring. I was glad to have Hermione and Electra around me. These two women were now the spiritual leaders of the Greeks. Hermione, under the guidance of her mother, had become a calm person who used reason to resolve her problems and was at peace with the world and the gods. During the fest, she announced the construction of a temple next to the one of Zeus in the name of her mother. She also took up the role of healer, as it was transmitted first from Leda to Helen and then from Helen to her. I was very proud for this woman who had understood the paths of life, was able to understand the will of the gods, and had learned from her mistakes.

Electra, though, was far from happy. She was still tormented by the violent deaths of her parents. She was feeling guilty for not being able to stop them and even more for having provoked the death of her mother. I knew I had to help her overcome it and find again her faith in life. She had to resume her duties and responsibilities as leader of her people and go back on the track of the gods. Orestes, her brother, had been purified and absolved. He could lead a new life now. But Electra's soul was still straying into a dark place full of ruins and spirits. I had to find a way to her soul and lead it out of its own condemnation to doom.

After Helen's funeral, Orestes, Electra, and Pylades headed back to Mycenae while Hermione, with her little son Tisamenus, stayed in Sparta to ensure all business ran smoothly and to launch the work for the new temple in the name of Helen. Odysseus and I asked for permission to go with Orestes. We claimed we wished to offer libations on the tombs of Agamemnon and Clytemnestra. The excuse sounded reasonable, and we were allowed to travel with them.

On the way I stayed as close as possible to Electra, hoping to know more about her, her violent past, and her deepest fears. But she was not ready to share any of these with me. She didn't aspire to any friendship with me, and she was mostly silent.

Odysseus, on the contrary, was by far more successful with Orestes, who opened up his heart and talked about his experiences throughout the time of his madness. He talked about the vision of his mother following him everywhere over the years—no matter how fast he ran and no matter how far he went. The same nightmare would come to him every time he closed his eyes from exhaustion: his mother in her white nightgown stained with blood, her long black hair loose on her shoulders, her beautiful black eyes fixed on him, her lips calling his name. The nightmare didn't let him sleep until his reason left him and he wished for his own death. He tried many times to kill himself. But he couldn't manage to achieve death, so he asked his friends to kill him, but they all refused and left him. He was not allowed to die—only to suffer for the death of his mother.

Electra stayed away when her brother was narrating his pathos. It was obvious to me that while he had been excused and reborn, she was still in the same nightmare that had been tormenting Orestes over thcte years. But she was unable to free herself, unable to forgive herself.

When I arrived at the Mycenaean palace, a feeling of immense pain overwhelmed me. I felt the need to cry, and Odysseus took my hand to show me he felt the same. The palace had nothing of its shine of the past. It reflected grief more than power. Orestes was mostly out with his guard and Pylades. He was reigning from the back of his horse, going from place to place, meeting people and distributing justice where it was needed. The palace was the realm of Electra, who was getting literally buried in it. She wished no meetings, no banquets, no visitors. She had declared continuous mourning for her father, and she had arranged for every sign of her mother to disappear from the palace. Orestes was taking the condition of his sister stoically, awaiting her awakening from the darkness.

The day came to offer libations, and all of us first went to Agamemnon's grave. Orestes, as the high priest and king of Mycenae, led the ceremony. We offered bread, milk, and honey. Orestes himself offered his best wine, while Electra offered her most beautiful shirt, which she had weaved for her father in the last year.

Then we moved on to Clytemnestra's tomb, but before we even got close, Electra started cursing us for offering anything to her adulterous, murderous mother. She urged us to go back to the palace, since this woman's name should have been written out of history for her deeds.

I tried to calm her and explain that it was not up to us to judge her, that these things were the will of the gods, and that we should continue with the libation. But she took the milk mug from my hands and threw it on the gravestone. "So you want to make the offering, Aunt Penelope? Here it is," she shouted as the mug broke and the milk was spilled.

She also tried to grab the wine mug from Orestes's hands, but he protected it, saying, "Sister, let me do what I have to. I am a king because of my father, but I'm a wise and just king because of my mother. With all your hate, you can do nothing to change that."

She stopped like a stroke of thunder, looked at him with hatred, turned, and ran into the palace.

We continued the ceremony, making the offerings to Clytemnestra. When a new mug of milk was given to me, I offered the milk, pouring it on the grave. A soft breeze hit my face and changed the direction of the milk, which stained my gown. No matter how I turned the mug, the milk was going on my gown and not on the grave. Everybody looked at me, and I turned to Odysseus, who took the mug from my hand and led me to sit on a bank close by. "She wants me to help Electra," I said. "I wish I knew how to do that."

"Maybe I know," said Orestes. "We have to go to the city of Hermione. Not far away from here. There, where the old women kill the cows in the sanctuary of the chthonic goddess, they once helped me meet Iphigenia, my sacrificed sister. No man is allowed in there—only Parthenos women, but they took pity on me when they saw me in my madness. I count on you, Aunt Penelope, to take her there and heal her."

In a week's time, we departed for Hermione, the city at the coast. We told Electra that Orestes needed to ask the chthonic goddess and god to spare the soul of his father from the doom of Tartarus. She would do anything for her dead father, so she followed. We took the boats in the morning from Tiryns, and we were there just before noon. We headed toward the temples on the hill. With us we had the four bulls required for the sacrifice, along with jars of milk, honey, and wine.

At a certain point, Orestes stopped and said, "Aunt Penelope and Electra, from now on, we men cannot follow. I authorize you to take my message to the lord of the dead and the chthonic goddess. May your libations and sacrifice bring peace to the soul of our father."

We continued. The temples appeared ever more mystic as we came closer. Closed gates. Ivy was coming out of the joints of the huge stones. We left the animals outside and pushed open the great gate, which squeaked as if to wake up the dead. The temple was dark inside, and it took our eyes a while to get used to it. It seemed empty, so we walked toward the center, hoping someone would be hiding in the darkness.

The temple was built around a chasm. Locals said that this was where Heracles brought Cerberus, Hades's terrible guardian dog, out from the underworld. As we reached the chasm, we saw the statues of the gods, Dimitra on the one end and Hades and Persephone on the other.

"A bloodcurdling place. Even the priestesses have abandoned it. How are we going to carry out the sacrifice, Aunt Penelope?" said Electra, eager to go on with the request of her brother.

"Someone will come, Electra. I'm sure…" Before I could go on, I saw it, and it left me speechless. My tiara from Sparta was on the statue. In fact, it was now held by Demetra. "So Clytemnestra brought it here," I thought loudly.

"No, my sister." I heard the voice as if the statue had talked to me. I looked around and saw her coming out from behind the statue.

An old woman, obviously a priestess, approached us. "I brought it here after the death of the great queen. The tiara had to go back to the chthonic goddess. But I'm sure you can have it back if you wish so, Penelope. You are the last Achaean high priestess."

"No," I said with firmness. "It's not about me anymore." I wanted to bring the point to Electra quickly and trigger the reactions that could liberate her from her torment. "It's about this young lady here. Princess Electra, daughter of the great queen and Agamemnon. She needs your help."

Electra sprang. "No, Aunty. It's about my brother, Orestes. He needs to be purified."

The old lady had come very close to her now and was watching skeptically. But her appearance made Electra step back for fear she would be touched. As she did so, she almost fell into the arms of a second old lady, who had come out of the shadows. "Such beautiful dark hair. Like your mother's," said the second priestess.

And a third one appeared, also, saying, "Look at her eyes. Aren't they the same as her mother's when she came here to ask our help to take revenge?"

Electra shouted, "What? You helped my mother kill my father? You horrible beasts!"

The ladies laughed. "Yes. She came to us half-mad for the loss of her daughter at Agamemnon's hand. Her hair was black and long. She cut it here in front of the statue of our lady Demetra, imploring her to punish him, to give him a terrible and humiliating death on the battlefield and to make it so that he would never return."

Now the third priestess talked. "She reminded the goddess of the disappearance of her own daughter. She reminded her of her grief, of her pain at not being able to find the kore."

The first priestess, pretending to be Clytemnestra, fell on her knees in front of the statue, crying and screaming. She opened her clothes so that her breasts came free, and then, with her arms up and wide open, she screamed, "Remember your sorrow, oh goddess? Your mourning darkened the earth. No cereals were coming from the soil, and the trees made no fruits. There was no food for years, and humanity seemed at the verge of extinction. Bring the same also to this earth. Punish all Achaeans for allowing this horrendous act to happen. Spread death to all and everything, and don't spare me. I cannot exist after that dreadful act."

I looked at Electra. She seemed shocked. "It was not right to kill my father," she shouted, with tears in her eyes.

But now the second priestess again took the floor. "I took her in my arms and told her, 'Come, my daughter. It is not decent to wish your own death. You have another three children to raise.' But that made her despair even more, saying…"

The third priestess took the floor again, and, pretending to be Clytemnestra, she shouted, "'Oh, my second daughter, Electra. How am I ever going to justify my miserable life when she learns how her sister died? How can I ever explain to her why she lives and Iphigenia died on the altar by the hand of her father? She will rightly assume I'm a failed mother. A woman who allows these atrocities in her own family. My beautiful Electra—in what world is she going to raise her kids? And my Orestes, my only son, alive after the death of my firstborn, son of Tantalus—what weight has been put on his shoulders? All the curse of the Atreides he has to bear alone. Whom is he supposed to kill, then? What a promise for a wretched life that even going down this chasm seems the better option.'"

Now Electra started crying and fell on her knees. "Mother," she cried, "Mother, forgive me. I didn't realize. Mother."

It was a moving scene, and the chasm fumes had given an even heavier meaning to all the scenes played by the old priestesses. We felt a soft motion of the earth under our feet, and I went to kneel to take Electra in my arms to help her up.

The fumes swirled around as if they wanted to take shape. The chasm lit up, and the fumes became dresses and then arms and hair and, in the end, a face. The face of my cousin Clytemnestra appeared, full of care and love for her little daughter, as if she had just hurt herself playing in the yard. "Stand up, my daughter. How much bitterness I have given you. I filled your life with hate to reach my objectives. I'm so sorry. It is all well now. I have found my sweet Iphigenia, and I'm well again. Your father regrets his acts, and he has renounced his greed. He is always with us now and not with Troy's war heroes. Orestes was spared death and is a just king, I hear. Now it is all right, as it was supposed to be. We only wish to hear you're happy, child—happy and at peace. Please do that for us," she said, and the fumes started disappearing. "Do that for Mommy" was the last we heard when the image dissolved and the chasm turned dark again.

The old priestesses opened the temple gates, and the sunlight chased the darkness. They went out and brought in the first bull. At the chasm, one of them took out a knife and, without hesitation, cut the throat of the bull, who seemed hobbled and incapable of resisting his own doom. Then they brought in the second bull and did the same, and then the third and the fourth. By the end, all the bulls had been killed, and all had fallen dead in the same direction.

"The signs are good, Princess," the first priestess told Electra. "A long and prosperous life. Remember to praise the chthonic goddess and make offerings to our temple."

The second priestess came and gave Electra the box with the tiara inside. "You are now the high priestess of the Achaeans," she said.

Electra, still sobbing, took it, nodded, and closed the lid. As we were going out, we heard the third one say, "Be just and righteous, then death looms."

Electra stopped for a moment, and then, without turning, she continued.

As we came out, I realized I was exhausted. My own life was coming to an end. Orestes, Pylades, and Odysseus ran toward us. Orestes embraced his sister and looked at me. I nodded to confirm the healing of his sister. Odysseus took my arm.

"Odysseus, take me back to Ithaka," I said. "My days are finishing, and I'd like so much to see my friends again."

Odysseus understood the message, and from Hermione we departed for our return trip to Ithaka.

μγ'

The trip was tiring. My forces had completely left me. I often thought I would not manage to finish it. Odysseus kept me company and tried to keep my spirits up, but I knew my days were numbered.

It took us more than three days to reach Ithaka. We survived only because we wanted to die together on our island, our kingdom. As we arrived, my wish was to be taken to the cave where I had met with my mother and the goddesses. It had been many years since I had last met them. I knew they were always around me, but I hadn't physically met them since they gave Odysseus back. It was the encounters with them that made me grow and mature during those difficult years of my reign, and now I wanted to go back to that assurance, to the warmth of their care, to the arms of my mother. I was old and tired and at the same time a child longing to be cuddled. I had worked hard to maintain the kingdom, to make ends meet, to give meaning to everything that happened, to stay rational when all seemed crazy. I just wanted to get my well-deserved rest, and Odysseus the same.

I insisted on going into the cave, although our guards told us that an earthquake had destroyed it, and it was very dangerous. Odysseus came with me while some of our guards went to call Telemachus, and some just stayed outside from fear of entering. Our old and trembling legs took us toward the room with the pool where I used to meet my company. Strangely, the cave was not dark anymore.

We arrived at the room with the pool, but we realized it had no roof anymore. It had collapsed during the earthquake, and one could see the fallen stones at the bottom of the pool, which was not golden anymore due to mineral deposits but greenish, since rain was coming in and changing the ecosystem.

Odysseus and I sat at the edge of the water, and I started telling him about my meetings with the goddesses. Suddenly, a group of ducks made their appearance, as if from nowhere. I counted seven of them, and I said, "How strange—exactly as many as there are goddesses."

"They must have found shelter in here since the collapse of the roof," Odysseus said.

"Yes, it must be like that," I murmured, and I put my head on his shoulder.

But then the ducks made an exact circle, and they left it open at just one post. They were swimming in circles, always faster, so fast that I couldn't see them anymore. And then an emerald-green ray propagated from the center of the circle. When they slowed down, the emerald-green ray was pointing up to the sky, going out of the opening and becoming sapphire blue. The ducks were not there anymore, but my friends—all of them, seven beautiful young women—were holding hands in a circle with one post open. Those with the free hands—my mother and Athena herself—made a sign for me to join them.

I looked at Odysseus, who didn't seem to be bothered at all, as if the seven goddesses were visible only to me. I stood up and told him that I had to join them, but then I realized that a part of me had never left my position next to Odysseus with my head lying on his shoulder.

I turned again toward my mother, who was smiling at me. "It's time, my daughter." Her words formed in my mind without her moving her lips.

I looked back at Odysseus, who was sitting quietly with his wife in his arms still laying her head on his shoulder. I then moved toward my mother with confidence, and as I touched the water, my old appearance fell off like a snake loses its old skin. And step by step, I was becoming more and more a young, beautiful woman like them.

As I arrived at the circle, I stopped and looked at all of them smiling with happiness. I knew that if I gave my hand, my life on earth would finish, and it felt so good because I wanted it to finish. I had given the world everything I could give, and I was proud of it.

I gave my hands first to my mother and then to Athena, who at the last moment turned behind me and took the hand of someone else. It was Odysseus, who had followed me without my noticing. Athena had given him the power to see us and follow us. He had also become the young Odysseus I had met so many years ago back in Sparta when he saved me from the thieves in the mountains.

She took his hand, and I took his other hand, and we started swirling fast and always faster, rising from the water and then from the cave's roof and always higher into the blue and into the history of mankind. When Telemachus arrived, he didn't find anything but the two bodies embracing each other, with my head still lying on Odysseus's shoulder. Our new life together had finally started.

End

Names of Goddesses and Gods

Apollo: god of music, arts, the oracles, and the sun

Artemis: virgin goddess of hunting, forests, and animals

Athena: virgin goddess of reason, wisdom, and victorious war

Demeter: goddess of agriculture and cereals

Eros: child god of love

Hera: goddess of marriage, wife of Zeus

Hestia: virgin goddess of fire and home

Leukothea: sea goddess helping sailors in distress

Metis: former goddess of wisdom, swallowed by Zeus

Persephone: daughter of Demeter and goddess of the underworld

Thetis: Nereid, goddess of the Mediterranean Sea

Zeus: god of gods

Names of People (as in Homer and Other Ancient Sources)

Achilles: hero of the Trojan War

Acrisius: grandfather of Odysseus on his father's side

Adamas: lord of Zakynthos and adviser to the palace of Ithaka

Aegisthus: husband of Clytemnestra after the murder of Agamemnon

Aethra: mother of Theseus and nanny of Helen

Agamemnon: king of Mycenae, husband of Clytemnestra

Aigyptius: a lord and elder of Ithaka and adviser to the palace of Ithaka

Ajax the Great: king of Salamis; hero of the Trojan War

Ajax the Lesser: king of Locris and hero of the Trojan War

Amphimachus: one of the boys of the academy and a suitor of Penelope

Amphitryon: son of Perseus, granduncle of Penelope

Anticlea: mother of Odysseus and mother-in-law of Penelope

Antilochus: son of Nestor and hero of the Trojan War

Antinous: one of the academy boys and later a suitor of Penelope

Aphareus: son of Perieres and king of Messene and uncle of Penelope

Arete: half sister of Icarius, aunt of Penelope

Arsinoe: daughter of Leucippus, princess of Messene, and cousin of Penelope

Autolycus: grandfather of Odysseus on his mother's side

Bateia: nymph, first wife of Oebalus and mother of Hippocoon and Arete

Callidice: queen of the Thesprotians

Calypso: nymph who lived on an island that could only be found if she wanted

Castor: cousin of Penelope, brother of Helen

Cephalus: great-grandfather of Odysseus, for whom Cephalonia was named

Chalcomedousa: grandmother of Odysseus, wife of Acrisius

Chrysothemis: last child of Clytemnestra and Agamemnon

Clytemnestra: queen of Mycenae, cousin of Penelope, and sister of Helen

Corianus: last son of Cycnus, king of Tenedos

Daunus: king of the Appulians in Italy

Deianeira: second wife of Heracles, who poisoned him

Deidamia: wife of Achilles and mother of Neoptolemus

Diomedes: king of Argos, hero of the Trojan War, king of the Appulians in Italy

Dolius: servant of Icarius who followed Penelope to Ithaka

Egialea: queen of Argos, wife of Diomedes

Electra: daughter of Clytemnestra and Agamemnon

Euippe: daughter of Daunus, wife of Diomedes in Appuglia

Eumaeus: swineherd and friend of Odysseus

Eumelus: king of Pherae in Thessaly, brother-in-law of Penelope

Eupithes: lord of Ithaka and part of the elders advisory group

Euriclea: nanny of Odysseus

Euridice: wife of Nestor, queen of Pylos

Eurydamas: one of the academy boys and later a suitor of Penelope

Eurymachus: one of the academy boys and later a suitor of Penelope

Eurytus: king of Oechalia in Thessaly

Glauca: queen of Salamis, wife of Ajax the Great

Gorgophone: grandmother of Penelope

Hagnes: nymph of Messene and sister of Neda

Helen: cousin and friend of Penelope

Hilaira: daughter of Leucippus, princess of Messene, and cousin of Penelope

Hippocoon: half brother of Icarius, uncle of Penelope

Hippodamia: wife of Pelops, queen of Elis

Icarius: father of Penelope, brother of Tyndareus, both of whom reigned over Sparta in the late Bronze Age

Idas: son of Aphareus and cousin of Penelope

Idomeneus: king of Crete; fought in Troy and died in Italy

Iole: daughter of Eurytus

Iphigenia: daughter of Clytemnestra and Agamemnon; sacrificed for the trojan war

Iphitus: son of Eurytus

Iphthimi: sister of Penelope

Kleokhareia: nymph of Lacedaemon

Laertes: father of Odysseus and father-in-law of Penelope

Leda: aunt of Penelope, mother of Helen

Leonteus: one of the suitors of Helen, prince of the Lapiths

Leucippus: son of Perieres, king of Messene, and uncle of Penelope

Leukos: foster son of Idomeneus, who sent Idomeneus to exile

Lynceus: son of Aphareus and cousin of Penelope

Machaon: prince from Thessaly, son of Asclepius, healer

Meda: queen of Crete, wife of Idomeneus

Meges: lord of Doulichion

Melissani: nymph of Cephalonia

Menelaus: king of Sparta, husband of Helen

Mentes: king of the Taphians

Mestor: lord of Ithaka and one of the elders

Minos: important king of Crete, long before Penelope's time

Neda: nymph of Messenia and Arcadia who helped save Zeus from his father Cronos

Neoptolemus: son of Achilles, king of Epirus

Nestor: king of Pylos, hero of the trojan war

Odysseus: husband of Penelope, king of Ithaka, hero of the trojan war

Oebalus: king of Sparta and father of Tyndareus and Icarius

Orestes: king of Mycenae, son of Clytemnestra and Agamemnon

Palamedes: exposed the trickery of Odysseus; killed by Odysseus during the trojan war

Patroclus: hero of the trojan war

Peleus: husband of Thetis and father of Achilles

Periboia: a nymph of Lacedaemon, and mother of Penelope
Perieres: king of Messene, son of king Cynortas of Sparta
Perseides: the descendants of Perseus
Perseus: famous hero, great-grandfather of Penelope
Philoctetes: Greek warrior in Troy who killed Paris
Phoebe: daughter of Leucippus, princess of Messene, and cousin of Penelope
Polites: friend of Odysseus who followed him in Troy
Pollux: cousin of Penelope, brother of Helen
Polybus: lord of Ithaka and one of the elders
Polycaste: first wife of Icarius
Polytherses: a lord of Same and elder adviser of the palace of Ithaka
Polyxo: queen of Rhodes Island, wife of Tlepolemus
Sthenelus: driver of Diomede's chariot
Tantalus: son of Thyestes
Taygete: nymph of Lacedaemon
Telemachus: son of Penelope and Odysseus
Tenes: king of Tenedos, son of Cycnus
Theisoa: nymph of Messenia and Arcadia, sister of Neda
Theseus: king of Athens, famous hero
Thyestes: brother of Atreas, king of Mycenae

Timandra: cousin of Penelope, sister of Helen

Tlepolemus: king of Rhodes who died in Troy

Tyndareus: uncle of Penelope, father of Helen

Names of Characters Invented for the Book

Armeria: servant woman from Sicily in the palace of Penelope, wife of Dolius

Autonoe: maid of Penelope

Cyanea: nanny of Helen and Penelope

Earine: nymph of Polylimnio in Pylos

Euarestos: teacher of Penelope in Sparta

Hippodamia: maid of Penelope

Nausos: Nestor's navigator

Paltibaal: teacher of Penelope

Phives: priest of Apollo in Ismarus

Polydorus: architect and builder friend of Odysseus and Penelope

Sotirios: herdsman of Idomeneus

Thekla: maid of Penelope

Names of Places

Acarnania: region of western Greece opposite to Ithaka

Acheron: river in Epirus that transported souls to the underworld

Aegina: island in the Saronic Gulf close to Athens

Amyclaes: palace city in Lacedaemon (currently Lakonia), Greece

Andania: sacred place in north Messenia where the mysteries were held

Aphrodisia: city founded by Diomedes in Apulia

Apulia: region of Italy

Arcadia: region of central Peloponnese

Argos: Greek city, home of Diomedes

Argos Hippion: city founded by Diomedes in Italy; today Arpi

Athens: famous city of Greece

Aulis: little city in Boeotia opposite to Euboea, where the Achaean fleet gathered before departing for Troy

Brendesium: city founded by Diomedes in Appulia, today Brindisi

Canysion: city founded by Diomedes in Appulia

Cephalonia: the main island of the Ithaka dominion

Crete: important Greek island, center of the Minoan civilization

Delphi: the main ancient Greek oracle

Dodona: the oldest ancient Greek oracle

Doulichion: island in the Ionian Sea; unclear which of today's islands it refers to

Echinae islands: sacred islands opposite to Elis

Eleusis: sacred city near Athens where the mysteries were held

Ephyra: place in Epirus with famous nekromanteion

Epirus: region of central Greece that faces the Ionian Sea

Evrotas: river in Lacedaemon, Greece

Gythion: beautiful little village at the gulf of Lacedaemon

Ismarus: Thracian city destroyed by the Greeks during the Trojan War

Ithaka: the island of Odysseus, in the Ionian Sea, that belonged in the dominion of Mycenae

Ithomi: mountain of Messenia Greece

Laganas: town and gulf of Zakynthos, Greek island

Lykaios: mountain at the border between Messenia and Arcadia
Meliboea: city of Philoctetes in Thessaly
Messene: city of central Messenia, took the name of the first queen of the region
Mycenae: most important city of the Mycenaean civilization, situated in Argolis, Greece; founded by Perseus and Andromeda
Pamisos: river of Messenia
Parnassus: mountain in central Greece
Parnon: mountain in eastern Lacedaemon, Greece
Pisa: the Bronze Age name of Olympia Greece
Pherae: ancient city in southeast Thessaly, Greece
Phthia: city in Thessaly, kingdom of Peleus and Achilles
Polylimnio: place of many lakes in a gorge close to Pylos
Pylos: Nestor's kingdom, today a small town of western Messenia
Rhodes: Greek island in the southeast Aegean
Salamis: island close to Athens
Same: island in Ionian Sea, probably today's Cephalonia
Scythia: region at the northern part of Black Sea
Sparta: famous city in Lacedaemon, Greece

Taphian islands: islands in the dominion of Ithaka

Taygetus: mountain in western Lacedaemon, Greece

Tegea: city in Arcadia

Tenedos: Greek island allied to Troy, destroyed by the Greeks

Zakynthos: island in Ionian Sea

Printed in Great Britain
by Amazon